INDIA'S GREATEST SHORT STORIES

GRAPEVINE INDIA

India's Greatest Short Stories

Grapevine India Publishers Pvt. Ltd.
16, Shanti Mohan House,
Ansari Road, Darya Ganj,
New Delhi - 110002
India
grapevineindiapublishers@gmail.com
contact@grapevineindia.com

First published by M/S Grapevine India Publishers India Ltd.

Printed and bound by Nutech Print Services - India

CONTENTS

Munshi Premchand

(1880-1936)

Idgah
(The Festival of Eid)

Eid comes after thirty days of Ramadan. The morning of Eid is so wonderful and beautiful! The sky has a pretty pink glow, the fields look festive, the trees look more vibrant. And the Sun! It is brighter and more dazzling than ever before, wishing the world a very happy Eid!

There is impatience in the village. Everyone is excited and up early. They have to visit the Eidgah mosque. One person finds a button missing from his shirt. He is rushing to the neighbour's place to ask for needle and thread. Another is hurrying to the oil-press to get oil for his hardened leather shoes. Many are feeding their oxen a lot of fodder, because by the time they will be back, it will already be afternoon. The Eidgah is three miles far from the village. There will be so many people to meet and chat with; they would certainly be late, probably will stay till midday.

The boys are more excited than the others. Some of them kept only one fast— and that only till noon. Some didn't even do that. But no one can deny them the joy of going to the Eidgah. Fasting is for the grown-ups and the aged. For the boys it is only the day of Eid. They have been talking about it all the time.

At long last the day has come. And now they are impatient

with people for not hurrying up. They have no concern with things that have to be done. They are not bothered whether or not there is enough milk and sugar for the vermicelli pudding. All they want is to eat the pudding. They have no idea why Abbajan is out of breath running to the house of Chaudhri Karim Ali. They don't know that if the Chaudhri were to change his mind he could turn the festive day of Eid into a day of mourning. Their pockets bulge with coins like the stomach of the pot-bellied Kubera, the Hindu God of Wealth. They are forever taking the treasure out of their pockets, counting and recounting it before putting it back.

Mahmood counts "One, two, ten, twelve"— he has twelve pice. Mohsin has "One, two, three, eight, nine, fifteen" pice. Out of this countless hoard they will buy countless things: toys, sweets, paper-pipes, rubber balls— and much else.

The happiest of the boys is Hamid. He is only four; poorly dressed, thin and famished-looking. His father died last year of cholera. Then his mother wasted away and, without anyone finding out what had ailed her she also died.

Now Hamid sleeps in Granny Ameena's lap and is as happy as a lark. She tells him that his father has gone to earn money and will return with sack loads of silver. And that his mother has gone to Allah to get lovely gifts for him.

This makes Hamid very happy. It is great to live on hope; for a child there is nothing like hope. A child's imagination can turn a mustard seed into a mountain. Hamid has no shoes on his feet; the cap on his head is soiled and tattered; its gold thread has turned black. Nevertheless Hamid is happy. He knows that when his father comes back with sacks full of silver and his mother with gifts from Allah he will be able to fulfil all his heart's desires. Then he will have more than Mahmood, Mohsin, Noorey and Sammi.In her hovel the unfortunate Ameena sheds bitter tears. It is Eid and she does not have even a handful of grain. Only if her Abid were there, it would have been a different kind of Eid!

Hamid goes to his grandmother and says, "Granny, don't you fret over me!I will be the first to get back. Don't worry!" Ameena is sad. Other boys are going out with their fathers. She is the only 'father' Hamid has. How can she let him go to the fair all by himself? What if he gets lost in the crowd? No, she must not lose her precious little soul!How can he walk three miles? He doesn't even have a pair of shoes. He will get blisters on his feet. If she went along with him she could pick him up now and then.

But then who would be there to cook the vermicelli? If only she had the money she could have bought the ingredients on the way back and quickly made the pudding. In the village it would take her many hours to get everything. The only way out was to ask someone for them.

The villagers leave in one party. With the boys is Hamid. They run on ahead of the elders and wait for them under a tree. Why do the oldies drag their feet? And Hamid is like one with wings on his feet. How could anyone think he would get tired? They reach the suburbs of the town. On both sides of the road are mansions of the rich enclosed all around by thick, high walls.In the gardens mango and leechee trees are laden with fruit.

A boy hurls a stone at a mango tree. The gardener rushes

out screaming abuses at them. By then the boys are furlongs out of his reach and roaring with laughter. What a silly ass they make of the gardener!

Then come big buildings: the law courts, the college and the club. How many boys would there be in this big college? No sir, they are not all boys! Some are grown-up men. They sport enormous moustaches. What are such grown-up men going on studying for? How long will they go on doing so? What will they do with all their knowledge? There are only two or three grown-up boys in Hamid's school. Absolute duds they are too! They get a thrashing every day because they do not work at all. These college fellows must be the same type— why else should they be there !And the Masonic Lodge. They perform magic there. It is rumoured that they make human skulls move about and do other kinds of weird things.

No wonder they don't let in outsiders! And the white folk play games in the evenings. Grown-up men, men with moustaches and beards playing games ! And not only they, but even their Memsahibs! That's the honest truth! You give my Granny that something they call a racket; she wouldn't know how to hold it.

And if she tried to wave it about she would collapse. Mahmood says, "My mother's hands would shake; I swear by Allah they would!" Mohsin says, "Mine can grind maunds of grain. Her hand would never shake holding a miserable racket. She draws hundreds of pitchers full of water from the well every day. My buffalo drinks up five pitchers. If a Memsahib had to draw one pitcher, she would go blue in the face." Mahmood interrupts, "But your mother couldn't run and leap about, could she?" "That's right," replies Mohsin, "she couldn't leap or jump. But one day our cow got loose and began grazing in the Chaudhri's fields.

My mother ran so fast after it that I couldn't catch up with her. Honest to God, I could not!" So we proceed to the stores of the sweet-meat vendors. All so gaily decorated!Who can eat all these delicacies?Just look! Every store has them piled up in mountain heaps. They say that after 1 1 nightfall, Jinns come and buy up everything. "My Abba says that at midnight there is a Jinn at every stall. He has all that remains weighed and pays in real rupees, just the sort of rupees we have," says Mohsin.

Hamid is not convinced. "Where would the Jinns come by rupees?" "Jinns are never short of money," replies Mohsin. "They can get into any treasury they want. Mister, don't you know no iron bars can stop them? They have all the diamonds and rubies they want. If they are pleased with anyone they will give him baskets full of diamonds. They are here one moment and five minutes later they can be in Calcutta." Hamid asks again, "Are these Jinns very big?" "Each one is as big as the sky," asserts Mohsin. "He has his feet on the ground, his head touches the sky. But if he so wanted, he could get into a tiny brass pot. "How do people make Jinns happy?" asks Hamid. "If anyone taught me the secret, I would make at least one Jinn happy with me."

"I do not know," replies Mohsin, "but the Chaudhri Sahib has a lot of Jinns under his control. If anything is stolen, he can trace it and even tell you the name of the thief. Jinns tell him everything that is going on in the world."Hamid understands how Chaudhri Sahib has come by his wealth and why people hold him in so much respect.

It begins to get crowded. Parties heading for the Eidgah are coming into town from different sides— each one dressed better than the other. Some on tongas and ekkas, some in motorcars. All wearing perfume; all bursting with excitement.Our small party of village rustics is not bothered about the poor show they make. They are a calm, contented lot. For village children everything in the town is strange. Whatever catches their eye, they stand and gape at it with wonder. Cars hoot frantically to get them out of the way, but they couldn't care less. Hamid is nearly run over by a car.

At long last the Eidgah comes in view. Above it are massive tamarind trees casting their shade on the cemented floor on which carpets have been spread. And there are row upon row of worshippers as far as the eye can see, spilling well beyond the mosque courtyard. Newcomers line themselves behind the others. Here neither wealth nor status matters because in the eyes of Islam all men are equal. Our villagers wash their hands and feet and make their own line behind the others. What a beautiful, heart-moving sight it is! What perfect coordination of movements ! A hundred thousand heads bow together in prayer! And then all together they stand erect; bow down and sit on their knees ! Many times they repeat these movements— exactly as if a hundred thousand electric bulbs were switched on and off at the same time again and again. What a wonderful spectacle it is!

The prayer is over. Men embrace each other. They descend on the sweet and toy- vendors' stores like an army moving to an assault. In this matter the grown-up rustic is no less eager than the boys. Look, here is a swing! Pay a pice and enjoy riding up to the heavens and then plummeting down to the earth. And here is the roundabout strung with wooden elephants, horses and camels! Pay one pice and have twenty-five rounds of fun.

Mahmood and Mohsin and Noorey and other boys mount the horses and camels. Hamid watches them from a distance. All he has are three pice. He couldn't afford to part with a third of his treasure for a few miserable rounds.They've finished with the roundabouts; now it is time for the toys. There is a row of stalls on one side with all kinds of toys; soldiers and milkmaids, kings and ministers, water-carriers and washerwomen and holy men. Splendid display! How lifelike! All they need are tongues to speak. Mahmood buys a policeman in khaki with a red turban on his head and a gun on his shoulder. Looks as if he is marching in a parade. Mohsin likes the water-carrier with his back bent under the weight of the water- bag. He holds the handle of the bag in one hand and looks pleased with himself.

Perhaps, he is singing. It seems as if the water is about to pour out of the bag. Noorey has fallen for the lawyer. What an expression of learning he has on his face ! A black gown over a long, white coat with a gold watch chain going into a pocket, a fat volume of some law book in his hand. Appears as if he has just finished arguing a case in a court of law.These toys cost two pice each. All Hamid has are three pice; how can he afford to buy such expensive toys? If they dropped out of his hand, they would be smashed to bits. If a drop of water fell on them, the paint would run. What would he do with toys like these? They'd be of no use to him. Mohsin says, "My water-carrier will sprinkle water every day, morning and evening." Mahmood says, "My policeman will guard my house. If a thief comes near, he will shoot him with his gun. Noorey says, "My lawyer will fight my cases." Sammi says, "My washer-woman will wash my clothes every day." Hamid pooh-poohs their toys-they're made of clay— one fall and they'll break in pieces. But his eyes look at them hungrily and he wishes he could hold them in his hands for just a moment or two. His hands stretch without his wanting to stretch them. But young boys are not givers, particularly when it is something new. Poor Hamid doesn't get to touch the toys.After the toys it is sweets. Someone buys sesame seed candy, others gulab-jammuns or halva. They smack their lips with relish.

Only Hamid is left out. The luckless boy has at least three pice; why doesn't he also buy something to eat? He looks with hungry eyes at the others. Mohsin says, "Hamid, take this sesame candy, it smells good."Hamid suspects it is a cruel joke; he knows Mohsin doesn't have so big a heart.

But knowing this Hamid goes to Mohsin. Mohsin takes a piece out of his leaf-wrap and holds it towards Hamid. Hamid stretches out his hand. Mohsin puts the candy in his own mouth. Mahmood, Noorey and Sammi clap their hands with glee and have a jolly good laugh. Hamid is crestfallen. Mohsin says, "This time I will let you have it.

I swear by Allah! I will give it to you. Come and take it." Hamid replies, "You keep your sweets. Don't I have the money?" "All you have are three pice," says Sammi. "What can you buy for three pice?"

Mahmood says, "Mohsin is a rascal. Hamid you come to me and I will give you gulcib-jammun."Hamid replies, "What is there to rave about sweets? Books are full of bad things about eating sweets." "In your heart you must be saying, 'If I could get it I would eat it,'" says Mohsin. "Why don't you take the money out of your pocket?" "I know what this clever fellow is up to," says Mahmood. "When we've spent all our money, he will buy sweets and tease us. After the sweet- vendors there are a few hardware stores and shops of real and artificial jewellery. There is nothing there to attract the boys' attention. So they go ahead— all of them except Hamid who stops to see a pile of tongs. It occurs to him that his granny does not have a pair of tongs. Each time she bakes chapattis, the iron plate burns her hands. If he were to buy her a pair of tongs she would be very pleased. She would never burn her fingers; it would be a useful thing to have in the house. What use are toys? They are a waste of money. You can have some fun with them but only for a very short time. Then you forget all about them.Hamid's friends have gone ahead. They are at a stall drinking sherbet.

How selfish they are! They bought so many sweets but did not give him one. And then they want him to play with them; they want him to do odd jobs for them.

Now if any of them asked him to do something, he would

tell them, "Go suck your lollipop, it will bum your mouth; it will give you a rash of pimples and boils; your tongue will always crave for sweets; you will have to steal money to buy them and get a thrashing in the bargain. It's all written in books. Nothing will happen to my tongs.

No sooner my granny sees my pair of tongs she will run up to take it from me and say, 'My child has brought me a pair of tongs,' and shower me with a thousand blessings. She will show it off to the neighbours' womenfolk. Soon the whole village will be saying, 'Hamid has brought his granny a pair of tongs, how nice he is!' No one will bless the other boys for the toys they have got for themselves. Blessings of elders are heard in the court of Allah and are immediately acted on. Because I have no money Mohsin and Mahmood adopt such airs towards me. I will teach them a lesson. Let them play with their toys and eat all the sweets they can. I will not play with toys. I will not stand any nonsense from anyone. And one day my father will return. And also my mother. Then I will ask these chaps, 'Do you want any toys? How many?' I will give each one a basket full of toys and teach them how to treat friends. I am not the sort who buys a pice worth of lollipops to tease others by sucking them myself. I know they will laugh and say Hamid has brought a pair of tongs. They can go to the Devil!"

Hamid asks the shopkeeper, "How much for this pair of tongs?" The shopkeeper looks at him and seeing no older person with him replies, "It's not for you." "Is it for sale or not?" "Why should it not be for sale? Why else should I have bothered to bring it here?" "Why then don't you tell me how much it is!" "It will cost you six pice." Hamid's heart sinks. "Let me have the correct price." "All right, it will be five pice, bottom price. Take it or leave it." Hamid steels his heart and says, "Will you give it to me for three?" And proceeds to walk away lest the shopkeeper screams at him. But the shopkeeper does not scream. On the contrary, he calls Hamid back and gives him the pair of tongs. Hamid carries it on his shoulder as if it were a gun and struts up proudly to show it to his friends. Let us hear what they have to say. Mohsin laughs and says, "Are you crazy? What will you do with the tongs?"

Hamid flings the tongs on the ground and replies, "Try and throw your water-carrier on the ground. Every bone in his body will break." Mahmood says, "Are these tongs some kind of toy?" "Why not?" retorts Hamid. "Place them across your shoulders and it is a gun; wield them in your hands and it is like the tongs carried by singing mendicants— they can make the same clanging as a pair of cymbals. One smack and they will reduce all your toys to dust. And much as your toys may try they could not bend a hair on the head of my tongs. My tongs are like a brave tiger."

Sammi who had bought a small tambourine asks, "Will you exchange them for my tambourine? It is worth eight pice." Hamid pretends not to look at the tambourine. "My tongs if they wanted to could tear out the bowels of your tambourine. All it has is a leather skin and all it can say is dhub, dhub. A drop of water could silence it forever. My brave pair of tongs can weather water and storms, without budging an inch." The pair of tongs wins over everyone to its side. But now no one has any money left and the fairground has been left far behind.

It is well past 9 a.m. and the sun is getting hotter every minute. Everyone is in a hurry to get home. Even if they talked their fathers into it, they could not get the tongs. This Hamid is a bit of a rascal. He saved up his money for the tongs. The boys divide into two factions. Mohsin, Mahmood, Sammi and Noorey on the one side, and Hamid by himself on the other. They are engaged in hot argument. Sammi has defected to the other side.But Mohsin, Mahmood and Noorey, though they are a year or two older than Hamid, are reluctant to take him on in debate. Right is on Hamid's side. Also it's moral force on the one side, clay on the other. Hamid has iron now calling itself steel, unconquerable and lethal. If a tiger was to spring on them the water-carrier would be out of his wits; Mister Constable would drop his clay gun and take to his heels; the lawyer would hide his face in his gown, lie down on the ground and wail as if his mother's mother had died.

But the tongs, the pair of tongs, Champion of India would leap and grab the tiger by its neck and gouge out its eyes. Mohsin puts all he has in his plea, "But they cannot go and fetch water, can they?" Hamid raises the tongs and replies, "One angry word of command from my tongs and your water-carrier will hasten to fetch the water and sprinkle it at any doorstep he is ordered to."Mohsin has no answer.

Mahmood comes to his rescue. "If we are caught, we are caught. We will have to do the rounds of the law courts in chains. Then we will be at the lawyer's feet asking for help."Hamid has no answer to this powerful argument. He asks, "Who will come to arrest us?" Noorey puffs out his chest and replies, "This policeman with the gun." Hamid makes a face and says with scorn, "This wretch come to arrest the Champion of India! Okay, let's have it out over a bout of wrestling, Far from catching them, he will be scared to look at my tongs in the face." Mohsin thinks of another ploy. "Your tongs' face will burn in the fire every day." He is sure that this will leave Hamid speechless. That is not so. Pat comes Hamid with the retort, "Mister, it is only the brave who can jump into a fire. Your miserable lawyers, policemen, and water-carriers will run like frightened women into their homes. Only this Champion of India can perform this feat of leaping into the fire." Mahmood has one more try, "The lawyer will have chairs to sit and tables for his things. Your tongs will only have the kitchen floor to lie on."

Hamid cannot think of an appropriate retort so he says whatever comes into his mind, "The tongs won't stay in the kitchen. When your lawyer sits on his chair my tongs will knock him down on the ground."It does not make sense but our three heroes are utterly squashed— almost as if a champion kite had been brought down from the heavens to the earth by a cheap, miserable paper imitation.

Thus Hamid wins the field. His tongs are the Champion of India. Neither Mohsin nor Mahmood, neither Noorey nor Sammi— nor anyone else can dispute the fact. The respect that a victor commands from the vanquished is paid to Hamid. The others have spent between twelve to sixteen pice each and bought nothing worthwhile. Hamid's three-pice worth has carried the day. And no one can deny that toys are unreliable things: they break, while Hamid's tongs will remain as they are for years.

The boys begin to make terms of peace. Mohsin says, "Give me your tongs for a while, you can have my water-carrier for the same time."Both Mahmood and Noorey similarly offer their toys. Hamid has no hesitation in agreeing to these terms. The tongs pass from one hand to another; and the toys are in turn handed to Hamid. How lovely they are! Hamid tries to wipe the tears of his defeated adversaries. "1 was simply pulling your leg, honestly 1 was. How can these tongs made of iron compare with your toys?" It seems that one or the other will call Hamid's bluff. But Mohsin's party are not solaced. The tongs have won the day and no amount of water can wash away their stamp of authority. Mohsin says, "No one will bless us for these toys."

Mahmood adds, "You talk of blessings! We may get a thrashing instead. My Amma is bound to say, 'Are these earthen toys all that you could find at the fair?'"Hamid has to concede that no mother will be as pleased with the toys as his granny will be when she sees the tongs. All he had was three pice and he has no reason to regret the way he has spent them. And now his tongs are the Champion of India and king of toys.

By eleven the village was again agog with excitement. All those who had gone to the fair were back at home. Mohsin's little sister ran up wrenched the water-carrier out of his hands and began to dance with joy. Mister Water-carrier slipped out of her hand, fell on the ground and went to paradise. The brother and sister began to fight; and both had lots to cry about. Their mother lost her temper because of the racket they were making and gave each two resounding slaps. Noorey's lawyer met an end befitting his grand status. A lawyer could not sit on the ground. He had to keep his dignity in mind. Two nails were driven into the wall, a plank put on them and a carpet of paper spread on the plank. The honourable counsel was seated like a king on his throne. Noorey began to wave a fan over him. He knew that in the law courts there were khus curtains and electric fans. So the least he could do was to provide a hand fan, otherwise the hot legal arguments might affect his lawyer's brains. Noorey was waving his fan made of bamboo leaf. We do not know whether it was the breeze or the fan or something else that brought the honourable counsel down from his high pedestal to the depths of hell and reduced his gown to mingle with the dust of which it was made.

There was much beating of breasts and the lawyer's bier was dumped on a dung heap. Mahmood's policeman remained. He was immediately put on duty to guard the village. But this police constable was no ordinary mortal who could walk on his own two feet. He had to be provided a palanquin. This was a basket lined with tatters of discarded clothes of red colour for the policeman to recline in comfort.Mahmood picked up the basket and started on his rounds. His two younger brothers followed him lisping, "Shopkeepers, keep awake!" But night has to be dark; Mahmood stumbled, the basket slipped out of his hand.

Mr. Constable with his gun crashed on the ground. He was short of one leg. Mahmood being a bit of a doctor knew of an ointment, which could quickly rejoin broken limbs. All it needed was the milk of a banyan sapling. The milk was brought and the broken leg reassembled.

But no sooner was the constable put on his feet the leg gave way. One leg was of no use because now he could neither walk nor sit. Mahmood became a surgeon and cut the other leg to the size of the broken one so the chap could at least sit in comfort. The constable was made into a holy man; he could sit in one place and guard the village. And sometimes he was like the image of the deity. The plume on his turban was scraped off and you could make as many changes in his appearance as you liked. And sometimes he was used for nothing better than weighing things. Now let's hear what happened to our friend Hamid.

As soon as she heard his voice, Granny Ameena ran out of the house, picked him up and kissed him. Suddenly she noticed the tongs in his hand. "Where did you find these tongs?" "I bought them." "How much did you pay for them?" "Three pice. Granny Ameena beat her breast. "You are a stupid child! It is almost noon and you haven't had anything to eat or drink. And what do you buy— tongs! Couldn't you find anything better in the fair than this pair of iron tongs?"Hamid replied in injured tones, "You bum your fingers on the iron plate. That is why I bought them." The old woman's temper suddenly changed to love— not the kind of calculated love, which wastes away in spoken words.

This love was mute, solid and seeped with tenderness. What a selfless child! What concern for others! What a big heart!

How he must have suffered seeing other boys buying toys and gobbling sweets ! How was he able to suppress his own feelings ! Even at the fair he thought of his old grandmother. Granny Ameena's heart was too full for words. And the strangest thing happened— stranger than the part played by the tongs was the role of Hamid the child playing Hamid the old man. And old Granny Ameena became Ameena the little girl. She broke down. She spread her apron and beseeched Allah's blessings for her grandchild. Big tears fell from her eyes. How was Hamid to understand what was going on inside her!

Kafan
(The Shroud)

1

(1a)

The father and the sun sat quietly by a burnt-out fire at the door of the hut. Inside, the son's young wife is writhing in pain; she is in labour. Now and then, her heart-wrenching scream would make them brace themselves, pressing their hands to their bosom. It was a cold winter night; there was desolation all around. The village was engulfed in darkness.

Ghisu said, "It looks like she won't live longer. She has been in pain for long. Go in , see how she is doing."

Madhav said painfully, " If she's going to die, why doesn't she die sooner? What is the use of going to see?"

"How hard-hearted you are! You've enjoyed your lives together for an year. And now such faithlessness?"

"Well, I can't stand to see her writhing and thrashing around."

It was a family of Chamars, and notorious in the whole village. If Ghisu worked for one day, then he rested for three. Madhav was such a slacker that if he worked for an hour, then he smoked his chilam for an hour. Thus nobody hired them on. If there was even a handful of grain in the house, they both swore off working. When they'd fasted for a couple of days, then Ghisu climbed trees and broke off branches, and Madhav sold the wood in the market; and as long as that money lasted, they both spent their time wandering idly around. *When their hunger grew intense, they again broke off branches, or looked for some work.* There was no shortage of work in the village. It was a village of farmers; for a hard-working man there were fifty jobs. But people only sent for those two when they were forced to content themselves with getting out of two men the work of one.

If only the two had been ascetics, then they wouldn't have needed any exercises in self-discipline to achieve contentment and patience. This was their very nature. Theirs was a strange life. Except for two or three clay pots, they had no goods at all in the house. Covering their nakedness with torn rags, free from the cares of the world, laden with debt-- they suffered abuse, they suffered blows too, but not grief. They were so poor that without the smallest hope of repayment, people used to lend them something or other. When peas or potatoes were in season, they would dig up peas or potatoes from the fields and roast and eat them, or break off five or ten stalks of sugarcane and suck them at night. Ghisu had spent sixty years of his life in this piousmanner, and Madhav, like a dutiful son, was following in his father's footsteps-- or rather, was making his name even more radiant.

(1b)

This time too, both were seated by the fire, roasting potatoes that they had dug up from somebody's field. Ghisu's wife had passed away long ago. Madhav's marriage had taken place the year before. Since this woman had come, she had laid the foundations of civilization in the family. *Grinding grain, cutting grass, she arranged for a couple of pounds of flour,* and kept filling the stomachs of those two shameless ones. After she came, they both grew even more lazy and indolent; indeed, they even began to swagger a bit. If someone sent for them to work, then with splendid indifference they demanded double wages. That woman was dying today in childbirth. And these two were perhaps waiting for her to die, so they could sleep in peace.

Pulling out a potato and peeling it, Ghisu said, "Go see what shape she's in. We'll have the fuss over a ghost-witch-- what else! And here even the exorcist demands a rupee-- *from whose house would we get one?*"

Madhav suspected that if he went into the hut, Ghisu would finish off most of the potatoes. He said, "I'm afraid to go in."

"What are you afraid of? I'm here, after all."

"Then you go and see, all right?"

"When my wife died, for three days I never even left her side. And then, won't she be ashamed in front of me? I've never seen her face-- and today I should see her naked body? She won't even have bodily ease: if she sees me, she won't be able to thrash around freely."

"I'm thinking, if a child is born-- what then? Dried ginger, brown sugar, oil-- there's nothing at all in the house."

"Everything will come. If Bhagwan gives a child-- those people who now aren't giving a paisa, will send for us and give us things. I've had nine sons. There was never anything in the house, but this is how we managed every time."

(1c)

A society in which those who labored night and day were not in much better shape than these two; a society in which compared to the peasants, those who knew how to exploit the peasants' weaknesses were much better off-- in such a society, the birth of this kind of mentality was no cause for surprise. We'll say that compared to the peasants, Ghisu was more insightful; and instead of joining the mindless group of peasants, he had joined the group of clever, scheming tricksters. Though indeed, he wasn't skilful in following the rules and customs of the tricksters. Thus while other members of his group became chiefs and headmen of villages, at him the whole village wagged its finger. But still, he did have the consolation that if he was in bad shape, at least he wasn't forced to do the back-breaking labor of the peasants, and others didn't take improper advantage of his simplicity and voicelessness.

Pulling out the potatoes, they both began to eat them burning hot. They had eaten nothing since the day before. They were too impatient to wait till the potatoes cooled. Both burned their tongues repeatedly. When the potatoes were peeled, their outer parts didn't seem so extremely hot. But the moment the teeth bit into them, the inner part burned the tongue and throat and roof of the mouth. Rather than keep that ember in the mouth, it was better to send it quickly along inward, where there was plenty of equipment for cooling it down. So they both swallowed very fast, although the attempt brought tears to their eyes.

(1d)

Then Ghisu remembered a landowner's wedding procession, in which he had taken part twenty years before. The repletion that had been vouchsafed to him in that feast was a memorable event in his life, and even today its memory was fresh. He said, "I'll never forget that feast. Never since then have I had that kind of food, or such a full stomach. The girl's family fed puris to everyone. As much as they wanted! Great and small, everyone ate puris-- ones made with real ghi! Chutney, raita, three kinds of green vegetables, a flavorful stew, yoghurt, chutney, sweets. How can I tell you now what relish there was in that feast! There was no limit. Whatever thing you want, just ask! And however much you want, eat! People ate so much, ate so much, that nobody could even drink any water. And there the servers were-- setting hot, round, sweet-smelling pastries before you! You refuse, saying you don't want it. You push away the tray with your hand. But that's how they are-- they just keep on giving it. And when everybody had wiped their mouths, then everybody got a pan as well. But how could I be in any shape for a pan? I couldn't stand up. I just staggered off and lay down on my blanket. He had a heart as big as the ocean, that landowner!"

Enjoying the story of these grand festivities, Madhav said,

"If only somebody would give us such a feast now!"

"As if anybody would feast anybody now! That was a different time. Now everybody thinks about economy-- 'don't spend money on weddings, don't spend money on religious festivals!'. Ask them-- what's this 'saving' of the poor people's wealth? There's no lack of 'saving'. But when it comes to spending, they think about economy!"

"You must have eaten twenty or so puris?"

"I ate more than twenty."

"I would have eaten up fifty."

"I couldn't have eaten less than fifty. I was hale and hearty. You're not half of what I was!"

After eating, they both drank some water, covered themselves with their dhotis, curled up, and went to sleep right there by the fire, as if two gigantic serpents lay coiled there.

And Budhiya was still moaning.

(2)

(2a)

In the morning, when Madhav went into the hut and looked, his wife had grown cold. Flies were buzzing on her face. Her stony eyes had rolled upward. Her whole body was covered with dust. In her stomach, the baby had died.

Madhav came running to Ghisu. Then they both together

began loudly lamenting and beating their breasts. When the neighbors heard the weeping and wailing, they came running. And following the ancient custom, they began to console the bereaved.

But this wasn't the occasion for an excessive show of grief. They had to worry about the shroud, and the wood. Money was as scarce in their house as meat in a raptor's nest.

Father and son went weeping to the village landlord. He hated the very sight of their faces. A number of times he had beaten them with his own hands-- for theft, or for not coming to work as they had promised. He asked, "What is it, Ghisua, why do you weep? Nowadays we don't even see you around. It seems that you no longer want to live in the village."

Ghisua fell prostrate on the ground, and said with tear-filled eyes, "Master, I'm in great trouble! Madhav's wife passed away last night. All day she was writhing in pain, Master; we two sat by her bed till midnight. Whatever medicines we could give her, we did. But she slipped away. Now we have no one to care for us, Master-- we're devastated-- our house is destroyed! I'm your slave. Now who but you will take care of her final rites? Whatever money we had at hand was used up on medicines. If the Master will show mercy, then she'll have the proper rites. To whose door should I come except yours?"

(2b)

The Landlord Sahib was a compassionate man. But to show compassion to Ghisu was to try to dye a black blanket. He felt like saying, "Get out of here! *Keep the corpse in your house and let it rot!* Usually you don't come even when you're called-- now when you want something, you come and flatter me! You treacherous bastard! You villain!" But this was not the occasion for anger or revenge. Willingly or not, he pulled out two rupees and flung them down. But he didn't open his lips to say a single word of consolation. He didn't even look in Ghisu's direction-- as if he'd discharged a duty.

When the Landlord Sahib gave two rupees, then how could the village merchants and money-lenders have the nerve to refuse? Ghisu knew how to beat the drum of the landlord's name. One gave two paisas, another gave four paisas. In an hour, Ghisu had collected the sum of five rupees in ready cash. Someone gave grain, someone else gave wood. And in the afternoon Ghisu and Madhav went to the market to get a shroud. Meanwhile, people began to cut the bamboo poles, and so on.

The sensitive-hearted women of the village came and looked at the body. They shed a few tears at its helplessness, and went away.

(3)

(3a)

When they reached the market, Ghisu said, "We've got enough wood to burn her, haven't we, Madhav?"

Madhav said, "Yes, there's plenty of wood. Now we need a shroud."

"So let's buy a light kind of shroud."

"Sure, what else! While the body is being carried along, night will come. At night, who sees a shroud?"

"What a bad custom it is that someone who didn't even get a rag to cover her body when she was alive, needs a new shroud when she's dead."

"After all, the shroud burns along with the body."

"What else is it good for? If we'd had these five rupees earlier, we would have given her some medicine."

Each of them inwardly guessed what the other was thinking. They kept wandering here and there in the market, until eventually evening came. [Sometimes they went to one cloth-seller's shop, sometimes to another. They looked at various kinds of fabric, they looked at silk and cotton, but nothing suited them.] The two arrived, by chance or deliberately, before a wine-house; and as if according to some prearranged decision, they went inside. For a little while they both stood there in a state of uncertainty. [Then Ghisu went to the counter and said, "Sir, please give us a bottle too."] *Ghisu bought one bottle of liquor, and some sesame sweets.* [After this some snacks came, fried fish came]. And they both sat down on the verandah and [peacefully] began to drink.

(3b)

After drinking a number of cups in a row, both became elevated.

Ghisu said, "What's the use of wrapping her in a shroud?

After all, it would only be burned. Nothing would go with her."

Looking toward the sky as if persuading the angels of his innocence, Madhav said, "It's the custom of the world-- why do these same people give thousands of rupees to the Brahmins? Who can tell whether a reward does or doesn't reach them in another world?"

"Rich people have wealth-- let them waste it! What do we have to waste?"

"But what will you tell people? Won't people ask where the shroud is?"

Ghisu laughed. "We'll say the money slipped out of my waistband-- we searched and searched for it, but it didn't turn up. [People won't believe it, but they'll still give the same sum again.]"

Madhav too laughed at this unexpected good fortune, *at defeating destiny in this way*. He said, "She was very good, the poor thing. Even as she died, she gave us a fine meal."

More than half the bottle had been finished. Ghisu ordered two sers of puris, a meat stew, and spiced liver and fried fish. There was a shop right next to the wine-house. Madhav ran over and brought everything back on two leaf-plates. The cost was fully one and a half rupees. Only a few paise were left.

(3c)

Both then sat eating puris, with all the majesty of a tiger in the jungle pursuing his prey. They had no fear of being called to account, nor any concern about disgrace. They had passed through these stages of weakness long ago. Ghisu said in a philosophical manner, "If my soul is being pleased, then won't she receive religious merit?"

Madhav bowed his head in pious confirmation. "Certainly she'll certainly receive it. Bhagwan, you are the knower of hearts-- take her to Heaven! We're both giving her our heartfelt blessing. The feast I've had today-- I haven't had its equal in my whole life!"

After a moment a doubt arose in Madhav's heart. He said, "How about it-- we'll go there too someday, won't we?"

Ghisu gave no answer to this childish question. *He looked reproachfully at Madhav.* [He didn't want the thought of heavenly matters to interfere with this bliss.]

"When she asks us, there, why we didn't give her a shroud, what will you say?"

"Oh, shut up!"

"She'll certainly ask."

"How do you know that she won't get a shroud? Do you consider me such a donkey? I've lived in this world for sixty years-- and have I just been loitering around? She'll get a shroud, and [a very good one]-- *a much better than we would have given*."

Madhav was not convinced. He said, "Who will give it? You've gobbled up the rupees! [It's me she'll ask-- I'm the one who put the sindur in the parting of her hair.]"

Ghisu grew irritated. "I tell you, she'll get a shroud. Why don't you believe me?"

"Who will give the money-- why don't you tell me?"

"The same people will give it who gave it this time. But they won't put the rupees into our hands. *And if somehow we get our hands on them, we'll sit here and drink again just like this, and they'll give the shroud a third time.*"

(3d)

As the darkness deepened and and the stars glittered more sharply, the tumult in the wine-house also increased. One person sang, another babbled, another embraced his companion, another pressed a glass to his friend's lips. Joy was in the atmosphere there. Intoxication was in the air. How many people become 'an ass with a glass'! *They came here only to taste the pleasure of self-forgetfulness.* More than liquor, the air here elevated their spirits. The disaster of life seized them and dragged them here. And for a while they forgot whether they were alive or dead-- or half-alive.

And these two, father and son, were still sipping with relish. Everyone's eyes had settled on them. How fortunate they were! They had a whole bottle between them.

After he had finished eating, Madhav picked up the leaf-plate of leftover puris and gave it to a beggar who was standing there looking at them with hungry eyes. And for the first time in his life he felt the pride and delight and thrill of giving.

Ghisu said, "Take it-- eat your fill, and give her your blessing. She whose earnings these are has died, but your blessing will certainly reach her. Bless her with every hair on your body-- these are the payment for very hard labor."

Madhav again looked toward the sky and said, "She'll go to Heaven-- she'll become the Queen of Heaven!"

(3e)

Ghisu stood up, and as if swimming in waves of joy he said, "Yes, son, she'll go to Heaven! She never tormented anyone, she never oppressed anyone; even while dying, she fulfilled the greatest desire of our lives. If she doesn't go to Heaven, then will those fat rich people go-- who loot the poor with both hands, and go to the Ganges to wash away their sin, and offer holy water in temples?"

This mood of piety too changed; variability is the special quality of intoxication. It was the turn of despair and grief. Madhav said, "But the poor thing suffered a great deal in her life. Even her death was so painful!" Covering his eyes with his hands, he began to weep, [and sobbed loudly].

Ghisu consoled him: "Why do you weep, son? Be happy that she's been liberated from this net of illusion. She's escaped from the snare; she was very fortunate that she was able to break the bonds of worldly illusion so quickly."

And both, standing there, began to sing, "Temptress! Why do your eyes flash, temptress?"

The whole wine-house was absorbed in the spectacle, and these two drinkers, deep in intoxication, kept on singing.

Then they both began to dance-- they leaped and jumped, fell down, flounced about, gesticulated, [strutted around]; and finally, overcome by drunkenness, they collapsed.

Boodhi Kaaki (The Old Aunt)

Old age is for the most part a backslide into infantilism. Old Kaki had lost all enthusiasm for life aside from her hankering for food; and was left with crying as the main methods for drawing in others' attention. Her senses, her eyes, her hands and feet had fallen into haggardness. She would stay lying on the floor the entire day; and if the householders accomplished something against her desires, or she didn't get her meals at the selected time or in satisfactory amount, or she was not given an offer of the eatables brought from the market, she would break into crying. Her wailing was no customary thing; it was a full-throated upheaval.

Her husband had departed long back. Her children had passed away when they were young. She had nobody with the exception of her nephew to rely on, and she had given all her property in his name. The nephew made tall guarantees around then however they ended up being fanciful green fields.

Although the income from the property was not less than hundred fifty to two hundred rupees per annum, old Kaki seldom got enough to eat. It is difficult to say who was at fault here; her nephew Pandit Budhiram, or his other-half Shrimati Roopa. Budhiram was gentle by nature, but only up to the point his own pocket remained untouched. Roopa was sharp-tongued, but she was God-fearing. Old Kaki didn't mind her harshness so much as Budhiram's gentleness.

Budhiram sometimes regretted his cruel behaviour, knowing well that he was able to wear the cloak of respectability only because of this very property. He wouldn't have minded if, through empty assurances and verbal sympathies, he had been able to make Kaki's life a little more bearable, but the very thought of incurring any additional expense supressed his good intentions. So much so that if Kaki opened up her tales of woe within the earshot of a visitor he would get inflamed and go inside and give her a dressing-down.

Boys seem to have a natural propensity to dislike old people; so Bhudhiram's sons, taking their cue from their parents, continually harassed Old Kaki. One would pinch her and run away, the other squirt a mouthful of water at her. Kaki would cry out, but since it was well-known that Kaki complained only when she was hungry, no one took notice of her outcries. And whenever the enraged Kaki started cursing the boys, Roopa appeared on the scene to silence her. Fearing this Kaki seldom used the tongue-lash, although this was a more effective means, than crying, to put an end to the boys' misdemeanour.

In the whole family it was Budhiram's little daughter Ladli who alone empathized with Kaki. Ladli, fearing her brothers, ate her sweets or roasted corn sitting beside Kaki; and although this strategy cost her dear because of Kaki's lust for food, this was the best protection against her brothers' injustices. This mutual self-interest had sown the seeds of sympathy between them.

2

It was evening time. Shehnai was playing at Bhudhiram's doorsteps. A group of children were enjoying the music with wonder-struck eyes. Guests, relaxing on charpais, were having their bodies kneaded and toned up by barbers. A balladeer was reciting the family's genealogy, and the appreciative applause from some admiring guests gave him the mistaken feeling that he himself was the object of their admiration. Two English-educated young men were indifferent to these goings-on. They considered it below their dignity to participate in such activities. The occasion was Budhiram's son Sukhram's engagement. A celebration was on. Women were singing inside the house. Roopa was busy supervising food preparations for the guests. Big kadais were placed on open-air fireplaces. Puris and kachoris were frying in one. In another, yet other dishes. In one cauldron a spicy curry was cooking. The aroma of ghee and spices was in the air all around.

Old Kaki was sitting in her unlighted room in a mood of dejection. The pleasing smell of cooking was unsettling her. She was wondering whether she would get her share of the puris. It was so late. No one had brought her any food. It seemed everyone had eaten and there was nothing left for her. She wanted to cry but fearing that this would be inauspicious she controlled herself.

Aha...what an appetizing smell! But no one cares for her. When she can't even get enough rotis, how can she hope to eat a stomach-full of puris? Her heart swelled with anguish. She was again on the verge of crying, but the fear of Roopa's temper stopped her.

Kaki remained lost in these disturbing thoughts for a long time. The fragrance of ghee and spices was making her lose control over herself. Her mouth was watering and the very thought of the taste of puris was sending ripples of joy in her heart. Whom should she call? Even Ladli had not come today. Even the two boys, who were always harassing her, were nowhere to be seen. At least she would have known what was going on.

Images of puris began to dance in her eyes: so brown, swelled-up, soft. Roopa must have eaten to her fill. The kachoris must be giving ajwain and cardamom flavours. If only she could take one puri in her hands to feel it! Why shouldn't she go and sit close to the kadai? She could imagine the crisp and sizzling puris being transferred from the kadai on to a tray. Flowers can be smelled even at home, but the pleasure of smelling them in the garden is very different. Having made up her mind thus, Kaki, crouching on her hands and feet, began to move slowly; and with great difficulty she crossed the threshold and crept close the kadai and sat down. Once there she felt the same satisfaction that a hungry dog feels while seated in front of someone eating.

At that time Roopa was over-stressed with work. Now she was in this room, now in that, now near the cooking area, then in the store. Someone came and said, 'The head cook is asking for "thandai".' She handed that over. Another came and said, 'The balladeer has come. Give him something.' She was taking out some uncooked ration when a third came and asked, 'When would the food be ready? And help me with the drum and manjeera.'

The poor woman was running everywhere, getting irritated, exasperated, yet unable to burst out. She was afraid that the neighbouring women might accuse her of losing her temper over small matters. Her throat was dry with thirst and her body scorched with heat yet she had no time to have a drink of water or fan herself for a moment.

And she was afraid that if she relaxed her watchfulness for a moment there would be no end to pilfering. It was in this state of mind that she saw Old Kaki sitting close to the kadai. She was infuriated and could no longer control her temper. She forgot that the neighbouring women were watching, or how the men sitting around would react.

Just as a frog jumps upon an earthworm, Roopa pounced upon Old Kaki and shook her with both hands and shouted: 'Shame on such a stomach. Is it a stomach or a furnace? Why couldn't you sit back in your room? The guests haven't eaten yet, no offering has been made to God, and you couldn't wait, and have come riding on our chests. Let such a tongue burn up. Had we not been feeding you every day I wonder what you would have done. Looking at you the villagers would accuse us of starving you. You torment us like an evil spirit and refuse to die. You're bent upon bringing us a bad name and shaming us. You eat so much and no one knows where it turns to ash. Go back to your room. You will eat when the family eats. You're not a goddess who should be fed before all others.'

Old Kaki lifted her head. She neither spoke nor cried. Quietly she crept back to her room.

3

The feast was ready. Leaf-plates were laid on the floor. The guests began to eat. The women started singing the song of the feast. The barbers and retainers of the guests were also eating, but they were seated at a distance from the guests. The custom required that no one should rise until the whole party had finished eating. A few educated guests were getting irritated for they thought the retainers were eating too much and taking too long to finish. They regarded this custom as meaningless.

Back in her room Old Kaki was ruing her conduct. She was not angry with Roopa but was regretting her own hasty behaviour. How could the householders eat before the guests had eaten? Why couldn't she restraint herself? She was insulted before everyone present. Now she won't go until she was called.

Having thus made up her mind she sat waiting to be called. But the pleasant smell of ghee was severely testing her patience. Each moment felt like an eon. The leaf-plates have been laid. The guests have arrived. The barbers are helping them wash their hands and feet. Now they have started eating. The song of the feast is being sung. Visualizing all this she lay down to console herself. Gradually she began to hum a tune. Then she felt she had been singing for too long. Were people still eating? She couldn't hear a sound. They must have gone away, having eaten. And no one has come to call her. Roopa must have been annoyed with her and won't send for her, assuming that she would come by herself. She was not a guest.

Kaki got ready to go. The belief that in a short while she would be servedpuris and spicy curry sent her taste buds humming. She weighed many options. 'First I would eat puris with curry, then with curds and shakkar;kachoris would taste lovely with raita. They may like it or not, I would feel no shame and ask them to serve me again and again. They might say I have no shame. Let them. I was getting to eat puris after so long. I wouldn't stop after eating only a mouthful.'

She came creeping into the courtyard. But what bad luck! Desire, as is its nature, had disoriented her sense of time.

The guests were still seated. Some were licking their fingers, some arching their eyes to see if others were still eating. Some were eyeing the puris lying uneaten on their plates, regretting they had not eaten them up. One was smacking his lips after eating curds but was too shy to ask for more. Just then Kaki came creeping amongst them. When they saw her some guests rose from their seats in a state of shock. They began to shout: 'Who's this old woman? Where has she come from? Be careful, she may not touch anyone.'

The moment he saw Kaki, Pandit Budhiram became red with anger. He dashed to the ground the trayful of puris he was holding; and just as a heartless money lender catches a dishonest and renegade debtor by his neck, he caught Kaki by her hands and dragged her into her unlighted room. The garden watered with hope was scorched dry with just one gust of hot wind. The guests had eaten. The family had eaten. The musicians, the washer men, the chamars - all had eaten, but no one thought of Kaki. Budhiram and Roopa had decided to punish her for her shameful conduct. They showed no compassion for Kaki's old age, her wretched existence, or her mental decline. Only Ladli was heart-broken for her.

Ladli loved Kaki very much. She was a simple minded girl with no trace of childish behaviour or prankishness. She had been dumbstruck when she saw her parents dragging Kaki away. This was too shocking for her. Why hadn't they fed Kaki? Would she have eaten all the puris? What if Kaki had eaten before the guests had been served? She wanted to go and commiserate with Kaki but couldn't do it for fear of her parents. She hadn't eaten her own share of puris, and hidden them in her doll's basket. She was impatient to carry these for Kaki. Kaki would get up at once on seeing her. She would be delighted to see the puris. She love her very much for this.

4

It was eleven in the night. Roopa was fast asleep in the courtyard. Ladli had been unable to sleep. The sweet pleasure of seeing Kaki eat puris wouldn't let her sleep. Her doll's basket lay by her side. When she was convinced that her mother was fast asleep she decided to get up. It was dark all around except for some light from the fireplaces. A dog was sleeping close by. Ladli looked up towards the neem tree. She felt as if Hanumanji was sitting up there. She could see his tail and mace very clearly. She shut her eyes out of fear. In the meantime the dog got up and ran off. This gave her some courage. She picked up her basket and walked towards Kaki's room.

5

The only thing Old Kaki remembered was that someone had dragged her by her hands and that she was being carried across a mountain. Her feet were repeatedly hitting against stones. Then someone had thrown her from atop the mountain and she had lost consciousness.

When she regained her senses she heard no sound of any movement. She realized that everyone had gone to sleep after eating. With this her own destiny had also been put to sleep. How would the night pass? Oh Ram, what should she eat? Her stomach was churning with hunger. No one cared for her. Would they get rich by keeping her hungry? These people had no compassion for an old woman who was going to die anytime. Why hurt her? All she does is eat a few rotis. Such treatment just for this! She was blind, disabled, deaf and deranged. If she had gone into the courtyard, Budhiram could have told her to wait till the guests had eaten. She was dragged and pushed. And just for these puris! Roopa insulted her before all; and even after such ill-treatment their hearts did not melt. They had fed everyone except her. And when they didn't feed her then, why would they do it now? With all these thoughts in her mind Kaki lay down. Her heart was filled with anguish but she didn't cry, thinking of the guests. All of a sudden she heard a voice. 'Get up, Kaki, I have brought puris for you.' Kaki recognized Laldli's voice. She got up at once, groped for Ladli with both hands and made her sit in her lap. Ladli gave her the puris.

'Has your Amma sent these?' Kaki asked.

'No, this's my share.'

Kaki pounced upon the puris. The basket was empty in five

minutes. Ladli asked, 'Kaki have you had your fill?'

Just as a light shower aggravates rather than mitigates the heat, the fewpuris spiked Kaki's craving, and she said, 'No, my daughter. Go to your mother and bring some more.'

Ladli said, 'Amma's asleep. If I wake her she would thrash me.'

Kaki fished around in the basket again. She found a few crumbs that were left there, and as she licked them she smacked her lips.

She was becoming desperate to eat some more puris. When the floodgates of patience are breached the gush of desire becomes uncontrollable. Just as the very thought of liquor sends the drunkards reeling, Kaki's ungratified heart was carried away. She forgot the distinction between what was proper or improper. Having lost her self-restraint she said to Ladli, 'Take me to the place where the guests were eating.'

Ladli could not guess her motive. She caught Kaki by her hands and took her there and made her sit among the leaf-plates on which lay the food leftover by the guests. The miserable, starved and unhinged old woman began to devour the leftovers from the leaf-plates lying scattered all over. Oh how tasty was the curd! How crisp, soft and well-salted were thekachoris! Although mentally unsettled, the old women knew that she was doing something that must never be done, that she was licking the leaf-plates left by the guests. But old age is the terminal stage of the sickness called insatiety where all the unfulfilled desires converge at one point. In the case of Old Kaki that point of convergence was her craving for food.

Just then Roopa woke up. She did not find Ladli by her side. She looked for her beside the cot fearing she might have slipped and fallen. When she looked around she saw Ladli standing beside the sullied leaf-plates and Old Kaki picking crumbs from there and eating. Roopa was stunned. She felt like someone watching a cow-slaughter. Nothing could be more shocking than to see a brahmin woman sifting through leftovers. Her husband's cousin's mother-in-law was behaving so despicably just for a few crumbs of puris! It was a terrifying sight. It was as if the earth had stopped spinning and the sky was reeling above them. Something cataclysmic was about to shake the world.

Roopa did not get angry, for anger had no place in this state of shock. Her eyes were filled with compassion as well as fear. Who was responsible for this sinful act? She lifted her hands towards heaven with a penitent heart and said, 'God, take pity on my children. Punish me for this sinful act, or I would be ruined.'

Roopa had never before realized her own selfish and unjust behavior with such clarity. She began to tell herself: How cruel I have been. Oh merciful God, forgive me. Today was my son's day of engagement. Hundreds of people feasted. I obeyed their commands like a slave. I spent hundreds of rupees to earn a good name for myself but could not feed the woman because of whom I have spent thousands of rupees. It is because of me this old woman is helpless. Roopa lit a lamp and went into her store room. She laid all the eatables in a tray and took it to the old woman.

It was already midnight. The sky was filled with stars and the gods were sitting there with heavenly dishes laid before them. But they wouldn't have felt the kind of pleasure Old Kaki felt when she saw the food laid before her. Roopa said to her with tearful eyes, 'Kaki, get up and eat. I committed a great blunder today. Don't take it ill. Pray to God to forgive me for my transgression.'

Just as innocent children forget neglect and thrashing after receiving a gift of sweets, Old Kaki was eating, forgetting everything. Good wishes were flowing out from every pore in her body, and Roopa was enjoying this heavenly sight.

Do Bailon Ki Katha (A Tale of Two Oxen)

1

The donkey is thought to be the most idiotic among creatures. At whatever point we need to call somebody a fool of the first water, we call him a jackass.

In any case, it isn't possible to decide if the donkey is really moronic, or it is his naivety and stony tolerance that has earned him this respect. A cow utilizes her horns, and a calved cow normally transforms into a tigress. The dog too is a humble creature, yet he too loses patience here and there.

Be that as it may, we have never observed or heard a donkey lose his temper. You may whip the poor fellow as much as you prefer, serve him the most spoiled grass, but then too you could never observe any indication of rebellion on his face. He may occasionally bray in joy in the long stretch of Baisakh, yet I have never seen a donkey in bliss.

A look of melancholy remains permanently etched on his face, which never changes in good or bad times. All the virtues that belong to the rishis and munis have touched their peak in him, and yet people call him stupid. We have never seen such a debasement of merit. May be simplicity is not something to be valued in this world. See, why the Indians are ill-treated in South Africa, and are not allowed to enter America! The poor fellows don't drink, save a few coins for bad times, work very hard, don't fight but instead keep quiet after uttering a few words. And yet they are maligned. It is said they have lowered the standards of living. Perhaps if they had learnt to hit back with a greater force, they would have been called civilized. Japan's example is before us. Just one victory has catapulted her into the class of civilized nations.

But the donkey has a younger brother, who is only slightly less donkeyish; and he is the ox. The sense in which we use the word 'donkey', we also use the phrase 'she-calf's great uncle'. Some people might call the ox is the first in stupidity, but I don't think that is so. The ox is sometimes aggressive, and sometimes he is headstrong. And he shows his resentment in many different ways. Therefore, to that extent, his status is lower than that of a donkey.

Jhuri, of the vegetable growers' caste, had two oxen, named Heera and Moti. Both belonged to the 'Pachchai' breed tall, handsome and sturdy. They had become friends. Both of them, sitting face to face or closeby, talked to each other in a sign language. How they understood each other we cannot say. Perhaps they possessed a special faculty which is denied to man, who claims to be the crown of the living world. Both expressed their love for each other by licking and smelling. Sometimes they locked their horns, not out of hostility but fun; like two friends engaged in a friendly combat, without which friendship would have looked dull and unreal, and not very trustworthy. Whenever both of them were yoked to the plough or a cart, they moved shaking their necks as if trying to take the maximum weight on their own necks. And when after the day's work they were unyoked, they relieved their weariness by licking each other. And when their fodder was put into the manger they stood up to eat together and when one stopped the other stopped too.

It so happened that one day Jhuri sent the pair to his in-laws. How could the oxen know why they had been sent away? They thought they had been sold. We cannot say whether or not the pair liked having been sold, but Jhuri's brother-in-law sweated between his teeth driving them homewards. If he goaded them from behind the two ran left or right, if he pulled them by their nose strap they pushed backwards. If he whipped them they lowered their horns and bellowed.

If God had given them speech, they would have asked Jhuri, 'Why are we being driven out? We have served you with all our devotion. If you had told us we were not working hard enough we could have worked harder. We were willing to die, serving you. We never complained about what you fed us. Ate whatever you gave us, with our heads down. And still you sold us to this cruel man.'

By the evening the pair reached their new destination. They had been hungry since morning, yet they did not lower their mouths into the manger. They were broken-hearted. What they thought was their home had been left behind. This new place, this new village, these new people – everything looked strange.

Both conferred in their sign language, looked at each other with slanted eyes, and lay down. When the village had gone to sleep, they broke their tether and made their way back home.

When Jhuri woke up in the morning he found both the oxen standing at the manger with the broken pieces of tether hanging round their necks. Their legs up to the knees were soiled with mud and both of them looked at Jhuri with an affectionate defiance.

Jhuri's heart was filled with love. He ran towards them and embraced them. This scene of embracing and kissing was a wonderful sight.

The family and the villagers came and stood around them clapping their hands in welcome. Although not something extraordinary, it was still a very special event in the village, and the boys of the village decided to honour the two animal heroes. One brought rotis, another gur, another seed cake and yet another fodder.

One of them said, 'These oxen are unique.'

Another agreed, 'They returned from so far unaided.'

The third said, 'They are not oxen. They were human beings in their previous life.'

No one dared refute this.

However, when Jhuri's wife saw them at the door, she became red with anger. She said, 'They are so ungrateful. Didn't work there even for a day and bolted.'

Jhuri could not stand this accusation and said, 'Why're they ungrateful? They were not fed properly. So they came back.'

The wife retorted, 'You alone know how to feed them, and others make them live on water.'

Jhuri hit back, 'Had they been fed they wouldn't have run back.'

The wife said, 'They ran back because people don't foolishly pamper their animals like you do. If they feed they make them work too. These two are shirkers, so they ran back. I will see how they get seed cake and wheat husk. I'll feed them only dry fodder, let them eat or not.'

And that is what happened. The attendant was strictly instructed to feed them only dry fodder.

When the oxen put their mouths into the manger to eat, they found the feed tasteless. No oil, no seedcake. What to eat! They looked at the door with expectant eyes.

Jhuri said to the attendant, 'Why don't you add some seed cake?'

'Malkin would kill me.'

'Do it without her knowing.'

'No, dada, later on you will throw the blame on me.'

2

The next day Jhuri's brother-in-law, Gaya, came again and

took the oxen away, this time yoking them to a cart.

Once or twice Moti tried to drive the cart into a ditch, but Heera pulled back. He was more forbearing.

In the evening when Gaya reached home he tethered them with a thick rope and thrashed them for their yesterday's escapade. He fed them only dry fodder, where to his own oxen he fed the usual diet including seed cake and pieces of dry rotis.

The duo had never been insulted like this. Jhuri had never touched them even with the lightest stick. Both of them would fly off merely at the click of his tongue. And here they had been thrashed. And this dry fodder now added insult to injury.

They didn't even look at the manger.

Next day Gaya yoked them to the plough. They refused to move even one step. Gaya thrashed them until he was tired. When Gaya hit repeatedly at Heera's muzzle, Moti became furious and broke loose and ran away with the plough. The plough, the rope and all the strappings were broken. Had there been no ropes round their necks, the two wouldn't have been caught.

Heera said in their sign language, 'No use running.'

Moti said, 'He nearly killed you. Now you'll get a big beating.'

'So what! Born an ox, you can't escape thrashing.'

Gaya was hurrying towards them with two men carrying

lathis.

Moti said, 'Should I give him a taste of his own medicine? He's coming here with lathis'

"No, brother, stop now.'

'If he thrashes me, I shall bring them down.'

'No, this is against our dharma.'

Moti was forced to restrain himself. Gaya came there and caught both of them and drove them back. Fortunately this time he did not resort to beating, otherwise Moti would have retaliated. Observing his mood, Gaya and his companions thought it wiser to be discrete.

Once again the two were served dry fodder. Both stood still. The family were eating their evening meal. Just then a small girl came out with tworotis and pushed them into their mouths. This did not alleviate their hunger, yet their hearts seemed satiated. Here too there was someone who was kind-hearted. The girl was Gaya's daughter. Her own mother was dead and the stepmother ill-treated her. That's why perhaps she had developed a soft corner for them.

Now both were yoked the whole day, beaten, but defiant. In the evening they were tethered to a stake. And the same little girl would come and feed them two rotis. As a result of this token of affection the two, in spite of the dry fodder they were fed, did not lose their strength. But their eyes, their hearts remained suffused with revolt.

One day Moti said, 'Heera, it's no longer possible to go on.'

'What do you want?'

'I'll toss one of them upon my horns.'

'But do you know that the sweet girl who feeds us with rotis is the owner's daughter. She would be orphaned.'

'Should I then toss up the wife? It is she who beats the girl.'

'But don't you know it's wrong to use violence against women?'

'But you don't show any way out. Should we break loose?'

'Yes, but how shall we cut this thick rope?'

'There's a way. Let's chew the rope first. Then it will snap with one jerk.'

At night, when the girl had fed them the two rotis, they began to chew their ropes. But the ropes were too thick to catch in the mouths. Poor fellows tried again and again but failed.

Suddenly the door opened and the same girl came out. Both of them began licking her hands, and raised their tails up. She patted their faces and said, 'I will untie you. Just run away from here, or these people will kill you. Today they are planning to put a halter through your noses.'

She untethered them. But the two stood still.

Moti asked, 'Why don't you move?'

Heera said that if they did, hell would be let loose on this girl. All would suspect her. Suddenly the girl began to shout, 'Oh dada, both the oxen are running away. Come, come quickly.'

Gaya came out in great confusion. The two oxen ran, chased by Gaya. Then Gaya returned to get some more villagers to help. This gave the pair a start and the two ran straight without knowing where they were going. They lost their way and now they found themselves in strange places. Then both of them stood at the edge of a field wondering what to do.

Heera said, 'Looks we have lost our way.'

'You ran like the mad. You should have brought him down.'

'If we had done that the people would have blamed us. If they don't follow their dharma, should we also do the same?'

Both were terribly hungry. They saw peas growing in the field and began to feed on them, wary of any danger.

When they had their fill, they felt they were free and began to frolic around. First they belched, then joined their horns and began to push one another. Moti pushed Heera so much that he fell into a ditch. Heera became angry, got up and recovered his balance and advanced towards Moti. When Moti saw that their frolic was leading to a fight he stepped aside.

3

Suddenly they saw a bull, bellowing and advancing towards them. Both the friends looked at him. He looked like an elephant. Fighting him was like inviting death, but not fighting was equally hazardous. He looked so terrible!

Moti said, 'We're in great danger. Think of a way out.'

Heera replied, 'He's drunk with pride. He won't listen to our entreaties.'

'Shouldn't we run away?'

'That would be cowardice.'

'Then die here. I'm going.'

'And if he chases you?'

'Then, think of a way out quickly.'

'The only way is for us to attack him together, I from front and you from rear. He won't be able to stand this two-prong attack. If he attacks me, you push your horns into his side. This is dangerous, but there's no other way.'

Both the friends attacked, risking their lives. The bull had no experience of fighting against two animals together. As he ran towards Heera, Moti attacked him from rear. When the bull turned towards Moti, Heera attacked him from the other side. The bull wanted to take them on one by one, but these two fought cleverly and did not give him that opportunity. When the bull made a decisive move to bring Heera down, Moti pushed his horn into his side.When he turned to attack Moti, Heera pushed his horn into the other flank. Wounded, the bull ran. The two now chased him and the poor fellow fell down, gasping for breath. Then the two let him go.

Both the friends were walking, relishing their victory.

Moti said in their sign language, 'I wanted to kill the fellow.'

Heera retorted, 'It's unfair to attack a fallen enemy.'

'This is hypocrisy. The enemy should be so hit that he can't rise again.'

'Think, how to reach home now?'

'Let's first eat something.'

The pea crop was right there. Moti entered the field against Heera's advice. They had just begun to eat when two men carrying lathis came running and closed on them. Heera was just on the edge and escaped. Moti could not run because his feet were caught in the soft soil that had been watered only recently. He was caught. When Heera saw this he came back to surrender. Both the oxen were now caught.

In the morning both the friends were locked up in the municipal yard for stray cattle, the Kanjihauz.

4

This was the first time ever in their lives that they did not get anything to eat for the whole day. They could not figure out the character of their new owner. Gaya was certainly better. There were buffaloes, sheep and goats, horses and donkeys here, but no one was being fed and all were lying half dead. A few had gone so weak they could hardly stand on their feet. The whole day the two friends kept staring at the gate, but they saw no trace of fodder. Then the two began to lick the salty mud on the walls, but this could not allay their hunger.

And when they did not get anything to eat, Heera became rebellious. He said to Moti, 'Now, I can't stand it anymore.'

Moti said, hanging his head down in dejection, 'It looks we are going to die.'

'Don't lose heart so soon. Think of a way to escape from here.'

'Come, let's bring down the wall.

'I won't be able to do anything now.'

'So this is all the toughness you have!'

'That's all gone.'

The wall of the municipal yard was built of mud. Heera rammed his horns into the wall and pushed. A piece of mud broke loose. This encouraged him. He ran again and again to the wall and drove his horns into it, and every time some chunks of mud came off the wall.

At that very time the chowkidar came there with a lantern, to count the animals. Observing Heera's wild behavior he squarely thrashed him with his lathi and then tethered him with a rope.

Moti said, 'So you got beaten up after all. What did you get?'

'But I applied all my strength.'

'What use was it? And now you're bound.'

'I'll keep doing it, in spite of all the ropes.'

'You will lose your life.'

'Who cares? We're going to die anyway. Just imagine if the wall had come down, so many lives would have been saved. So many are locked up here! All are almost lifeless. If this continues for some more days, they will die.'

'That is true. All right, I'll join you.'

Moti also thrust his horns into the same place. A chunk of mud came off. Encouraged, he began to dig his horns into the wall with all his force. He persisted and after about two hours half the wall came down.

As soon as the wall collapsed, all the half-dead animals suddenly came alive. The three mares were the first to bolt; then the goats, and then the buffaloes. But the donkeys stayed put.

Heera asked, 'Why don't you run away?'

One of the donkeys said, 'What if we're caught again?'

'So what? Now you have a chance to escape.'

'We're afraid. We shall keep lying here.'

It was past midnight. The donkeys were still undecided. Moti was busy cutting his friend's rope. And when he failed, Heera said, 'You go and leave me here. We might meet somewhere.'

Moti replied tearfully, 'Do you think I am so selfish. We have been together for so long. And now you want me to leave you when you're in trouble.'

Heera said, 'You will get a severe beating. They will think you are responsible for this.'

Moti replied with pride, 'I don't care if I am thrashed for what we have done. We have at least saved nine or ten lives. They will bless us.'

Saying this Moti drove the two donkeys out with his horns. Then he came and lay down close to his friend.

There is no need to describe the hullabaloo raised when the munshi, the chowkidar and other employees came there. Enough to say that Moti was given a sound beating and was bound with a rope like his friend.

5

For one full week the two friends remained bound in the kanjihauz. They were given nothing to eat, only water once a day. They had become so weak that their backbones had become prominent.

One day they heard a drum beat in front of the kanjihauz, and by the afternoon about fifty to sixty people had assembled there. Then the two friends were brought out. People came, looked at them and turned away uninterested. Who would buy such emaciated cattle?

Suddenly a bearded man, red-eyed and cruel looking, came there and started talking to the munshi, while prodding their haunches with his fingers. Both the friends were terrified at the very look of the man. They were in no doubt who he was and why he was interested in them. Both looked at each other and lowered their heads.

Heera said, 'Why did we run awayfrom Gaya.? Now we would lose our lives.'

Moti said irreverently, 'They say God is kind to all. Why doesn't He take pity on us?'

'For God it's the same whether we live or die. It's all right. We'll stay with this man for sometime. Once God came to our rescue in the shape of that small girl, won't he come again?'

'This man will use his chopper on us. You'll see.'

'Why worry? Our flesh, our skin, our bones, our horns all would be of some use to people.'

Having been sold, the two friends went with the bearded man. They were shivering in every limb.They were unable to walk steadily, but they continued to move driven by fear. The moment they slowed down they were hit with a stick.

On their way they saw a herd of cattle grazing in a green field. All the animals were happy, shiny skinned, quick-footed. One was jumping. Another sitting and leisurly chewing the cud. What a peaceful life! But how selfish they were! They were unmindful that two of their brothers were in the clutches of an executioner.

Suddenly they realized that this route was familiar to them. Yes, this was the route Gaya had taken to drive them to his village. The same fields, the same garden, the same villages. Now they began to move faster. All their weariness was gone. Lo and be hold, it was their own village. This was the same well where they used to drive the water-wheel.

Moti said, 'We're close to our home.'

Heera said, 'By God's blessing.'

'I'll run home now.'

'He won't let you.'

'I'll push him down.'

'No, no. Let's run up to our pen.'

Both of them ran towards their fold jumping like calves. Both of them came and stood there. The stout man also came there chasing them.

Jhuri was basking in the sun. The moment he saw the oxen he ran towards them and embraced them one by one. Their eyes were filled with tears of joy. One of them was licking Jhuri's hand.

The stout man came and caught the oxen by their ropes.

Jhuri said, 'These're my oxen.'

'How? I bought them in an auction from the kanjihauz.'

'I think you have stolen them. Just go away. These're my oxen. They can be bought only if I sell them. No one has the right to sell my oxen.'

'I'll go and report to the police.'

'These are my oxen. The proof is they have come to my doors.'

The bearded man tried to forcibly take away the oxen. At that very moment Moti advanced towards him lowering his horns. The man drew back. Moti chased him and the man began to run. Moti ran after him. Once outside the village the man stopped and started threatening, cursing and throwing stones. And Moti stood facing him. The villagers were having fun laughing at the show.

When the man had gone away, Moti returned in a triumphant mood.

Heera said, 'I was afraid you would kill him.'

"If he had caught me, I would certainly have hit him.'

'He won't come now.'

'If he comes, I'll teach him a lesson.'

'Suppose he gets you shot?'

'I'll die but won't be of any use to him.'

'No one values our lives.'

'Just because we're so simple!'

In a short while their manger was filled with fodder, seedcake and grain, and both of them began to eat.

Jhuri was standing there patting them, and dozens of boys were enjoying the sight. The whole village was in a state of excitement.

Just then Jhuri's wife came and kissed their faces.

Thakur Ka Kuan (Thakur's Well)

Jhokhu conveyed the lota to his mouth however the water smelled badly. He said to Gangi, 'What sort of water is this? It stinks so much! My throat is burning and you give me water that is unfit to drink.'

Each evening Gangi filled the water containers. The well was far off and it was hard for her to make several excursions. She'd brought this water yesterday and there'd been no terrible stench till then. How might it be there now? She brought the lota to her nostrils and it unquestionably smelled foul. Without a doubt some creature much likely had fallen into the well and died. In any case, she didn't know where else she could get any water.

No one would let her walk up to the Thakur's well. Even while she was far off, people would start yelling at her. At the other end of the village, the shopkeeper had a well but even there they wouldn't let her draw water. For people like herself there wasn't any well in the village. Jhokhu, who'd been sick for several days, held back his thirst for a little while. Then he said, 'I'm so thirsty I can't stand it. Bring me the water, I'll hold my nose and drink a little.

Gangi did not give it to him. His sickness would get worse from drinking bad water-that much she knew. But she didn't know that by boiling the water it would be made safe. She said, 'How can you drink it? Who knows what kind of beast has died in it! I'll go and get you some water from the well.' Surprised, Jokhu stared at her. 'Where can you get more water?' The Thakur and the shopkeeper both have wells. Won't they let me fill just one lota!'

'You'll come back with your arms and legs broken, that's all. You'd better just sit down and keep quiet. The Brahman will give a curse, the Thakur will beat you with a stick, and that money-lending shopkeeper takes five for every one he gives. Do you think people like that are going to let you draw water from their wells.' Harsh truth was in these words and Gangi could not deny it. But she wouldn't let him drink that stinking water.

By nine at night the dead-tired field hands were fast asleep. Gangi reached the Thakur's property to get water from his well. The dim glow of a small oil lamp lit up the well. Gangi sat hidden behind the wall and began to wait for the right moment. Everybody in the village drank the water from his well. It was closed to nobody; only those unlucky ones like herself could not use their buckets here.

Gangi [suddenly felt very angry.] Why was she so low and those others so high! Because they wore a thread around their necks? There wasn't one of them in the village who wasn't rotten. They stole, they cheated, they lied in court, [then how were they so high and mighty?] She heard people approaching the well and her heart began to pound. If anybody saw her, she'd get an awful kicking out of it. She grabbed her bucket and rope and crept away to hide in the dark shadows of a tree. Two women had come to draw water and they were talking. One said: 'There they were eating and they order us to get more water.' 'The men folk get jealous if they think they see us sitting around taking it easy.'

'That's right, and you'll never see them pick up the pitcher and fetch it themselves.' They just order us to get it as though we were slaves.' After they had filled their buckets and left, Gangi came out from the shadow of the tree and drew close to the well platform. The idlers had left, the Thakur had shut his door and gone inside to the courtyard to sleep. Gangi took a moment to sigh with relief. On every side, the field was clear. Gangi tiptoed up on to the well platform. Never before had she felt such a sense of triumph.

She looped the rope around the bucket. Like some soldier stealing into the enemy's fortress at night she peered cautiously on every side. If she were caught now, the slightest hope of mercy or leniency won't be there. Finally, with a prayer to the gods, she mustered her courage and cast the bucket into the well. Slowly, slowly it sank in the water. There was not the slightest sound. Gangi yanked it back up with all her might to the rim of the well. No strong-armed athlete could have dragged it up more swiftly.

She had just stooped to catch it and set it on the wall when suddenly the Thakur's door opened. The jaws of a tiger could not have terrified her more. The rope escaped from her hand. With a crash the bucket fell into the water, the rope after it, and for a few seconds there were sounds of splashing.

Yelling 'Who's there' Who's there?' the Thakur came toward the well and Gangi jumped from the platform and ran way as fast as she could. When she reached home, Jokhu, with the lota at his mouth, was drinking that filthy, stinking water.

Jurmana
(Penalty)

Munshi Khairat Ali Khan was the inspector of Sanitation and many sweeper ladies relied upon him. He was good-hearted and was respected - not the sort who cut their compensation, reproved them or fined them.

However, he went on frequently reproaching and rebuffing Alarakkhi. She was not a shirker, nor saucy or messy; she was likewise not in any manner ugly. During these chilly days she would be out with her sweeper before it was light and go on perseveringly clearing the street until nine. In any case, all the same, she would be punished. Huseni, her husband, would assist her with the work as well when he got the chance, yet it was in Alarakkhi's destiny that she would have been fined. For others pay-day was an event to celebrate, for Alarakkhi it was a time to cry.

On that day it was as though her heart had broken. Who could tell how much would be deducted! Like students awaiting the results of their examinations, over and over again she would speculate on the amount of the deduction.

Whenever she got so tired that she'd sit down a moment to catch her breath, precisely then the Inspector would arrive riding in his ekka. No matter how much she'd say, 'Please, Excellency, I'll go back to work again,' he would jot her name down in his book without listening. A few days later the very same thing would happen again. If she bought a few cents worth of candy from the sweets-vendor and started to eat it, just at that moment the Inspector would drop on her from the devil knew where and once more write her name down in his book. Where could he have been hiding?

The minute she began to rest the least bit he was upon her like an evil spirit. If he wrote her name down on only two days, how much would the penalty be then! God knew. More than eight annas? If only it weren't a whole rupee!With her head bowed she'd go to collect her pay and find even more deducted than she'd estimated. Taking her money with trembling hands she'd go home, her eyes full of tears. There was no one to turn to, no one who'd listen.

Today was pay-day again. The past month her unweaned daughter had suffered from coughing and fever.The weather had been exceptionally cold. Partly because of the cold, partly because of the little girl's crying she was kept awake the whole night. Several times she'd come to work late. Khan Sahib had noted down her name, and this time she would be fined half her pay. It was impossible to say how much might be deducted.

Early in the morning she picked up the baby, took her broom and went to the street.But the naughty creature wouldn't let herself be put down. Time after time Alarakkhi would threaten her with the arrival of the Inspector. 'He's on his way and he'll beat me and as for you, he'll cut off your nose and ears! 'The child was willing to sacrifice her nose and ears but not to be put down. At last, when Alarakkhi had failed to get rid of her with threats and coaxing alike, she set her down and left her crying and wailing while she started to sweep.

But the little wretch wouldn't sit in one place to cry her heart out; she crawled after her mother time and time again, caught her sari, clung to her legs, then wallowed around on the ground and a moment later sat up to start crying again. 'Shut up!' Alarakkhi said, brandishing the broom. 'If you don't, I'll hit you with the broom and that'll be the end of you. That bastard of an Inspector's going to show up at any moment.'She had hardly got the words out of her mouth when inspector Khairat Ali Khan dismounted from his bicycle directly in front of her. She turned pale, her heart began to thump. 'Oh God, may my head fall off if he heard me! Right in front of me and I didn't see him. Who could tell he'd come on his bicycle today? He's always come in his ekka.

'The blood froze in her veins, she stood holding the broom as though paralyzed. Angrily the Inspector said, 'Why do you drag the kid after you to work! Why didn't you leave it at home!' 'She's sick, Excellency' Alarakkhi said timidly. 'Who's at home to leave her with!' 'What's the matter with her?'

'She has a fever, Huzoor.'

'And you make her cry by leaving her? Don't you care if she lives? 'How can I do my work if I carry her?'

'Why don't you ask for leave!' 'If my pay is cut, Huzoor,

what will we have to live on?' 'Pick her up and take her home.When Huseni comes back send him here to finish the sweeping. She picked up the baby and was about to go when he asked, 'Why were you abusing me!' Alarakkhi felt all her breath knocked out of her. If you'd cut her there wouldn't have been any blood. Trembling she said, 'No, Huzoor, may my head fall off if I was abusing you. And she burst into tears.

In the evening Huseni and Alarakkhi went to collect her pay. She was very downcast. 'Why so sad?'Huseni tried to console her. 'The pay's going to be cut, so let them cut it. I swear on your life from now on I won't touch another drop of booze or toddy.'

'I'm afraid I'm fired. Damn my tongue! How could I....'

'If you're fired, then you're fired, but let Allah be merciful to him. Why go on crying about it?'

'You've made me come for nothing. Everyone of those women will laugh at me. 'If he's fired you, won't we ask on what grounds! And who heard you abuse him' Can there be so much injustice that he can fire anyone he pleases! If I'm not heard I'll complain to the panchayat, I'll beat my head on the headman's gate--'

'If our people stuck together like that would Khan Sahib ever dare fine us so much" 'No matter how serious the sickness there's a medicine for it, silly.'

But Alarakkhi was not set at rest. Dejection covered her face like a cloud. When the Inspector heard her abuse him why didn't he even scold her? Why didn't he ~re her on the spot! She wasn't able to work it out, he actually seemed kind. She couldn't manage to understand this mystery. She was afraid. He had decided to fire her- that must have been why he was so nice.She'd heard that a man about to be hanged is given a fine last meal, they have to give him anything he wants-so surely the Inspector was going to dismiss her.

They reached the municipal office building. The pay began to be distributed. The sweeper women were first. Whoever's name was called would go running and taking her money call down undeserved blessings on the Inspector and go away. Alarakkhi's name was always called after Champa's. Today she was passed over. After Champa, Jahuran's name was called, and she always followed Alarakkhi.

In despair she looked at Huseni.The women were watching her and beginning to whisper. One after another the names were called and Alarakkhi went on looking at the trees across the way.Suddenly startled, she heard her name. Slowly she stood up and walked ahead with the slow tread of a new bride.

The paymaster put the full amount of six rupees in her hand. She was stupefied. Surely the paymaster was mistaken! In these three years she had never once got her full pay. And now to get even half would have been a windfall.She stood there for a second in case the paymaster should ask for the money back.

When he asked her, 'Why are you standing here now, why don't you move along!' she said softly, 'But it's the full amount.' Puzzled the paymaster looked at her and said,

'What else do you want--do you want to get less!' 'There's no penalty deducted?' 'No, today there aren't any deductions. She came away but in her heart she was not content. She was full of remorse for having abused the Inspector.

Mukti Marg
(The Road to Salvation)

Whenever Jhingur looked at his cane fields, it kind of intoxicated him. He had three bighas of land which would win him a simple 600 rupees of livelihood. What's more, if God made sure that the rates went up, at that point who could complain. Both his bullocks were old so he'd purchase another match at the Batesar fair. On the off chance that he could snare on to another two bighas, so much the better. For what reason would it occur to him to stress over money?

He was persuaded that no one was better than himself- thus there was hardly anybody in the village he hadn't fought with.

One evening when he was sitting with his son in his lap, shelling peas, he saw a nock of sheep coming towards him. He said to himself, 'The sheep path doesn't come that way. Can't those sheep go along the bank? What's the idea, coming over here? They'll trample and gobble up the crop. I bet it's Buddhu the shepherd-- just look at his nerve! He can see me here but he won't drive his sheep back. What good will it do me to put up with this? If I try to buy a ram from him he actually asks for five rupees, and everybody sells blankets for four rupees but he won't settle for less than five.

By now the sheep were close to the cane-field. Jhingur yelled, 'Arrey, where do you think you're taking those sheep, you?' Buddhu said meekly, 'Chief, they're coming by way of the boundary embankment. If I take them back around it will mean a couple of miles extra.' 'And I'm supposed to let you trample my held to save you a detour! Why didn't you take them by way of some other boundary path! Do you think I'm some bull-skinning nobody or has your money turned your head' Turn 'em back!'

'Chief, just let them through today. If I ever come back this way again you can punish me any way you want.'

'I told you to get them out. If just one of them crosses the line you're going to be in a pack of trouble. 'Chief,' Buddhu said, 'if even one blade of grass gets under my sheep's feet you can call me anything you want.'

Although Buddhu was still speaking meekly he had decided that it would be a loss of face to turn back. 'If I drive the flock back for a few little threats: he thought, 'how will I graze my sheep?'

And Buddhu was a tough man too. He owned 240 sheep and he was able to get eight annas per night to leave them in people's fields to manure them, and he sold their milk as well and made blankets from their wool. He thought, 'Why's he getting so angry! What can he do to me? I'm not his servant.'

When the sheep got a whiff of the green leaves they became restless and they broke into the field. Beating them with his stick Buddhu tried to push them back across the boundary line but they just broke in somewhere else.

In a fury Jhingur said, 'You're trying to force your way through here but I'll teach you a lesson!' He put down his son and grabbing up his cudgel he began to whack the sheep. Not even a washer man would have beaten his donkey so cruelly. He smashed legs and backs and while they bleated Buddhu stood silent watching the destruction of his army. After this carnage among the host of sheep Jhingur said with the pride of victory, 'Now move on straight! And don't ever think about coming this way again.' Looking at his wounded sheep, Buddhu said, Jhingur, you've done a dirty job. You're going to regret it.'

When Jhingur came home and told his family about the battle, they started to give him advice. 'Jhingur, you've got yourself into real trouble! You knew what to do but you acted as though you didn't. Don't you realize what a tough customer Buddhu is! Even now it's not too late--go and make peace, otherwise the whole village will come to grief along with you.

Jhingur thought it over. He began to regret that he'd stopped Buddhu at all. If the sheep had eaten up a little of his crop it wouldn't have ruined him.Jhingur didn't enjoy the idea of going to Buddhu's house but urged on by the others he set out. It was the dead of winter, foggy, with the darkness settling in everywhere. He had just come out of the village when suddenly he was astonished to see a fire blazing over in the direction of his cane-held. His heart started to hammer. A field had caught fire! He ran wildly, hoping it wasn't his own field, but as he got closer this deluded hope died. He'd been struck by the very misfortune he'd set out to avert.

Buddhu had started the fire and was ruining the whole village because of him. As he ran it seemed to him that today his held was a lot nearer than it used to be, as though the fallow land between had ceased to exist. When he finally reached his field the fire had assumed dreadful proportions. Jhingur began to wail. The villagers were running and ripping up stalks of millet to beat the tire.

Among the men Buddhu was the most valiant fighter; with his dhoti tucked up around his waist he leapt into the fiery gulfs as though ready to subdue the enemy or die, and he'd emerge after many a narrow escape. In the end it was the men who triumphed, but the triumph amounted to defeat. The whole village's sugarcane crop was burned to ashes and with the cane all their hopes as well. It was no secret who had started the fire. But no one dared say anything about it.There was no proof and what was the point of a case without any evidence!

As for Jhingur, it had become difficult for him to show himself out of his house. Wherever he went he had to listen to abuse. People said right to his face, 'You were the cause of the fire! You ruined us, if you hadn't fought with Buddhu would all this have happened?' Jhingur was even more grieved by these taunts than by the destruction of his crop, and he would stay in his house the whole day.Jhingur thought and thought and decided that Buddhu had to be put in a situation exactly like his own. Buddhu had ruined him and he was wallowing in comfort, so Jhingur would ruin Buddhu too.Since the day of their terrible quarrel Buddhu had ceased to come by Jhingur's. Jhingur decided to cultivate an intimacy with him; he wanted to show him he had no suspicion at all that Buddhu started the fire.

One day, on the pretext of getting a blanket, he went to Buddhu, who greeted him with every courtesy and honour--for a man offers the hookah even to an enemy and won't let him depart without making him drink milk and syrup. These days Jhingur was earning a living by working in a jute-wrapping mill. Usually he got several days wages at once.

Only by means of Buddhu's help could he meet his daily expenses between times. So it was that Jhingur re-established a friendly footing between them.Spring came and the peasants were getting the fields ready for planting cane. Buddhu was doing a fine business. Everybody wanted his sheep. There were always a half dozen men at his door fawning on him, and he lorded it over everybody.He doubled the price of hiring out his sheep to manure the field; if anybody objected he'd say bluntly, 'Look, brother, I'm not shoving my sheep on you. If you don't want them, don't take them.

But I can't let you have them for a pice less than I said. 'The result was that everybody swarmed around him, despite his rudeness, just like priests after some pilgrim. Buddhu's house also began to grow.

A veranda was built in front of the door, six rooms replaced the former two. In short, the house was done over from top to bottom.

Buddhu got the wood from a peasant, from another the cow dung cakes for the kiln fuel to make the tiles; somebody else gave him the bamboo and reeds for the mats. He had to pay for having the walls put up but he didn't give any cash even for this; he gave some lambs. Such is the power of Lakshmi: the whole job--and it was quite a good house, all in all--was put up for nothing. They began to prepare for a house-warming.Jhingur was still labouring all day with but getting enough to half fill his belly, while gold was raining on Buddhu's house. If Jhingur was angry, who could blame him! Nobody could put up with such injustice.

One day Jhingur went out walking in the direction of the untouchable tanners' settlement. He called for Harihar, who came out, greeting him with 'Ram Ram!' and filled the hookah. They began to smoke.

Harihar, the leader of the tamers, was ? mean fellow and there wasn't a peasant who didn't tremble at the sight of him. After smoking a bit, Jhingur said, 'No singing for the spring festival these days! We haven't heard you. 'What festival? The belly can't take a holiday. Tell me, how are you getting on lately?' 'Getting by,' Jhingur said. 'Hard times mean a hard life. If I work all day in the mill there's a tire in my stove. But these days only Buddhu's making money. He doesn't have room to store it! He's built a new house, bought more sheep. Now there's a big hiss about his house-warming. He's sent paan to the headmen of all the seven villages around to invite everybody to it.' Then Jhingur and Harihar began to whisper, plotting their course of action--the method, the time and all the steps.

When Jhingur left he was strutting-- he'd already overcome his enemy, there was no way for Buddhu to escape now. On his way to work the next day he stopped by Buddhu's house. Buddhu asked him, 'Aren't you working today?' 'I'm on my way, but I came by to ask you if you wouldn't let my calf graze with your sheep. The poor thing's dying tied up to the post while I'm away all day, she doesn't get enough grass and fodder to eat.' 'Brother, I don't keep cows and buffaloes. You know the tanners, they're all killers. That Harihar killed my two cows, I don't know what he fed them. Since then I've vowed never again to keep cattle. But yours is just a calf, there'd be no profit to anyone in harming her. Bring her over whenever you want.'

Then he began to show Jhingur the arrangements for the house-warming. Ghee, sugar, flour and vegetables were all on hand.

All they were waiting for was the Satyanarayan ceremony. Jhingur's eyes were popping. When he came home after work the first thing he did was bring his calf to Buddhu's house. That night the ceremony was performed and a feast offered to the Brahmans. The whole night passed in lavishing hospitality on the priests. Buddhu had no opportunity to go to look after his flock of sheep. The feasting went on until morning.

Buddhu had just got up and had his breakfast when a man came and said, 'Buddhu, while you've been sitting around here, out there in your hock the calf has died.

You're a fine one! The rope was still around its neck.'When Buddhu heard this it was as though he'd been punched.

Jhingur, who was there having some breakfast too, said,' Oh God, my calf? Come on, I want to see her! But listen, I never tied her with a rope. I brought her to the flock of sheep and went back home. When did you have her tied with a rope, Buddhu'' 'God's my witness, I never touched any rope! I haven't been back to my sheep since then.' 'If you didn't, then who put the rope on her!' Jhingur said. 'You must have done it and forgotten it.' '

And it was in your flock,' one of the Brahmans said. 'People are going to say that whoever tied the rope, that heifer died because of Buddhu's negligence.'Harihar came along just then and said, 'I saw him tying the rope around the calf's neck last night.'

'Me?' Buddhu said. 'Wasn't that you with your stick over your shoulder tying up the heifer!'

'And you're an honest fellow, I suppose!' Buddhu said. 'You saw me tying her up?'

'Why get angry with me, brother! Let's just say you didn't tie her up, if that's what you want.'

'We will have to decide about it: one of the Brahmans said. 'A cow slaughterer should be stoned--it's no laughing matter. 'Maharaj,' Jhingur said, 'the killing was accidental.' 'What's that got to do with it!' the Brahman said. 'It's set down that no cow is ever to be done to death in any way.' 'That's right, 'Jhingur said, 'Just to tie a cow up is a fiendish act. 'In the Scriptures it's called the greatest sin,' the Brahman said. 'Killing a cow is no less than killing a Brahman.' 'That's right, 'Jhingur said. 'The cow's got a high place, that's why we respect her, isn't it' The cow is like a mother. But Maharaj, it was an accident--figure out something to get the poor fellow off.'Buddhu stood listening while the charge of murder was brought against him like the simplest thing in the world. He had no doubt it was Jhingur's plotting, but if he said a thousand times that he hadn't put the rope on the calf nobody would pay any attention to it. They'd say he was trying to escape the penance.

The outcome was that Buddhu was charged with the death of a cow; the Brahman had got very incensed about it too and he determined the manner of compensation.

The punishment consisted of three months of begging in the streets, then a pilgrimage to the seven holy places, and in addition the price for five cows and feeding 500 Brahmans. Stunned, Buddhu listened to it. He began to weep, and after that the period of begging was reduced by one month.

Apart from this he received no favour. There was no one to appeal to, no one to complain to. He had to accept the punishment. He gave up his sheep to God's care. His children were young and all by herself what could his wife do! The poor fellow would stand in one door after another hiding his face and saying, 'Even the gods are banished for cow-slaughter!' He received alms but along with them he had to listen to bitter insults.Whatever he picked up during the day he'd cook in the evening under some tree and then go to sleep right there. He did not mind the hardship, for he was used to wandering all day with his sheep and sleeping beneath trees, and his food at home hadn't been much better than this, but he was ashamed of having to beg, especially when some harridan would taunt him with, 'You've found a fine way to earn your bread!' That sort of thing hurt him profoundly but what could he do? He came home after two months. His hair was long, and he was as weak as though he were sixty years old.During the two months many of his sheep had been stolen. When the children took them to graze the other villagers would hide one or two sheep away in a field or hue and afterwards slaughter them and eat them. The boys, poor lads, couldn't catch a single one of them, and even when they saw, how could they fight' The whole village was banded together. It was an awful dilemma.

Helpless, Buddhu sent for a butcher and sold the whole flock to him for 500 rupees. He took 200 rupees and started out on his pilgrimage. The rest of the money he set aside for feeding the Brahmans. When Buddhu left, his house was burgled twice, but by good fortune the family woke up and the money was saved. It was Savan, the month of rains, with everything green. Jhingur, who had no bullocks now, had rented out his field to sharecroppers.

Buddhu had been heed from his penitential obligations and along with them his delusions about wealth. Neither one of them had anything left; neither could be angry with the other--there was nothing left to be angry about. Because the jute mill had closed down Jhingur went to work with pick and shovel in town where a very large rest house for pilgrims was being built. There were a thousand labourers on the job.

Every seventh day Jhingur would take his pay home and after spending the night there go back the next morning. Buddhu came to the same place looking for work. Once when he was going with a shallow pan on his head to get mortar Jhingur saw him. 'Ram Ram' they said to one another and Jhingur filled the pan. Buddhu picked it up. For the rest of the day they went about their work in silence. At the end of the day Jhingur asked, 'Are you going to cook something?' 'How can I eat if I don't?' Buddhu said. 'I eat solid food only once a day, 'Jhingur said. 'I get by just drinking water with ground meal in it in the evenings. Why fuss!' 'Pick up some of those sticks lying around,' Buddhu said. 'I brought some flour from home. I had it ground there---it costs a lot here in town. I'll knead it on the hat side of this rock. Since you won't eat food I cook I'll get it ready and you cook it.' 'But there's no frying pan.'

'There are lots of frying pans: Buddhu said. 'I'll scour out one of these mortar trays.'

The fire was lit, the flour kneaded. Jhingur cooked the chapatties, Buddhu brought the water. They both ate the bread with salt and red pepper. Then they filled the bowl of the hookah. They both lay down on the stony ground and smoked. Buddhu said, 'I was the one who set tire to your cane-field.'

Jhingur said light-heartedly, 'I know. After a little while he. said, 'I tied up the heifer and Harihar fed it something. In the same light-hearted tone Buddhu said, 'I know. Then the two of them went to sleep.

Poos ki Raat (January Night)

Halku came in and said to his wife, "The Landlord has come! Get the money you put aside, I'll give him the cash. Munni had been cleaning. She turned and said, 'But there is just three rupees. If you are going to give him this money, how will we buy the blanket? How are you going to get past these January nights in the fields! Tell him that we will pay him after the harvest, not at this moment.

For a minute Halku stood wavering. January was just round the corner. Without a blanket he couldn't in any way, survive in the fields during night time. Be that as it may, the proprietor wouldn't be put off, he'd insult him and threaten him. Trying to persuade her Halku said, 'Go ahead, give it to me. I'll think of some other plan later.'

Munni was angry. She said, "You've already tried. Some other plan". You just tell me what other plan can be found. Is somebody going to give you a blanket! What I say is, give up this tenant farming! The work's killing you, whatever you harvest goes to pay up the arrears. Were we born just to keep paying off debts! Earn some money for your own belly, give up that kind of farming. I won't give you the money, I won't!, Sadly Halku said, 'Then I'll have to put up with his abuse.'Losing her temper, Munni said, 'Why should he abuse you--is this his kingdom?' But as she said it her brews relaxed from the frown. The bitter truth in Halku's words came charging at her like a wild beast. She went to the niche in the wall, took out the rupees and handed them over to Halku.

Halku took the money and went outside looking as though he were tearing his heart out and giving it away. He'd saved the rupees from his work, pice by pice, for his blanket.

Today he was going to throw it away. With every step his head sank lower under the burden of his poverty.

A dark January night. In the sky even the stars seemed to be shivering. At the edge of his field, underneath a shelter of cane leaves, Halku lay on a bamboo cot wrapped up in his old burlap shawl, shivering. Underneath the cot his friend, Jabra the dog, was whimpering with his muzzle pressed into his belly. Neither one of them was able to sleep. Halku curled up drawing his knees close against his chin and said, 'Cold, Jabra! Didn't I tell you, in the house you could lie in the paddy straw! So why did you come out here!, Now you'll have to bear the cold, there's nothing I can do.

You thought I was coming out here to eat puris and sweets and you came running on ahead of me. Now you can moan all you want.' Jabra wagged his tail without getting up.Halku reached out his hand and patted Jabra's cold back. He got up, took some embers hem the pit and filled his pipe. Jabra got up too. Smoking, Halku said, 'If you smoke the cold's just as bad, but at least you feel a little betters'

Jabra looked at him with eyes overgrowing with love. 'You

have to put up with just one more cold night. Tomorrow I'll spread some straw. When you bed down in that you won't feel the cold.' Jabra put his paws on Halku's knees and brought his muzzle close.

Halku felt his warm breath.After he finished smoking Halku lay down and made up his mind that however things were he would sleep now. But in only one minute his he began to pound. He turned from side to side, but like some kind of witch the cold weather continued to torment him. When he could no longer bear it he gently picked Jabra up and, patting his he; got him to fall asleep in his lap. The dog's body gave off some kind of stink but Halku, hugging him tight, experienced a happiness he hadn't felt for months.Jabra probably thought he was in heaven, and in Halku's innocent heart there no resentment of his smell. He embraced him with the very same affection he would have felt for a brother or a friend.

Suddenly Jabra picked up the noise of some animal. This special intimacy had produced a new alertness in him that disdained the onslaught of the wind. Springing up, he ran out of the shelter and began to bark. Halku whistled and called him several times.

But Jabra would not come back to him. He went on barking while he ran around through the furrows of the field. He would come back for a moment, then dash off again at once.Another hour passed. The night fanned up the cold with the wind. Halku sat up and bringing both knees tight against his chest hid his face between them, but the cold was just as biting. It seemed is though all his blood had frozen, that ice rather than blood filled his veins.

He leaned back to look at the skies. How much of the night was still left! Only a stone's throw from Halku's field there was a mango grove. Halku thought, 'If I go and get a pile of leaves I can make a tire of them and keep warm. If anybody sees me gathering the leaves in the dead of night they'll think it's a ghost. Of course there's a chance some animal's hidden in my field waiting, but I can't stand sitting here any longer.' He ripped up some stalks from a nearby field, made a broom out of them and picking up a lighted cow dung cake went toward the grove.Jabra watched him coming and ran to him wagging his tail. Halku said, 'I couldn't stand it any more, Jabra. Come along, let's go into the orchard and gather leaves to warm up with. When we're toasted we'll come back and sleep. The night's still far from over.' Jabra barked his agreement and trotted on toward the orchard.

Suddenly a gust carried the scene of henna blossoms to him. 'Where's that sweet smell coming from, Jabra?' Jabra had found a bone lying somewhere and he was chewing on it.

Halku set his fire down on the ground and began to gather the leaves. In a little while he had a great heap. His hands were frozen, his bare feet numb. In a little while the fire was burning merrily. The dames leapt upward licking at the overhanging branches. In the flickering light the immense trees of the grove looked as though they were carrying the vast darkness on their heads. In the blissful sea of darkness the firelight seemed to pitch and toss like a boat. Halku sat before the fire and let it warm him.

After a while he took off his shawl and tucked it behind him, then he spread out both feet as though challenging the cold to do its worst. Victorious over the immense power of the winter, he could not repress his pride in his triumph.

He said to Jabra, 'Well, Jabra, you're not cold now, are you!' Jabra barked as though to say, 'How could I feel cold now!' The leaves were all burned up. Darkness covered the orchard again. Under the ashes a few embers smouldered. Halku wrapped himself up in his shawl again and sat by the warm ashes humming a tune. The fire had warmed him , through but as the cold began to spread he felt drowsy. Jabra gave a loud bark and ran toward the field.

Halku realized chat this meant a pack of wild animals had probably broken into the field. They might be nilgai. He distinctly heard the noise of their moving around. Then it seemed to him they must be grazing; he began to hear the sound of nibbling. He thought, 'No, with Jabra around no animal can get into the field, he'd rip it to shreds. I must have been mistaken. Now there's no sound at all. How could I have been mistaken!' He shouted, 'Jabra! Jabra!' Jabra went on barking and did not come to him.

Then again there was the sound of munching and crunching in the field. He could not have been mistaken this time. It really hurt to think about getting up from where he was. It was so comfortable there that it seemed intolerable to go to the field in this cold and chase after animals. He didn't stir. He shouted at the top of his lungs, 'Hillo! Hillo! Hillo!' Jabra started barking again. There were animals eating his held just when the crop was ready. What a fine crop it was! And these cursed animals were destroying it. With a firm resolve he got up and took a few steps.

But suddenly a blast of wind pierced him with a sting like a scorpion's so that he went back and sat again by the extinguished ~re and stirred up the ashes to warm his chilled body.

Jabra was barking his lungs out, the nilgai were devastating his field and Halku went on sitting peacefully near the warm ashes. His drowsiness held him motionless as though with ropes. Wrapped in his shawl he fell asleep on the warmed ground near the ashes.

When he woke in the morning the sun was high and Munni was saying, 'Do you think you're going to sleep all day! You came out here and had a fine time while the whole field was being flattened!' Halku got up and said, 'Then you've just come from the field!' 'Yes, it's all ruined. And you could sleep like that! Why did you bother to put up the shelter anyway?'

Halku sought an excuse. 'I nearly died and just managed to get through the night and you worry about your crop. I had such a pain in my belly I can't describe it.'Then the two of them walked to the edge of their land.

He looked: the whole field had been trampled and Jabra was stretched out underneath the shelter as though he were dead. They continued to stare at the ruined field. Munni's face was shadowed with grief but Halku was content. Munni said, 'Now you'll have to hire yourself out to earn some money to pay off the rent and taxes.'With a contented smile Halku said, 'But I won't have to sleep nights out here in the cold.'

Bade Bhai Sahab
(Big Brother)

My older brother was five years older than me yet just three grades ahead. He'd started his schooling at the same age I had yet he didn't like being hasty in an essential issue like education. He needed to establish a firm foundation for that great structure, so he took two years to complete one year's work; sometimes he even took three. In case that the foundations weren't well-made, how could the building persevere?

I was nine years old, he was fourteen. He had full right by precedence to oversee and instruct me. And I was supposed to follow his orders by law.

His disposition was that of a studious kid. He was mostly found sitting with a book open in front of him. Sometimes, for leisure and to rest his mind, he would draw pictures of birds, dogs and cats in the back of his notebooks.

Occasionally he would write a name, word or a sentence ten or twenty times. He might copy a couplet out several times in beautiful letters or create new words which made no rhyme or reason. I wasn't really very keen about studying.

To pick up a book and sit with it for an hour was a tremendous effort. As soon as I found a chance I'd leave the hostel and go to the field and play marbles or fly paper kites or sometimes just meet a chum--what could be more fun? But as soon as I came back into the room and saw my brother's scowling face I was petrified. His first question would be, 'Where were you!' Always this question, always asked in the same tone and the only answer I had was silence. I don't know why I couldn't manage to say that I'd just been outside playing.

My silence was an acknowledgement of guilt and my brother's only remedy for this was to greet me with indignant words. 'If you study English this way you'll be studying your whole life and you won't get one word right! Studying English is no laughing matter that anyone who wants to can learn. You've got to wear out your eyes morning and night and use every ounce of energy, then maybe you'll master the subject. And even then it's just to say you have a smattering of it.

Even great scholars can't write proper English, to say nothing of being able to speak it. End I ask you, how much of a blockhead are you chat you can't learn a lesson from looking at me? You've seen with your own eyes how much I grind. No matter how many shows and carnivals there may be have you ever seen me going to watch them?Every day there are cricket and hockey matches but I don't go near them. I keep on studying all the time, and even so it takes me two years or even three for one grade. So, how do you expect to pass when you waste your time playing like this? Why waste our dad's hard-earned money?'

Hearing a dressing-down like this I'd start to cry. My brother was an expert in the art of giving advice. He'd say such sarcastic words, overwhelm me with such good counsel that my spirits would collapse, my courage disappear. I'd think, 'Why don't I run away from school and go back home! Why should I spoil my life fiddling with work that's beyond my capacity? '

But after an hour or two the cloud of despair would clear away and I'd resolve to study with all my might. I'd draw up a schedule on the spot. How could I start work without first making an outline, working out a plan! In my timetable the heading of play was entirely absent. Get up at the crack of dawn, wash hands and face at six, eat a snack, sit down and study.

From six to eight English eight to nine arithmetic, nine to nine-thirty history, then meal-time and afterwards off to school. A half hour's rest at 3.30 when I got back from school, geography from four to five, grammar from five to six, then a half hour's wall; in front of the hostel, six-thirty to seven English composition, then supper, translation from eight to nine, Hindi from nine to ten, from ten to eleven miscellaneous, then to bed. But it's one thing to draw up a schedule, another to follow it.

It began to be neglected from the very first day. The inviting green expanse of the playground, the balmy winds, the commotion on the football field, the exciting stratagems of prisoner's-base, the speed and flurries of volleyball would all draw me mysteriously and irresistibly. As soon as I was there I forgot everything: the life-destroying schedule, the books that strained your eyes--I couldn't remember them at all.

And then my big brother would have an occasion for sermons and scolding. I would stay well out of his way, try to keep out of his sight, come into the room on tiptoe so he wouldn't know. But if he spotted me I'd just about die. The yearly exams came round: my brother failed, I passed and was first in my class. Only two year's difference was left between him and me.

Now I could be a little proud of myself and indeed my ego expanded. My brother's sway over me was over. I began to take part freely in the games, my spirits were running high. One day when I'd spent the whole morning playing stickball and came back exactly at meal-time, he said, with all the air of pulling out a sword to rush at me: 'I see you've passed this year and you're first in your class, and you've got stuck up about it. But my dear brother, even great men live to regret their pride, and who are you compared to them?

You must have read about what happened to Ravan.Just to pass an exam isn't anything, the real thing is to develop your mind. Understand the significance of what you read. Ravan was master of the earth. Such kings are called 'Rulers of the World'. All the kings of the earth paid taxes to him. Great divinities were his slaves, even the gods of fire and water.

But what happened to him in the end?Pride completely finished him off, destroying even his name. There wasn't anybody left to perform all his funeral rites properly. A man can commit any sin he wants but he'd better not be proud. When he turns proud he loses both this world and the next. You've just been promoted one grade and your head's turned by it. 'Don't assume that because I failed I'm stupid and you're smart.

When you reach my class you'll sweat right through lour teeth when you have to bite into algebra and geometry and study English history--it's not easy to memorize these king's names. There were eight Henrys--do you think it's easy to remember all the things that happened in each Henry's time? If you write Henry the Eighth instead of Henry the Seventh you get a zero. There were dozens of James, dozens of Williams and scores of Charles! You get dizzy with them, your mind's in a whirl.

Those poor fellows didn't have names enough to go around. After every name they have to put second, third, fourth and fifth. If anybody'd asked me I could have reeled off thousands of names. And as for geometry, well God help you! If you write a c b instead of a b c your whole answer is marked wrong. If you bring this Perpendicular line down on that line it will be twice the base line. I ask you, what's the point of that! If it isn't twice as long it's four times as long or half as long, what do I care! But you've got to pass so you've got to memorize all.

'They say, "Write an essay on punctuality no less than four pages long." So now you open up your notebook in front of you, take your pen and [hate] the whole business.

Who doesn't know that punctuality's a very good thing!A man's life is organized according to it, others love him for it and his business prospers from it. How can you write four pages on something so trifling! Do I need four pages for what I can describe in one sentence! It's not economizing time, it's wasting it. We want a man to say what he has to say quickly and then get moving. It's a contradiction for them to ask us to write concisely. Write a concise essay on punctuality in no less than four pages. All right! If four pages is concise then maybe otherwise they'd ask us to write one or two hundred pages. Run fast and walk slow at the same time. Is that all mixed up or isn't it! When you get into my class, you'll really take a beating, and then you'll find out what's what.

Just because you got a first division this time you're all puffed up--so pay attention to what I say. What if I failed, I'm still older than you, I have more experience of the world. Take what I say to heart or you'll be sorry.

It was almost time for school, otherwiseI don't know when this medley of sermons would have ended. I didn't have much appetite that day. If I got a scolding like this when I passed, maybe if I'd failed I would have had to pay with my life.My brother's terrible description of studying in the ninth grade really scared me. I'm surprised I didn't run away from school and go home. But even a scolding like this didn't change my distaste for books a bit, I didn't miss one chance to play. I also studied, but much less.

Well, anyway, just enough to complete the day's assignment and not be disgraced in class. But the confidence I'd gained in myself disappeared and then I began to lead a life like a thief.

Then it was the yearly exams again and it so happened that once more I passed and my brother failed again. I hadn't done much work; but somehow or other I was in the first division. I myself was astonished.

My brother had just about killed himself with work, memorizing every word in the course, studying till ten at night and starting again at four in the morning, and from six until 9.30 before going to school. He'd grown pale. But the poor fellow failed again and I felt sorry for him. When he heard the results he broke down and cried and so did I. My pleasure in passing was cut by half. There was only one grade left between my brother and me.

The evil thought crossed my mind that if he failed just once more I'd be at the same level as him and then what grounds would he have for lecturing me! But I violently rejected this unworthy idea.After all, he'd scolded me only with the intention of helping me.

At the time it was really bad, but maybe it was only as a result of his advice that I'd passed so easily and with such good marks. Now my brother had become much gentler toward me. Several times when he found occasion to scold me he did it without losing his temper. Perhaps he himself was beginning to understand that he no longer had the right to tell me o~-or at least not so much as before.My independence grew. I began to take unfair advantage of his toleration, I half started to imagine that I'd pass next time whether I studied or not, my luck was high.As a result, the little I'd studied before because of my brother, even that ceased. I found a new pleasure in flying kites and now I spent all my time at the sport.

Still, I minded my manners with my brother and concealed my kite-flying from him. In preparation for the kite tournament I was secretly busy solving such problems as how best to secure the string and how to apply the paste mixed with ground glass in it to cut the other fellows' kites off their strings. I didn't want to let my brother suspect that my respect for him had in any way diminished.

One day, far from the hostel, I was running along like mad trying to grab hold of a kite.A whole army of boys came racing out to welcome it with long, thick bamboo rods. Nobody was aware who was in front or in back of him. Suddenly I collided with my brother, who was probably coming back from the market.He grabbed my hand and said angrily, 'Aren't you ashamed to be running with these ragamuffins after a one-paisa kite;' Have you forgotten that you're not in a low grade any more! You're in the eighth now, one behind me. A man's got to have some regard for his position, after all. 'I'm sorry to see you have so little sense.

You're smart, there's no doubt of that, but what use is it if it destroys your self-respect? You must have assumed, 'I'm just one grade behind my brother so now he doesn't have any right to say anything to me."

But you're mistaken. I'm five years older than you and even if you come into my grade today that difference of five years between us not even God--to say nothing of you--can remove. I'm five years older than you and always will be.The experience I have of life and the world you can never catch up with even if you get an M.A. and a D.Litt. and even a Ph.D. Understanding doesn't come from reading books. Our mother never passed any grade and

Dad probably never went beyond the fifth, but even if we studied the wisdom of the whole world mother and father would always have the right to explain to us and to correct us.

Not just because they're our parents but because they'll always have more experience of the world. Maybe they don't know what kind of government they've got in America or how many constellations there are in the sky, but there are a thousand things they know more about than you or me. God forbid, but if I should fall sick today then you'd be [at your wit's end].

You wouldn't be able to think of anything except sending a telegram to Dad. But in your place he wouldn't send anybody a telegram or get upset or be all flustered.

First of all he'd diagnose the disease himself and try the remedy; then if it didn't work he'd call some doctor. But you and I don't even know how to make our allowance last through the month.We spend what father sends us and then we're penniless again.

But as much as you and I spend today, Dad's maintained himself honourably and in good reputation the greater part of his life and brought up a family on half of it. So brother, don't be so proud of having almost caught up with me and being independent now. I'll see that you don't go off the track. If you don't mind, then (showing me his fist) I can use this too.I know you don't like hearing all this. I was thoroughly shamed by this new approach of his. I had truly come to know my own insignificance and a new respect for my brother was born in my heart.With tears in my eyes, I said, 'No, no, what you say is completely true and you have the right to say it.'

My brother embraced me and said, 'I don't forbid you to fly kites. I'd like to too. But what can I do? If I go off- the track myself then how can I watch out for you! That's my responsibility.'Just then by chance a kite that had been cut loose passed over us with its string dangling down. A crowd of boys were chasing after it. My brother is very tall and leaping up he caught hold of the string and ran at top speed toward the hostel and I ran close behind him.

Vidhwans (Catastrophe)

In Banaras District there is a town called Bira in which an old, childless widow used to live. She was a Gond lady named Bhungi and she didn't possess either a piece of land or a house to live in. Her exclusive source of income was a parching oven. The village people usually have one meal a day of dried grains, so there was dependably a swarm around Bhungi's stove.

Whatever grain she was paid for drying she would grind or fry and eat it. She dozed in a corner of a same little shack that shielded the oven. In the dawn, she'd get up and go out to assemble dry leaves from all around to make her fire. She would stack the leaves alongside the stove, and light the fire after twelve.

But on the days when she had to parch grain for Pandit Udaybhan Pandey, the owner of the village, she went to bed hungry. She was obliged to work without pay for Pandit Udaybhan Pandey She also had to fetch water for his house. And, for this reason, from time to time the oven was not lit. She lived in the Pandit's village, therefore he had full authority to make her do any sort of odd job.In his opinion if she received food for working from him, how could it be considered as work done without pay? He was doing her a favour, in fact, by letting her live in the village at all.It was spring, a day on which the fresh grain was fried and eaten and given as a gift. No fire was lit in the houses Bhungi's oven was being put to good use today.

There was a crowd worthy of a village fair around her. She had scarcely opportunity to draw a breath. Because of the customer's impatience, squabbles kept breaking out.

Then two servants arrived, each carrying a heaped basket of grain from Pandit Udaybhan with the order to parch it right away. When Bhungi saw the two baskets she was alarmed.It was already after twelve and even by sunset, she would not have time to parch so much grain. Now she would have to stay at the oven parching until after dark for no payment.In despair she took the two baskets. One of the flunkeys said menacingly, 'Don't waste any time or you'll be sorry.' With this command the servants went away and

Bhungi began to parch the grain. It's no laughing matter to parch a whole maund of grain. She had to keep stopping from the parching in order to keep the oven fire going. So by sundown not even half the work was done. She was afraid Panditji's men would be coming. She began to move her hands all the more frantically.Soon the servants returned and said, 'Well, is the grain parched?' Feeling bold, Bhungi said, 'Can't you see? I'm parching it now.'

'The whole day's gone and you haven't finished any more grain than this! Have you been roasting it or spoiling it? This is completely uncooked! How's it going to be used for food? It's the ruin of us! You'll see what Panditji does to you for this.'

The result was that that night the oven was dug up and Bhungi was left without a means of livelihood. Bhungi now had no means of support. The villagers suffered a good deal too from the destruction of the oven. In many houses even at noon, cooked cereal was no longer available.

People went to Panditji and asked him to give the order for the old woman's oven to be rebuilt and the fire once more lighted, but he paid no attention to them. He could not suffer a loss of face.

A few people who wished her well urged her to move to another village. But her heart would not accept this suggestion. She had spent her fifty miserable years in this village and she loved every leaf on every tree. Here she had known the sorrows and pleasures of life; she could not give it up now in the last days. The very idea of moving distressed her. Sorrow in this village was preferable to happiness in another.A month went by. Very early one morning Pandit Udaybhan, taking his little band of servants with him, went out to collect his rents. Now when he looked toward the old woman's oven he fell into a violent rage: it was being made again.

Bhungi was energetically rebuilding it with balls of clay Most likely she'd spent the night at this work and wanted to finish it before the sun was high. She knew that she was going against the Pandit's wishes, but she hoped that he had forgotten his anger by then. But alas, the poor creature had gown old without growing wise.

Suddenly Panditji shouted, 'By whose order?' Bewildered, Bhungi saw that he was standing before her.He demanded once again, 'By whose order are you building it?' In a flight she said, 'Everybody said I should build it and so I'm building it.'

'I'll have it smashed again. 'With this he kicked the oven. The wet clay collapsed in a heap. He kicked at the trough again but she ran in front of it and took the kick in her side. Rubbing her ribs she said, 'Maharaj, you're not afraid of anybody but you ought to fear God. What good does it do you to ruin me like this!Do you think gold is going to grow out of this small piece of land! For your own good, I'm telling you, don't torment poor people, don't be the death of me. 'You're not going to build any oven here again. 'If I don't how am I going to be able to eat!' 'I'm not responsible for your belly.'

'But if I do nothing except chores for you where will I go for food!'

'If you're going to stay in the village you'll have to do my chores. 'I'll do them when I've built my over?. I can't do your work just for the sake of staying in the village. 'Then don't, just get out of the village. 'How can I! I've grown old in this hut. My in-laws and their grandparents lived in this same hut.

Except for Yama, king of death, nobody's going to force me out of it now. 'Excellent, now you're quoting Scripture!' Pandit Udaybhan said. 'lf you'd worked hard I might have let you stay, but after this I won't rest until I've had you thrown out. 'To his attendants he said, 'Go get a pile of leaves right away and set fire to the whole thing; we'll show her how to make an oven.In a moment there was a tremendous racket. The names leapt towards the sky, the blaze spread wildly in all directions till the villagers came clustering around this mountain of fire.

Hopelessly, Bhungi stood by her oven watching the conflagration. Suddenly, with a violent dash, she hurled herself into the names. They came running from everywhere but no one had the courage to go into the mouth of the blaze.In a matter of seconds her withered body was completely consumed.

At that moment the wind rose with a gust. The liberated flames began to race toward the east. There were some peasants' huts near the oven which were engulfed by the fierce flames. Fed in this way, the blaze spread even further. Panditji's barn was in its path and it pounced upon it.By now the whole village was in a panic. They began to band together to put out the fire but the sprinkle of water acted like oil on it and the flames kept mounting higher.

Pandit Udaybhan's splendid mansion was swallowed up; while he watched, it tossed like a ship amid wild waves and disappeared in the sea of fire. The sound of lamentation that broke out amidst the ashes was even more pitiful than Bhungi's grievous cries.

Rabindranath Tagore

(1861-1941)

Kabuliwallah (The Fruitseller From Kabul)

My little daughter who is five years of age cannot live without jabbering. I truly believe that in all her life she has not been quiet for a moment. Her mom is often bugged by this, and would stop her babble, but I would not. To see Mini silent is unnatural, and I can't bear with it for long. And so my own conversation with her is always exciting.

One morning, for example, when I was amidst the seventeenth chapter of my new novel, my little Mini snuck into the room, and putting her hand into mine, said to me, "Father! Ramdayal the doorkeeper calls a crow a krow! He knows nothing, does he?"

Before I could explain to her the differences of language in this world, she was embarked on the full tide of another subject. "What do you think, Father? Bhola says there is an elephant in the clouds, blowing water out of his trunk, and that is why it rains!"

And then, darting off anew, while I sat still making ready some reply to this last saying, "Father! what relation is Mother to you?"

"My dear little sister in the law!" I murmured involuntarily to myself, but with a grave face contrived to answer: "Go and play with Bhola, Mini! I am busy!"

The window of my room overlooks the road. The child had seated herself at my feet near my table, and was playing softly, drumming on her knees. I was hard at work on my seventeenth chapter, where Protrap Singh, the hero, had just caught Kanchanlata, the heroine, in his arms, and was about to escape with her by the third story window of the castle, when all of a sudden Mini left her play, and ran to the window, crying, "A Kabuliwallah! a Kabuliwallah!" Sure enough in the street below was a Kabuliwallah, passing slowly along. He wore the loose soiled clothing of his people, with a tall turban; there was a bag on his back, and he carried boxes of grapes in his hand.

I cannot tell what were my daughter's feelings at the sight of this man, but she began to call him loudly. "Ah!" I thought, "he will come in, and my seventeenth chapter will never be finished!" At which exact moment the Kabuliwallah turned, and looked up at the child. When she saw this, overcome by terror, she fled to her mother's protection, and disappeared. She had a blind belief that inside the bag, which the big man carried, there were perhaps two or three other children like herself. The pedlar meanwhile entered my doorway, and greeted me with a smiling face.

So precarious was the position of my hero and my heroine, that my first impulse was to stop and buy something, since the man had been called. I made some small purchases, and a conversation began about Abdurrahman, the Russians, the English, and the Frontier Policy.

As he was about to leave, he asked: "And where is the little girl, sir?"

And I, thinking that Mini must get rid of her false fear, had her brought out.

She stood by my chair, and looked at the Kabuliwallah and his bag. He offered her nuts and raisins, but she would not be tempted, and only clung the closer to me, with all her doubts increased.

This was their first meeting.

One morning, however, not many days later, as I was leaving the house, I was startled to find Mini, seated on a bench near the door, laughing and talking, with the great Kabuliwallah at her feet. In all her life, it appeared; my small daughter had never found so patient a listener, save her father. And already the corner of her little sari was stuffed with almonds and raisins, the gift of her visitor, "Why did you give her those?" I said, and taking out an eight-anna bit, I handed it to him. The man accepted the money without demur, and slipped it into his pocket.

Alas, on my return an hour later, I found the unfortunate coin had made twice its own worth of trouble! For the Kabuliwallah had given it to Mini, and her mother catching sight of the bright round object, had pounced on the child with: "Where did you get that eight-anna bit? "

"The Kabuliwallah gave it me," said Mini cheerfully.

"The Kabuliwallah gave it you!" cried her mother much shocked. "Oh, Mini! how could you take it from him?"

I, entering at the moment, saved her from impending disaster, and proceeded to make my own inquiries.

It was not the first or second time, I found, that the two had met. The Kabuliwallah had overcome the child's first terror by a judicious bribery of nuts and almonds, and the two were now great friends.

They had many quaint jokes, which afforded them much amusement. Seated in front of him, looking down on his gigantic frame in all her tiny dignity, Mini would ripple her face with laughter, and begin: "O Kabuliwallah, Kabuliwallah, what have you got in your bag?"

And he would reply, in the nasal accents of the mountaineer: "An elephant!" Not much cause for merriment, perhaps; but how they both enjoyed the witticism! And for me, this child's talk with a grown-up man had always in it something strangely fascinating.

Then the Kabuliwallah, not to be behindhand, would take his turn: "Well, little one, and when are you going to the father-in-law's house?"

Now most small Bengali maidens have heard long ago about the father-in-law's house; but we, being a little new-fangled, had kept these things from our child, and Mini at this question must have been a trifle bewildered. But she would not show it, and with ready tact replied: "Are you going there?"

Amongst men of the Kabuliwallah's class, however, it is well known that the words father-in-law's house have a double meaning. It is a euphemism for jail, the place where we are well cared for, at no expense to ourselves. In this sense would the sturdy pedlar take my daughter's question. "Ah," he would say, shaking his fist at an invisible policeman, "I will thrash my father-in-law!" Hearing this, and picturing the poor discomfited relative, Mini would go off into peals of laughter, in which her formidable friend would join.

These were autumn mornings, the very time of year when kings of old went forth to conquest; and I, never stirring from my little corner in Calcutta, would let my mind wander over the whole world. At the very name of another country, my heart would go out to it, and at the sight of a foreigner in the streets, I would fall to weaving a network of dreams, --the mountains, the glens, and the forests of his distant home, with his cottage in its setting, and the free and independent life of far-away wilds.

Perhaps the scenes of travel conjure themselves up before me, and pass and repass in my imagination all the more vividly, because I lead such a vegetable existence, that a call to travel would fall upon me like a thunderbolt.

In the presence of this Kabuliwallah, I was immediately transported to the foot of arid mountain peaks, with narrow little defiles twisting in and out amongst their towering heights. I could see the string of camels bearing the merchandise, and the company of turbaned merchants, carrying some of their queer old firearms, and some of their spears, journeying downward towards the plains. I could see--but at some such point Mini's mother would intervene, imploring me to "beware of that man."

Mini's mother is unfortunately a very timid lady. Whenever she hears a noise in the street, or sees people coming towards the house, she always jumps to the conclusion that they are either thieves, or drunkards, or snakes, or tigers, or malaria or cockroaches, or caterpillars, or an English sailor. Even after all these years of experience, she is not able to overcome her terror. So she was full of doubts about the Kabuliwallah, and used to beg me to keep a watchful eye on him.

I tried to laugh her fear gently away, but then she would turn round on me seriously, and ask me solemn questions.

Were children never kidnapped?

Was it, then, not true that there was slavery in Kabul?

Was it so very absurd that this big man should be able to carry off a tiny child?

I urged that, though not impossible, it was highly improbable. But this was not enough, and her dread persisted. As it was indefinite, however, it did not seem right to forbid the man the house, and the intimacy went on unchecked.

Once a year in the middle of January Rahmun, the Kabuliwallah, was in the habit of returning to his country, and as the time approached he would be very busy, going from house to house collecting his debts. This year, however, he could always find time to come and see Mini. It would have seemed to an outsider that there was some conspiracy between the two, for when he could not come in the morning, he would appear in the evening.

Even to me it was a little startling now and then, in the corner of a dark room, suddenly to surprise this tall, loose-garmented, much bebagged man; but when Mini would run in smiling, with her, "O! Kabuliwallah! Kabuliwallah!" and the two friends, so far apart in age, would subside into their old laughter and their old jokes, I felt reassured.

One morning, a few days before he had made up his mind to go, I was correcting my proof sheets in my study. It was chilly weather. Through the window the rays of the sun touched my feet, and the slight warmth was very welcome. It was almost eight o'clock, and the early pedestrians were returning home, with their heads covered. All at once, I heard an uproar in the street, and, looking out, saw Rahmun being led away bound between two policemen, and behind them a crowd of curious boys. There were blood-stains on the clothes of the Kabuliwallah, and one of the policemen carried a knife.

Hurrying out, I stopped them, and enquired what it all meant. Partly from one, partly from another, I gathered that a certain neighbour had owed the pedlar something for a Rampuri shawl, but had falsely denied having bought it, and that in the course of the quarrel, Rahmun had struck him. Now in the heat of his excitement, the prisoner began calling his enemy all sorts of names, when suddenly in a verandah of my house appeared my little Mini, with her usual exclamation: "O Kabuliwallah! Kabuliwallah!" Rahmun's face lighted up as he turned to her. He had no bag under his arm today, so she could not discuss the elephant with him. She at once therefore proceeded to the next question: "Are you going to the father-in-law's house?" Rahmun laughed and said: "Just where I am going, little one!" Then seeing that the reply did not amuse the child, he held up his fettered hands. " Ali," he said, " I would have thrashed that old father-in-law, but my hands are bound!"

On a charge of murderous assault, Rahmun was sentenced to some years' imprisonment.

Time passed away, and he was not remembered. The accustomed work in the accustomed place was ours, and the thought of the once-free mountaineer spending his years in prison seldom or never occurred to us. Even my light-hearted Mini, I am ashamed to say, forgot her old friend. New companions filled her life. As she grew older, she spent more of her time with girls. So much time indeed did she spend with them that she came no more, as she used to do, to her father's room. I was scarcely on speaking terms with her.

Years had passed away. It was once more autumn and we had made arrangements for our Mini's marriage. It was to take place during the Puja Holidays. With Durga returning to Kailas, the light of our home also was to depart to her husband's house, and leave her father's in the shadow.

The morning was bright. After the rains, there was a sense of ablution in the air, and the sun-rays looked like pure gold. So bright were they that they gave a beautiful radiance even to the sordid brick walls of our Calcutta lanes. Since early dawn to-day the wedding-pipes had been sounding, and at each beat my own heart throbbed. The wail of the tune, Bhairavi, seemed to intensify my pain at the approaching separation. My Mini was to be married to-night.

From early morning noise and bustle had pervaded the house. In the courtyard the canopy had to be slung on its bamboo poles; the chandeliers with their tinkling sound must be hung in each room and verandah. There was no end of hurry and excitement. I was sitting in my study, looking through the accounts, when some one entered, saluting respectfully, and stood before me. It was Rahmun the Kabuliwallah. At first I did not recognise him. He had no bag, nor the long hair, nor the same vigour that he used to have. But he smiled, and I knew him again.

"When did you come, Rahmun?" I asked him.

"Last evening," he said, "I was released from jail."

The words struck harsh upon my ears. I had never before talked with one who had wounded his fellow, and my heart shrank within itself, when I realised this, for I felt that the day would have been better-omened had he not turned up.

"There are ceremonies going on," I said, "and I am busy. Could you perhaps come another day?"

At once he turned to go; but as he reached the door he hesitated, and said: "May I not see the little one, sir, for a moment?" It was his belief that Mini was still the same. He had pictured her running to him as she used, calling "O Kabuliwallah! Kabuliwallah!" He had imagined too that they would laugh and talk together, just as of old. In fact, in memory of former days he had brought, carefully wrapped up in paper, a few almonds and raisins and grapes, obtained somehow from a countryman, for his own little fund was dispersed.

I said again: "There is a ceremony in the house, and you will not be able to see any one to-day."

The man's face fell. He looked wistfully at me for a moment, said "Good morning," and went out. I felt a little sorry, and would have called him back, but I found he was returning of his own accord. He came close up to me holding out his offerings and said: "I brought these few things, sir, for the little one. Will you give them to her?"

I took them and was going to pay him, but he caught my hand and said: "You are very kind, sir! Keep me in your recollection. Do not offer me money!--You have a little girl, I too have one like her in my own home. I think of her, and bring fruits to your child, not to make a profit for myself."

Saying this, he put his hand inside his big loose robe, and brought out a small and dirty piece of paper. With great care he unfolded this, and smoothed it out with both hands on my table. It bore the impression of a little band. Not a photograph. Not a drawing. The impression of an ink-smeared hand laid flat on the paper. This touch of his own little daughter had been always on his heart, as he had come year after year to Calcutta, to sell his wares in the streets.

Tears came to my eyes. I forgot that he was a poor Kabuli fruit-seller, while I was--but no, what was I more than he? He also was a father. That impression of the hand of his little Parbati in her distant mountain home reminded me of my own little Mini.

I sent for Mini immediately from the inner apartment. Many difficulties were raised, but I would not listen. Clad in the red silk of her wedding-day, with the sandal paste on her forehead, and adorned as a young bride, Mini came, and stood bashfully before me.

The Kabuliwallah looked a little staggered at the apparition. He could not revive their old friendship. At last he smiled and said: "Little one, are you going to your father-in-law's house?"

But Mini now understood the meaning of the word "father-in-law," and she could not reply to him as of old. She flushed up at the question, and stood before him with her bride-like face turned down.

I remembered the day when the Kabuliwallah and my Mini had first met, and I felt sad. When she had gone, Rahmun heaved a deep sigh, and sat down on the floor. The idea had suddenly come to him that his daughter too must have grown in this long time, and that he would have to make friends with her anew. Assuredly he would not find her, as he used to know her. And besides, what might not have happened to her in these eight years?

The marriage-pipes sounded, and the mild autumn sun streamed round us. But Rahmun sat in the little Calcutta lane, and saw before him the barren mountains of Afghanistan.

I took out a bank-note, and gave it to him, saying: "Go back to your own daughter, Rahmun, in your own country, and may the happiness of your meeting bring good fortune to my child!"

Having made this present, I had to curtail some of the festivities. I could not have the electric lights I had intended, nor the military band, and the ladies of the house were despondent at it. But to me the wedding feast was all the brighter for the thought that in a distant land a long-lost father met again with his only child.

The Postmaster

The postmaster initially took up his duties in the town of Ulapur. In spite of the fact that the town was a little one, there was an indigo processing plant close by, and the proprietor, an Englishman, had figured out how to get a post office built up.

Our postmaster was from Calcutta. He felt like a fish out of water in this remote village. His office and family room were in a dull covered shed, not a long way from a green, muddy pond, encompassed on all sides by a thick growth of weed.

The men employed in the indigo factory had no leisure; moreover, they were hardly desirable companions for decent folk. Nor is a Calcutta boy an adept in the art of associating with others. Among strangers he appears either proud or ill at ease. At any rate, the postmaster had but little company; nor had he much to do.

At times he tried his hand at writing a verse or two. That the movement of the leaves and the clouds of the sky were enough to fill life with joy ¬such were the sentiments to which he sought to give expression. But God knows that the poor fellow would have felt it as the gift of a new life, if some genie of the Arabian Nights had in one night swept away the trees, leaves and all, and replaced them with a macadamised road, hiding the clouds from view with rows of tall houses.

The postmaster's salary was small. He had to cook his own meals, which he used to share with Ratan, an orphan girl of the village, who did odd jobs for him.

When in the evening the smoke began to curl up from the village cowsheds, and the crickets chirped in every bush; when the mendicants of the Baul sect sang their shrill songs in their daily meeting-place, when any poet, who had attempted to watch the movement of the leaves in the dense bamboo thickets, would have felt a ghostly shiver run down his back, the postmaster would light his little lamp, and call out "Ratan."

Ratan would sit outside waiting for this call, and, instead of coming in at once, would reply, "Did you call me, sir?"

"What are you doing?" the postmaster would ask.

"I must be going to light the kitchen fire," would be the answer.

And the postmaster would say: "Oh, let the kitchen fire be for awhile; light me my pipe first."

At last Ratan would enter, with puffed-out cheeks, vigorously blowing into a flame a live coal to light the tobacco. This would give the postmaster an opportunity of conversing. "Well, Ratan," perhaps he would begin, "do you remember anything of your mother?" That was a fertile subject. Ratan partly remembered, and partly didn't. Her father had been fonder of her than her mother; him she recollected more vividly. He used to come home in the evening after his work, and one or two evenings stood out more clearly than others, like pictures in her memory. Ratan would sit on the floor near the postmaster's feet, as memories crowded in upon her. She called to mind a little brother that she had ¬and how on some bygone cloudy day she had played at fishing with him on the edge of the pond, with a twig for a make-believe fishing-rod. Such little incidents would drive out greater events from her mind. Thus, as they talked, it would often get very late, and the postmaster would feel too lazy to do any cooking at all. Ratan would then hastily light the fire, and toast some unleavened bread, which, with the cold remnants of the morning meal, was enough for their supper.

On some evenings, seated at his desk in the corner of the big empty shed, the postmaster too would call up memories of his own home, of his mother and his sister, of those for whom in his exile his heart was sad, ¬memories which were always haunting him, but which he could not talk about with the men of the factory, though he found himself naturally recalling them aloud in the presence of the simple little girl. And so it came about that the girl would allude to his people as mother, brother, and sister, as if she had known them all her life. In fact, she had a complete picture of each one of them painted in her little heart.

One noon, during a break in the rains, there was a cool soft breeze blowing; the smell of the damp grass and leaves in the hot sun felt like the warm breathing of the tired earth on one's body. A persistent bird went on all the afternoon repeating the burden of its one complaint in Nature's audience chamber.

The postmaster had nothing to do. The shimmer of the freshly washed leaves, and the banked-up remnants of the retreating rain-clouds were sights to see; and the postmaster was watching them and thinking to himself: "Oh, if only some kindred soul were near ¬just one loving human being whom I could hold near my heart!" This was exactly, he went on to think, what that bird was trying to say, and it was the same feeling which the murmuring leaves were striving to express. But no one knows, or would believe, that such an idea might also take possession of an ill-paid village postmaster in the deep, silent mid-day interval of his work.

The postmaster sighed, and called out "Ratan." Ratan was then sprawling beneath the guava-tree, busily engaged in eating unripe guavas. At the voice of her master, she ran up breathlessly, saying: "Were you calling me, Dada?" "I was thinking," said the postmaster, "of teaching you to read." And then for the rest of the afternoon he taught her the alphabet.

Thus, in a very short time, Ratan had got as far as the double consonants.

It seemed as though the showers of the season would never end. Canals, ditches, and hollows were all overflowing with water. Day and night the patter of rain was heard, and the croaking of frogs. The village roads became impassable, and marketing had to be done in punts.

One heavily clouded morning, the postmaster's little pupil had been long waiting outside the door for her call, but, not hearing it as usual, she took up her dog-eared book, and slowly entered the room. She found her master stretched out on his bed, and, thinking that he was resting, she was about to retire on tip-toe, when she suddenly heard her name ¬"Ratan!" She turned at once and asked: "Were you sleeping, Dada?" The postmaster in a plaintive voice said: "I am not well. Feel my head; is it very hot?"

In the loneliness of his exile, and in the gloom of the rains, his ailing body needed a little tender nursing. He longed to remember the touch on the forehead of soft hands with tinkling bracelets, to imagine the presence of loving womanhood, the nearness of mother and sister. And the exile was not disappointed. Ratan ceased to be a little girl. She at once stepped into the post of mother, called in the village doctor, gave the patient his pills at the proper intervals, sat up all night by his pillow, cooked his gruel for him, and every now and then asked: "Are you feeling a little better, Dada?"

It was some time before the postmaster, with weakened body, was able to leave his sick-bed. "No more of this," said he with decision. "I must get a transfer." He at once wrote off to Calcutta an application for a transfer, on the ground of the unhealthiness of the place.

Relieved from her duties as nurse, Ratan again took up her old place outside the door. But she no longer heard the same old call. She would sometimes peep inside furtively to find the postmaster sitting on his chair, or stretched on his bed, and staring absent-mindedly into the air. While Ratan was awaiting her call, the postmaster was awaiting a reply to his application. The girl read her old lessons over and over again, ¬her great fear was lest, when the call came, she might be found wanting in the double consonants. At last, after a week, the call did come one evening. With an overflowing heart Ratan rushed into the room with her ¬"Were you calling me, Dada?"

The postmaster said: "I am going away to-morrow, Ratan."

"Where are you going, Dada?"

"I am going home."

"When will you come back?"

"I am not coming back."

Ratan asked no other question. The postmaster, of his own accord, went on to tell her that his application for a transfer had been rejected, so he had resigned his post and was going home.

For a long time neither of them spoke another word. The lamp went on dimly burning, and from a leak in one corner of the thatch water dripped steadily into an earthen vessel on the floor beneath it.

After a while Ratan rose, and went off to the kitchen to prepare the meal; but she was not so quick about it as on other days. Many new things to think of had entered her little brain. When the postmaster had finished his supper, the girl suddenly asked him: "Dada, will you take me to your home?"

The postmaster laughed. "What an idea!" said he; but he did not think it necessary to explain to the girl wherein lay the absurdity.

That whole night, in her waking and in her dreams, the postmaster's laughing reply haunted her ¬"What an idea!"

On getting up in the morning, the postmaster found his bath ready. He had stuck to his Calcutta habit of bathing in water drawn and kept in pitchers, instead of taking a plunge in the river as was the custom of the village. For some reason or other, the girl could not ask him about the time of his departure, so she had fetched the water from the river long before sunrise, that it should be ready as early as he might want it. After the bath came a call for Ratan. She entered noiselessly, and looked silently into her master's face for orders. The master said: "You need not be anxious about my going away, Ratan; I shall tell my successor to look after you." These words were kindly meant, no doubt: but inscrutable are the ways of a woman's heart!

Ratan had borne many a scolding from her master without complaint, but these kind words she could not bear. She burst out weeping, and said: "No, no, you need not tell anybody anything at all about me; I don't want to stay on here."

The postmaster was dumbfounded. He had never seen Ratan like this before.

The new incumbent duly arrived, and the postmaster, having given over charge, prepared to depart. Just before starting he called Ratan and said: "Here is something for you; I hope it will keep you for some little time." He brought out from his pocket the whole of his month's salary, retaining only a trifle for his travelling expenses. Then Ratan fell at his feet and cried: "Oh, Dada, I pray you, don't give me anything, don't in any way trouble about me," and then she ran away out of sight.

The postmaster heaved a sigh, took up his carpet bag, put his umbrella over his shoulder, and, accompanied by a mancarrying his many-coloured tin trunk, he slowly made for the boat.

When he got in and the boat was under way, and the rain-swollen river, like a stream of tears welling up from the earth, swirled and sobbed at her bows, then he felt a pain at heart; the grief-stricken face of a village girl seemed to represent for him the great unspoken pervading grief of Mother Earth herself. At one time he had an impulse to go back, and bring away along with him that lonesome waif, forsaken of the world. But the wind had just filled the sails, the boat had got well into the middle of the turbulent current, and already the village was left behind, and its outlying burning-ground came in sight.

So the traveller, borne on the breast of the swift-flowing river, consoled himself with philosophical reflections on the numberless meetings and partings going on in the world ¬on death, the great parting, from which none returns.

But Ratan had no philosophy. She was wandering about the post office in a flood of tears. It may be that she had still a lurking hope in some corner of her heart that her Dada would return, and that is why she could not tear herself away. Alas for our foolish human nature! Its fond mistakes are persistent. The dictates of reason take a long time to assert their own sway. The surest proofs meanwhile are disbelieved. False hope is clung to with all one's might and main, till a day comes when it has sucked the heart dry and it forcibly breaks through its bonds and departs. After that comes the misery of awakening, and then once again the longing to get back into the maze of the same mistakes.

The Castaway

Towards night the tempest was at its climax. From the tremendous storm of rain, the crash of thunder, and the recurring flashes of lightning, you may imagine that a clash of the divine beings and evil spirits was raging in the skies. Dark clouds waved like the Flags of Doom. The Ganges was lashed into a fierceness, and the trees of the gardens on either bank groaned and sighed.

In a shut room of one of the riverside houses at Chandernagore, a couple was seated on a quilt on the floor, eagerly engaged in a conversation. An earthen lamp burned alongside them.

The husband, Sharat, was saying: "I wish you would stay on a few days more; you would then be able to return home quite strong again."

The wife, Kiran, was saying: "I have quite recovered already. It will not, cannot possibly, do me any harm to go home now."

Every married person will at once understand that the conversation was not quite so brief as I have reported it. The matter was not difficult, but the arguments for and against did not advance it towards a solution. Like a rudderless boat, the discussion kept turning round and round the same point; and at last threatened to be overwhelmed in a flood of tears.

Sharat said: "The doctor thinks you should stop here a few days longer."

Kiran replied: "Your doctor knows everything!"

"Well," said Sharat, "you know that just now all sorts of illnesses are abroad. You would do well to stop here a month or two more."

"And at this moment I suppose every one in this place is perfectly well!"

What had happened was this: Kiran was a universal favourite with her family and neighbours, so that, when she fell seriously ill, they were all anxious. The village wiseacres thought it shameless for her husband to make so much fuss about a mere wife and even to suggest a change of air, and asked if Sharat supposed that no woman had ever been ill before, or whether he had found out that the folk of the place to which he meant to take her were immortal. Did he imagine that the writ of Fate did not run there? But Sharat and his mother turned a deaf ear to them, thinking that the little life of their darling was of greater importance than the united wisdom of a village. People are wont to reason thus when danger threatens their loved ones. So Sharat went to Chandernagore, and Kiran recovered, though she was still very weak. There was a pinched look on her face which filled the beholder with pity, and made his heart tremble, as he thought how narrowly she had escaped death.

Kiran was fond of society and amusement; the loneliness of her riverside villa did not suit her at all. There was nothing to do, there were no interesting neighbours, and she hated to be busy all day with medicine and dieting. There was no fun in measuring doses and making fomentations. Such was the subject discussed in their closed room on this stormy evening.

So long as Kiran deigned to argue, there was a chance of a fair fight. When she ceased to reply, and with a toss of her head disconsolately looked the other way, the poor man was disarmed. He was on the point of surrendering unconditionally when a servant shouted a message through the shut door.

Sharat got up and on opening the door learnt that a boat had been upset in the storm, and that one of the occupants, a young Brahmin boy, had succeeded in swimming ashore at their garden.

Kiran was at once her own sweet self and set to work to get out some dry clothes for the boy. She then warmed a cup of milk and invited him to her room.

The boy had long curly hair, big expressive eyes, and no sign yet of hair on the face. Kiran, after getting him to drink some milk asked him all about himself.

He told her that his name was Nilkanta, and that he belonged to a theatrical troupe. They were coming to play in a neighbouring villa when the boat had suddenly foundered in the storm. He had no idea what had become of his companions. He was a good swimmer and had just managed to reach the shore.

The boy stayed with them. His narrow escape from a

terrible death made Kiran take a warm interest in him. Sharat thought the boy's appearance at this moment rather a good thing, as his wife would now have something to amuse her, and might be persuaded to stay on for some time longer. Her mother-in-law, too, was pleased at the prospect of profiting their Brahmin guest by her kindness. And Nilkanta himself was delighted at his double escape from his master and from the other world, as well as at finding a home in this wealthy family.

But in a short while Sharat and his mother changed their opinion, and longed for his departure. The boy found a secret pleasure in smoking Sharat's hookahs; he would calmly go off in pouring rain with Sharat's best silk umbrella for a stroll through the village, and make friends with all whom he met. Moreover, he had got hold of a mongrel village dog which he petted so recklessly that it came indoors with muddy paws, and left tokens of its visit on Sharat's spotless bed. Then he gathered about him a devoted band of boys of all sorts and sizes, and the result was that not a solitary mango in the neighbourhood had a chance of ripening that season.

There is no doubt that Kiran had a hand in spoiling the boy. Sharat often warned her about it, but she would not listen to him. She made a dandy of him with Sharat's cast-off clothes, and gave him new ones also. And because she felt drawn towards him, and had a curiosity to know more about him, she was constantly calling him to her own room. After her bath and midday meal Kiran would be seated on the bedstead with her betel-leaf box by her side; and while her maid combed and dried her hair, Nilkanta would stand in front and recite pieces out of his repertory with appropriate gesture and song, his elf-locks waving wildly. Thus the long afternoon hours passed merrily away. Kiran would often try to persuade Sharat to sit with her as one of the audience, but Sharat, who had taken a cordial dislike to the boy, refused; nor could Nilkanta do his part half so well when Sharat was there. His mother would sometimes be lured by the hope of hearing sacred names in the recitation; but love of her mid-day sleep speedily overcame devotion, and she lay lapped in dreams.

The boy often got his ears boxed and pulled by Sharat, but as this was nothing to what he had been used to as a member of the troupe, he did not mind it in the least. In his short experience of the world he had come to the conclusion that, as the earth consisted of land and water, so human life was made up of eatings and beatings, and that the beatings largely predominated.

It was hard to tell Nilkanta's age. If it was about fourteen or fifteen, then his face was too old for his years; if seventeen or eighteen, then it was too young. He was either a man too early or a boy too late. The fact was that, joining the theatrical band when very young, he had played the parts of Radhika, Damayanti, and Sita, and a thoughtful Providence so arranged things that he grew to the exact stature that his manager required, and then growth ceased.

Since every one saw how small Nilkanta was, and he himself felt small, he did not receive due respect for his years. Causes, natural and artificial, combined to make him sometimes seem immature for seventeen years, and at other times a mere lad of fourteen but far too knowing even for seventeen. And as no sign of hair appeared on his face, the confusion became greater. Either because he smoked or because he used language beyond his years, his lips puckered into lines that showed him to be old and hard; but innocence and youth shone in his large eyes. I fancy that his heart remained young, but the hot glare of publicity had been a forcing-house that ripened untimely his outward aspect.

In the quiet shelter of Sharat's house and garden at Chandernagore, Nature had leisure to work her way unimpeded. Nilkanta had lingered in a kind of unnatural youth, but now he silently and swiftly overpassed that stage. His seventeen or eighteen years came to adequate revelation. No one observed the change, and its first sign was this, that when Kiran treated him like a boy, he felt ashamed. When the gay Kiran one day proposed that he should play the part of lady's companion, the idea of woman's dress hurt him, though he could not say why. So now, when she called for him to act over again his old characters, he disappeared.

It never occurred to Nilkanta that he was even now not much more than a lad-of-all-work in a strolling company. He even made up his mind to pick up a little education from Sharat's factor. But, because he was the pet of his master's wife, the factor could not endure the sight of him. Also, his restless training made it impossible for him to keep his mind long engaged; sooner or later, the alphabet did a misty dance before his eyes. He would sit long enough with an open book on his lap, leaning against a champak bush beside the Ganges. The waves sighed below, boats floated past, birds flitted and twittered restlessly above. What thoughts passed through his mind as he looked down on that book he alone knew, if indeed he did know. He never advanced from one word to another, but the glorious thought, that he was actually reading a book, filled his soul with exultation. Whenever a boat went by, he lifted his book, and pretended to be reading hard, shouting at the top of his voice. But his energy dropped as soon as the audience was gone.

Formerly he sang his songs automatically, but now their tunes stirred in his mind. Their words were of little import and full of trifling alliteration. Even the feeble meaning they had was beyond his comprehension; yet when he sang —

Twice-born bird, ah! wherefore stirred

To wrong our royal lady?

Goose, ah, say why wilt thou slay

Her in forest shady?

then he felt as if transported to another world and to fear other folk. This familiar earth and his own poor life became music, and he was transformed. That tale of the goose and the king's daughter flung upon the mirror of his mind a picture of surpassing beauty. It is impossible to say what he imagined himself to be, but the destitute little slave of the theatrical troupe faded from his memory.

When with evening the child of want lies down, dirty and hungry, in his squalid home, and hears of prince and princess and fabled gold, then in the dark hovel with its dim flickering candle, his mind springs free from its bonds of poverty and misery and walks in fresh beauty and glowing raiment, strong beyond all fear of hindrance, through that fairy realm where all is possible.

Even so, this drudge of wandering players fashioned himself and his world anew, as he moved in spirit amid his songs. The lapping water, rustling leaves, and calling birds; the goddess who had given shelter to him, the helpless, the God-forsaken; her gracious, lovely face, her exquisite arms with their shining bangles, her rosy feet as soft as flower-petals; all these by some magic became one with the music of his song. When the singing ended, the mirage faded, and the Nilkanta of the stage appeared again, with his wild elf-locks. Fresh from the complaints of his neighbour, the owner of the despoiled mango-orchard, Sharat would come and box his ears and cuff him. The boy Nilkanta, the misleader of adoring youths, went forth once more, to make ever new mischief by land and water and in the branches that are above the earth.

Shortly after the advent of Nilkanta, Sharat's younger brother, Satish, came to spend his college vacation with them. Kiran was hugely pleased at finding a fresh occupation. She and Satish were of the same age, and the time passed pleasantly in games and quarrels and reconciliations and laughter and even tears. Suddenly she would clasp him over the eyes from behind with vermilion-stained hands, or she would write "monkey" on his back, or else she would bolt the door on him from the outside amidst peals of laughter. Satish in his turn did not take things lying down; he would steal her keys and rings; he would put pepper among her betel, he would tie her to the bed when she was not looking.

Meanwhile, heaven only knows what possessed poor Nilkanta. He was suddenly filled with a bitterness which he must avenge on somebody or something. He thrashed his devoted boy-followers for no fault, and sent them away crying. He would kick his pet mongrel till it made the skies resound with its whinings. When he went out for a walk, he would litter his path with twigs and leaves beaten from the roadside shrubs with his cane.

Kiran liked to see people enjoying good fare. Nilkanta had an immense capacity for eating, and never refused a good thing however often it was offered. So Kiran liked to send for him to have his meals in her presence, and ply him with delicacies, happy in the bliss of seeing this Brahmin boy eat to satiety. After Satish's arrival she had much less spare time on her hands, and was seldom present when Nilkanta's meals were served. Before, her absence made no difference to the boy's appetite, and he would not rise till he had drained his cup of milk and rinsed it thoroughly with water.

But now, if Kiran was not present to ask him to try this and that, he was miserable, and nothing tasted right. He would get up, without eating much, and say to the serving-maid in a choking voice: "I am not hungry." He thought in imagination that the news of his repeated refusal, "I am not hungry," would reach Kiran; he pictured her concern, and hoped that she would send for him, and press him to eat. But nothing of the sort happened. Kiran never knew and never sent for him; and the maid finished whatever he left. He would then put out the lamp in his room, and throw himself on his bed in the darkness, burying his head in the pillow in a paroxysm of sobs. What was his grievance? Against whom? And from whom did he expect redress? At last, when no one else came, Mother Sleep soothed with her soft caresses the wounded heart of the motherless lad.

Nilkanta came to the unshakable conviction that Satish was poisoning Kiran's mind against him. If Kiran was absent-minded, and had not her usual smile, he would jump to the conclusion that some trick of Satish had made her angry with him. He took to praying to the gods, with all the fervour of his hate, to make him at the next rebirth Satish, and Satish him. He had an idea that a Brahmin's wrath could never be in vain; and the more he tried to consume Satish with the fire of his curses, the more did his own heart burn within him. And upstairs he would hear Satish laughing and joking with his sister-in-law.

Nilkanta never dared openly to show his enmity to Satish. But he would contrive a hundred petty ways of causing him annoyance. When Satish went for a swim in the river, and left his soap on the steps of the bathing-place, on coming back for it he would find that it had disappeared. Once he found his favourite striped tunic floating past him on the water, and thought it had been blown away by the wind.

One day Kiran, desiring to entertain Satish, sent for Nilkanta to recite as usual, but he stood there in gloomy silence. Quite surprised, Kiran asked him what was the matter. But he remained silent. And when again pressed by her to repeat some particular favourite piece of hers, he answered: "I don't remember," and walked away.

At last the time came for their return home. Everybody was busy packing up. Satish was going with them. But to Nilkanta nobody said a word. The question whether he was to go or not seemed to have occurred to nobody.

The subject, as a matter of fact, had been raised by Kiran, who had proposed to take him along with them. But her husband and his mother and brother had all objected so strenuously that she let the matter drop. A couple of days before they were to start, she sent for the boy, and with kind words advised him to go back to his own home.

So many days had he felt neglected that this touch of kindness was too much for him; he burst into tears. Kiran's eyes were also brimming over. She was filled with remorse at the thought that she had created a tie of affection, which could not be permanent.

But Satish was much annoyed at the blubbering of this overgrown boy. "Why does the fool stand there howling instead of speaking?" said he. When Kiran scolded him for an unfeeling creature, he replied: "My dear sister, you do not understand. You are too good and trustful. This fellow turns up from the Lord knows where, and is treated like a king. Naturally the tiger has no wish to become a mouse again. And he has evidently discovered that there is nothing like a tear or two to soften your heart."

Nilkanta hurriedly left the spot. He felt he would like to be a knife to cut Satish to pieces; a needle to pierce him through and through; a fire to burn him to ashes. But Satish was not even scared. It was only his own heart that bled and bled.

Satish had brought with him from Calcutta a grand inkstand. The inkpot was set in a mother-of-pearl boat drawn by a German-silver goose supporting a penholder. It was a great favourite of his, and he cleaned it carefully every day with an old silk handkerchief. Kiran would laugh, and tapping the silver bird's beak would say —

Twice-born bird, ah! wherefore stirred

To wrong our royal lady?

and the usual war of words would break out between her and her brother-in-law.

The day before they were to start, the inkstand was missing and could nowhere be found. Kiran smiled, and said: "Brother-in-law, your goose has flown off to look for your Damayanti."

But Satish was in a great rage. He was certain that Nilkanta had stolen it—for several people said they had seen him prowling about the room the night before. He had the accused brought before him. Kiran also was there. "You have stolen my inkstand, you thief!" he blurted out. "Bring it back at once." Nilkanta had always taken punishment from Sharat, deserved or undeserved, with perfect equanimity. But, when he was called a thief in Kiran's presence, his eyes blazed with a fierce anger, his breast swelled, and his throat choked. If Satish had said another word, he would have flown at him like a wild cat and used his nails like claws.

Kiran was greatly distressed at the scene, and taking the boy into another room said in her sweet, kind way: "Nilu, if you really have taken that inkstand give it to me quietly, and I shall see that no one says another word to you about it." Big tears coursed down the boy's cheeks, till at last he hid his face in his hands, and wept bitterly. Kiran came back from the room and said: "I am sure Nilkanta has not taken the inkstand." Sharat and Satish were equally positive that no other than Nilkanta could have done it.

But Kiran said determinedly: "Never."

Sharat wanted to cross-examine the boy, but his wife refused to allow it.

Then Satish suggested that his room and box should be searched. And Kiran said: "If you dare do such a thing I will never forgive you. You shall not spy on the poor innocent boy." And as she spoke, her wonderful eyes filled with tears. That settled the matter and effectually prevented any further molestation of Nilkanta.

Kiran's heart overflowed with pity at this attempted outrage on a homeless lad. She got two new suits of clothes and a pair of shoes, and with these and a banknote in her hand she quietly went into Nilkanta's room in the evening. She intended to put these parting presents into his box as a surprise. The box itself had been her gift.

From her bunch of keys she selected one that fitted and noiselessly opened the box. It was so jumbled up with odds and ends that the new clothes would not go in. So she thought she had better take everything out and pack the box for him. At first knives, tops, kite-flying reels, bamboo twigs, polished shells for peeling green mangoes, bottoms of broken tumblers and such like things dear to a boy's heart were discovered. Then there came a layer of linen, clean and otherwise. And from under the linen there emerged the missing inkstand, goose and all.

Kiran, with flushed face, sat down helplessly with the inkstand in her hand, puzzled and wondering.

In the meantime, Nilkanta had come into the room from behind without Kiran knowing it. He had seen the whole thing and thought that Kiran had come like a thief to catch him in his thieving,—and that his deed was out. How could he ever hope to convince her that he was not a thief, and that only revenge had prompted him to take the inkstand, which he meant to throw into the river at the first chance? In a weak moment he had put it in the box instead. "He was not a thief," his heart cried out, "not a thief!" Then what was he? What could he say? That he had stolen, and yet he was not a thief? He could never explain to Kiran how grievously wrong she was. And then, how could he bear the thought that she had tried to spy on him?

At last Kiran with a deep sigh replaced the inkstand in the box, and, as if she were the thief herself, covered it up with the linen and the trinkets as they were before; and at the top she placed the presents, together with the banknote which she had brought for him.

The next day the boy was nowhere to be found. The villagers had not seen him; the police could discover no trace of him. Said Sharat: "Now, as a matter of curiosity, let us have a look at his box." But Kiran was obstinate in her refusal to allow that to be done.

She had the box brought up to her own room; and taking out the inkstand alone, she threw it into the river.

The whole family went home. In a day the garden became desolate. And only that starving mongrel of Nilkanta's remained prowling along the river-bank, whining and whining as if its heart would break.

Subha

At the point when the young girl was given the name of Subhashini, who could have speculated that she would turn out to be dumb? Her two elder sisters were Sukeshini and Suhasini, and for consistency her father named his youngest ydaughter Subhashini. She was called Subha.

Her two elder sisters had been married with the standard cost and trouble, and now the youngest one lay like a quiet burden upon the heart of her parents. All the world assumed that, since she didn't talk, therefore she did not feel; it examined her future and its own anxiousness openly when she was around. She had understood from the time when she was very young, that God had sent her like a curse on her family, so she pulled back herself from ordinary folks and attempted to live aloof. If only they would all overlook her she believed she could bear with it all.

But who can forget pain? Night and day her parents' minds were aching on her account. Especially her mother looked upon her as a deformity in herself. To a mother a daughter is a more closely intimate part of herself than a son can be; and a fault in her is a source of personal shame. Banikantha, Subha's father, loved her rather better than his other daughters; her mother regarded her with aversion as a stain upon her own body.

If Subha lacked speech, she did not lack a pair of large

dark eyes, shaded with long lashes; and her lips trembled like a leaf in response to any thought that rose in her mind.

When we express our thought in words, the medium is not found easily. There must be a process of translation, which is often inexact, and then we fall into error.

But black eyes need no translating; the mind itself throws a shadow upon them. In them thought opens or shuts, shines forth or goes out in darkness, hangs steadfast like the setting moon or like the swift and restless lightning illumines all quarters of the sky. They who from birth have had no other speech than the trembling of their lips learn a language of the eyes, endless in expression, deep as the sea, clear as the heavens, wherein play dawn and sunset, light and shadow. The dumb have a lonely grandeur like Nature's own. Wherefore the other children almost dreaded Subha and never played with her. She was silent and companionless as noontide.

The hamlet where she lived was Chandipur. Its river, small for a river of Bengal, kept to its narrow bounds like a daughter of the middle class. This busy streak of water never overflowed its banks, but went about its duties as though it were a member of every family in the villages beside it. On either side were houses and banks shaded with trees. So stepping from her queenly throne, the river-goddess became a garden deity of each home, and forgetful of herself performed her task of endless benediction with swift and cheerful foot.

Banikantha's house looked out upon the stream. Every hut and stack in the place could be seen by the passing boatmen. I know not if amid these signs of worldly wealth any one noticed the little girl who, when her work was done, stole away to the waterside and sat there. But here Nature fulfilled her want of speech and spoke for her. The murmur of the brook, the voice of the village folk, the songs of the boatmen, the crying of the birds and rustle of trees mingled and were one with the trembling of her heart. They became one vast wave of sound which beat upon her restless soul. This murmur and movement of Nature were the dumb girl's language; that speech of the dark eyes, which the long lashes shaded, was the language of the world about her. From the trees, where the cicalas chirped, to the quiet stars there was nothing but signs and gestures, weeping and sighing.

And in the deep mid-noon, when the boatmen and fisher-folk had gone to their dinner, when the villagers slept and birds were still, when the ferry-boats were idle, when the great busy world paused in its toil and became suddenly a lonely, awful giant, then beneath the vast impressive heavens there were only dumb Nature and a dumb girl, sitting very silent,—one under the spreading sunlight, the other where a small tree cast its shadow.

But Subha was not altogether without friends. In the stall were two cows, Sarbbashi and Panguli. They had never heard their names from her lips, but they knew her footfall. Though she had no words, she murmured lovingly and they understood her gentle murmuring better than all speech. When she fondled them or scolded or coaxed them, they understood her better than men could do. Subha would come to the shed and throw her arms round Sarbbashi's neck; she would rub her cheek against her friend's, and Panguli would turn her great kind eyes and lick her face. The girl paid them three regular visits every day and others that were irregular. Whenever she heard any words that hurt her, she would come to these dumb friends out of due time. It was as though they guessed her anguish of spirit from her quiet look of sadness. Coming close to her, they would rub their horns softly against her arms, and in dumb, puzzled fashion try to comfort her.

Besides these two, there were goats and a kitten; but Subha had not the same equality of friendship with them, though they showed the same attachment. Every time it got a chance, night or day, the kitten would jump into her lap, and settle down to slumber, and show its appreciation of an aid to sleep as Subha drew her soft fingers over its neck and back.

Subha had a comrade also among the higher animals, and it is hard to say what were the girl's relations with him; for he could speak, and his gift of speech left them without any common language. He was the youngest boy of the Gosains, Pratap by name, an idle fellow.

After long effort, his parents had abandoned the hope that he would ever make his living. Now losels have this advantage, that, though their own folk disapprove of them, they are generally popular with every one else. Having no work to chain them, they become public property. Just as every town needs an open space where all may breathe, so a village needs two or three gentlemen of leisure, who can give time to all; then, if we are lazy and want a companion, one is to hand.

Pratap's chief ambition was to catch fish. He managed to waste a lot of time this way, and might be seen almost any afternoon so employed. It was thus most often that he met Subha.

Whatever he was about, he liked a companion; and, when one is catching fish, a silent companion is best of all. Pratap respected Subha for her taciturnity, and, as every one called her Subha, he showed his affection by calling her Su. Subha used to sit beneath a tamarind, and Pratap, a little distance off, would cast his line. Pratap took with him a small allowance of betel, and Subha prepared it for him. And I think that, sitting and gazing a long while, she desired ardently to bring some great help to Pratap, to be of real aid, to prove by any means that she was not a useless burden to the world. But there was nothing to do. Then she turned to the Creator in prayer for some rare power, that by an astonishing miracle she might startle Pratap into exclaiming: "My! I never dreamt our Su could have done this!"

Only think, if Subha had been a water nymph, she might have risen slowly from the river, bringing the gem of a snake's crown to the landing-place. Then Pratap, leaving his paltry fishing, might dive into the lower world, and see there, on a golden bed in a palace of silver, whom else but dumb little Su, Banikantha's child? Yes, our Su, the only daughter of the king of that shining city of jewels! But that might not be, it was impossible. Not that anything is really impossible, but Su had been born, not into the royal house of Patalpur, but into Banikantha's family, and she knew no means of astonishing the Gosains' boy.

Gradually she grew up. Gradually she began to find herself. A new inexpressible consciousness like a tide from the central places of the sea, when the moon is full, swept through her. She saw herself, questioned herself, but no answer came that she could understand.

Once upon a time, late on a night of full moon, she slowly opened her door and peeped out timidly. Nature, herself at full moon, like lonely Subha, was looking down on the sleeping earth. Her strong young life beat within her; joy and sadness filled her being to its brim; she reached the limits even of her own illimitable loneliness, nay, passed beyond them. Her heart was heavy, and she could not speak. At the skirts of this silent troubled Mother there stood a silent troubled girl.

The thought of her marriage filled her parents with an anxious care. People blamed them, and even talked of making them outcasts. Banikantha was well off; they had fish-curry twice daily; and consequently he did not lack enemies. Then the women interfered, and Bani went away for a few days. Presently he returned and said: "We must go to Calcutta."

They got ready to go to this strange country. Subha's heart was heavy with tears, like a mist-wrapt dawn. With a vague fear that had been gathering for days, she dogged her father and mother like a dumb animal. With her large eyes wide open, she scanned their faces as though she wished to learn something. But not a word did they vouchsafe. One afternoon in the midst of all this, as Pratap was fishing, he laughed: "So then, Su, they have caught your bridegroom, and you are going to be married! Mind you don't forget me altogether!" Then he turned his mind again to his fish. As a stricken doe looks in the hunter's face, asking in silent agony: "What have I done to you?" so Subha looked at Pratap. That day she sat no longer beneath her tree. Banikantha, having finished his nap, was smoking in his bedroom when Subha dropped down at his feet and burst out weeping as she gazed towards him. Banikantha tried to comfort her, and his cheek grew wet with tears.

It was settled that on the morrow they should go to Calcutta. Subha went to the cow-shed to bid farewell to her childhood's comrades. She fed them with her hand; she clasped their necks; she looked into their faces, and tears fell fast from the eyes which spoke for her. That night was the tenth of the moon. Subha left her room, and flung herself down on her grassy couch beside her dear river. It was as if she threw her arms about Earth, her strong silent mother, and tried to say: "Do not let me leave you, mother. Put your arms about me, as I have put mine about you, and hold me fast."

One day in a house in Calcutta, Subha's mother dressed her up with great care. She imprisoned her hair, knotting it up in laces, she hung her about with ornaments, and did her best to kill her natural beauty. Subha's eyes filled with tears. Her mother, fearing they would grow swollen with weeping, scolded her harshly, but the tears disregarded the scolding. The bridegroom came with a friend to inspect the bride. Her parents were dizzy with anxiety and fear when they saw the god arrive to select the beast for his sacrifice. Behind the stage, the mother called her instructions aloud, and increased her daughter's weeping twofold, before she sent her into the examiner's presence. The great man, after scanning her a long time, observed: "Not so bad."

He took special note of her tears, and thought she must have a tender heart. He put it to her credit in the account, arguing that the heart, which to-day was distressed at leaving her parents, would presently prove a useful possession. Like the oyster's pearls, the child's tears only increased her value, and he made no other comment.

The almanac was consulted, and the marriage took place on an auspicious day. Having delivered over their dumb girl into another's hands, Subha's parents returned home. Thank God! Their caste in this and their safety in the next world were assured! The bridegroom's work lay in the west, and shortly after the marriage he took his wife thither.

In less than ten days every one knew that the bride was dumb! At least, if any one did not, it was not her fault, for she deceived no one. Her eyes told them everything, though no one understood her. She looked on every hand, she found no speech, she missed the faces, familiar from birth, of thosc who had understood a dumb girl's language. In her silent heart there sounded an endless, voiceless weeping, which only the Searcher of Hearts could hear.

The Hungry Stones

My cousin and myself were coming back to Calcutta from our Puja trip when we met the man in a train. From his dress and bearing we took him at first for an up-nation Mahomedan, however we were confused as we heard him talk. He talked upon all subjects so assertively that you may think the Disposer of All Things counseled him consistently in all that He did. Up to this point we had been happy, as we didn't realize that mystery and inconceivable powers which were at work, that the Russians had advanced closer to us, that the English had profound and mysterious strategies, that confusions among the local chiefs had reached a crucial stage.

In any case, our new friend said with a wily grin: "There happen more things in paradise and earth, Horatio, than are accounted for in your daily papers."

As we had never stirred out of our homes before, the demeanour of the man struck us dumb with wonder. Be the topic ever so trivial, he would quote science, or comment on the Vedas, or repeat quatrains from some Persian poet; and as we had no pretence to a knowledge of science or the Vedas or Persian, our admiration for him went on increasing, and my kinsman, a theosophist, was firmly convinced that our fellow-passenger must have been supernaturally inspired by some strange "magnetism" or "occult power," by an "astral body" or something of that kind. He listened to the tritest saying that fell from the lips of our extraordinary companion with devotional rapture, and secretly took down notes of his conversation. I fancy that the extraordinary man saw this, and was a little pleased with it.

When the train reached the junction, we assembled in the waiting room for the connection. It was then 10 P.M., and as the train, we heard, was likely to be very late, owing to something wrong in the lines, I spread my bed on the table and was about to lie down for a comfortable doze, when the extraordinary person deliberately set about spinning the following yarn. Of course, I could get no sleep that night.

When, owing to a disagreement about some questions of administrative policy, I threw up my post at Junagarh, and entered the service of the Nizam of Hydria, they appointed me at once, as a strong young man, collector of cotton duties at Barich.

Barich is a lovely place. The Susta "chatters over stony ways and babbles on the pebbles," tripping, like a skilful dancing girl, in through the woods below the lonely hills. A flight of 150 steps rises from the river, and above that flight, on the river's brim and at the foot of the hills, there stands a solitary marble palace. Around it there is no habitation of man—the village and the cotton mart of Barich being far off.

About 250 years ago the Emperor Mahmud Shah II. had built this lonely palace for his pleasure and luxury. In his days jets of rose-water spurted from its fountains, and on the cold marble floors of its spray-cooled rooms young Persian damsels would sit, their hair dishevelled before bathing, and, splashing their soft naked feet in the clear water of the reservoirs, would sing, to the tune of the guitar, the ghazals of their vineyards.

The fountains play no longer; the songs have ceased; no longer do snow-white feet step gracefully on the snowy marble. It is but the vast and solitary quarters of cess-collectors like us, men oppressed with solitude and deprived of the society of women. Now, Karim Khan, the old clerk of my office, warned me repeatedly not to take up my abode there. "Pass the day there, if you like," said he, "but never stay the night." I passed it off with a light laugh. The servants said that they would work till dark and go away at night. I gave my ready assent. The house had such a bad name that even thieves would not venture near it after dark.

At first the solitude of the deserted palace weighed upon me like a nightmare. I would stay out, and work hard as long as possible, then return home at night jaded and tired, go to bed and fall asleep.

Before a week had passed, the place began to exert a weird fascination upon me. It is difficult to describe or to induce people to believe; but I felt as if the whole house was like a living organism slowly and imperceptibly digesting me by the action of some stupefying gastric juice.

Perhaps the process had begun as soon as I set my foot in the house, but I distinctly remember the day on which I first was conscious of it.

It was the beginning of summer, and the market being dull

I had no work to do. A little before sunset I was sitting in an arm-chair near the water's edge below the steps. The Susta had shrunk and sunk low; a broad patch of sand on the other side glowed with the hues of evening; on this side the pebbles at the bottom of the clear shallow waters were glistening. There was not a breath of wind anywhere, and the still air was laden with an oppressive scent from the spicy shrubs growing on the hills close by.

As the sun sank behind the hill-tops a long dark curtain fell upon the stage of day, and the intervening hills cut short the time in which light and shade mingle at sunset. I thought of going out for a ride, and was about to get up when I heard a footfall on the steps behind. I looked back, but there was no one.

As I sat down again, thinking it to be an illusion, I heard many footfalls, as if a large number of persons were rushing down the steps.

A strange thrill of delight, slightly tinged with fear, passed through my frame, and though there was not a figure before my eyes, methought I saw a bevy of joyous maidens coming down the steps to bathe in the Susta in that summer evening. Not a sound was in the valley, in the river, or in the palace, to break the silence, but I distinctly heard the maidens' gay and mirthful laugh, like the gurgle of a spring gushing forth in a hundred cascades, as they ran past me, in quick playful pursuit of each other, towards the river, without noticing me at all. As they were invisible to me, so I was, as it were, invisible to them.

The river was perfectly calm, but I felt that its still, shallow, and clear waters were stirred suddenly by the splash of many an arm jingling with bracelets, that the girls laughed and dashed and spattered water at one another, that the feet of the fair swimmers tossed the tiny waves up in showers of pearl.

I felt a thrill at my heart—I cannot say whether the excitement was due to fear or delight or curiosity. I had a strong desire to see them more clearly, but naught was visible before me; I thought I could catch all that they said if I only strained my ears; but however hard I strained them, I heard nothing but the chirping of the cicadas in the woods. It seemed as if a dark curtain of 250 years was hanging before me, and I would fain lift a corner of it tremblingly and peer through, though the assembly on the other side was completely enveloped in darkness.

The oppressive closeness of the evening was broken by a sudden gust of wind, and the still surface of the Suista rippled and curled like the hair of a nymph, and from the woods wrapt in the evening gloom there came forth a simultaneous murmur, as though they were awakening from a black dream. Call it reality or dream, the momentary glimpse of that invisible mirage reflected from a far-off world, 250 years old, vanished in a flash. The mystic forms that brushed past me with their quick unbodied steps, and loud, voiceless laughter, and threw themselves into the river, did not go back wringing their dripping robes as they went. Like fragrance wafted away by the wind they were dispersed by a single breath of the spring.

Then I was filled with a lively fear that it was the Muse

that had taken advantage of my solitude and possessed me—the witch had evidently come to ruin a poor devil like myself making a living by collecting cotton duties. I decided to have a good dinner—it is the empty stomach that all sorts of incurable diseases find an easy prey. I sent for my cook and gave orders for a rich, sumptuous moghlai dinner, redolent of spices and ghi.

Next morning the whole affair appeared a queer fantasy. With a light heart I put on a sola hat like the sahebs, and drove out to my work. I was to have written my quarterly report that day, and expected to return late; but before it was dark I was strangely drawn to my house—by what I could not say—I felt they were all waiting, and that I should delay no longer. Leaving my report unfinished I rose, put on my sola hat, and startling the dark, shady, desolate path with the rattle of my carriage, I reached the vast silent palace standing on the gloomy skirts of the hills.

On the first floor the stairs led to a very spacious hall, its roof stretching wide over ornamental arches resting on three rows of massive pillars, and groaning day and night under the weight of its own intense solitude. The day had just closed, and the lamps had not yet been lighted. As I pushed the door open a great bustle seemed to follow within, as if a throng of people had broken up in confusion, and rushed out through the doors and windows and corridors and verandas and rooms, to make its hurried escape.

As I saw no one I stood bewildered, my hair on end in a kind of ecstatic delight, and a faint scent of attar and unguents almost effected by age lingered in my nostrils. Standing in the darkness of that vast desolate hall between the rows of those ancient pillars, I could hear the gurgle of fountains plashing on the marble floor, a strange tune on the guitar, the jingle of ornaments and the tinkle of anklets, the clang of bells tolling the hours, the distant note of nahabat, the din of the crystal pendants of chandeliers shaken by the breeze, the song of bulbuls from the cages in the corridors, the cackle of storks in the gardens, all creating round me a strange unearthly music.

Then I came under such a spell that this intangible, inaccessible, unearthly vision appeared to be the only reality in the world—and all else a mere dream. That I, that is to say, Srijut So-and-so, the eldest son of So-and-so of blessed memory, should be drawing a monthly salary of Rs. 450 by the discharge of my duties as collector of cotton duties, and driving in my dog-cart to my office every day in a short coat and soia hat, appeared to me to be such an astonishingly ludicrous illusion that I burst into a horse-laugh, as I stood in the gloom of that vast silent hall.

At that moment my servant entered with a lighted kerosene lamp in his hand. I do not know whether he thought me mad, but it came back to me at once that I was in very deed Srijut So-and-so, son of So-and-so of blessed memory, and that, while our poets, great and small, alone could say whether inside of or outside the earth there was a region where unseen fountains perpetually played and fairy guitars, struck by invisible fingers, sent forth an eternal harmony, this at any rate was certain, that I collected duties at the cotton market at Banch, and earned thereby Rs. 450 per mensem as my salary. I laughed in great glee at my curious illusion, as I sat over the newspaper at my camp-table, lighted by the kerosene lamp.

After I had finished my paper and eaten my moghlai dinner, I put out the lamp, and lay down on my bed in a small side-room. Through the open window a radiant star, high above the Avalli hills skirted by the darkness of their woods, was gazing intently from millions and millions of miles away in the sky at Mr. Collector lying on a humble camp-bedstead. I wondered and felt amused at the idea, and do not knew when I fell asleep or how long I slept; but I suddenly awoke with a start, though I heard no sound and saw no intruder—only the steady bright star on the hilltop had set, and the dim light of the new moon was stealthily entering the room through the open window, as if ashamed of its intrusion.

I saw nobody, but felt as if some one was gently pushing me. As I awoke she said not a word, but beckoned me with her five fingers bedecked with rings to follow her cautiously. I got up noiselessly, and, though not a soul save myself was there in the countless apartments of that deserted palace with its slumbering sounds and waiting echoes, I feared at every step lest any one should wake up. Most of the rooms of the palace were always kept closed, and I had never entered them.

I followed breathless and with silent steps my invisible guide—I cannot now say where. What endless dark and narrow passages, what long corridors, what silent and solemn audience-chambers and close secret cells I crossed!

Though I could not see my fair guide, her form was not

invisible to my mind's eye,—an Arab girl, her arms, hard and smooth as marble, visible through her loose sleeves, a thin veil falling on her face from the fringe of her cap, and a curved dagger at her waist! Methought that one of the thousand and one Arabian Nights had been wafted to me from the world of romance, and that at the dead of night I was wending my way through the dark narrow alleys of slumbering Bagdad to a trysting-place fraught with peril.

At last my fair guide stopped abruptly before a deep blue screen, and seemed to point to something below. There was nothing there, but a sudden dread froze the blood in my heart-methought I saw there on the floor at the foot of the screen a terrible negro eunuch dressed in rich brocade, sitting and dozing with outstretched legs, with a naked sword on his lap. My fair guide lightly tripped over his legs and held up a fringe of the screen. I could catch a glimpse of a part of the room spread with a Persian carpet—some one was sitting inside on a bed—I could not see her, but only caught a glimpse of two exquisite feet in gold-embroidered slippers, hanging out from loose saffron-coloured paijamas and placed idly on the orange-coloured velvet carpet. On one side there was a bluish crystal tray on which a few apples, pears, oranges, and bunches of grapes in plenty, two small cups and a gold-tinted decanter were evidently waiting the guest. A fragrant intoxicating vapour, issuing from a strange sort of incense that burned within, almost overpowered my senses.

As with trembling heart I made an attempt to step across the outstretched legs of the eunuch, he woke up suddenly with a start, and the sword fell from his lap with a sharp clang on the marble floor. A terrific scream made me jump, and I saw I was sitting on that camp-bedstead of mine sweating heavily; and the crescent moon looked pale in the morning light like a weary sleepless patient at dawn; and our crazy Meher Ali was crying out, as is his daily custom, "Stand back! Stand back!!" while he went along the lonely road.

Such was the abrupt close of one of my Arabian Nights; but there were yet a thousand nights left.

Then followed a great discord between my days and nights. During the day I would go to my work worn and tired, cursing the bewitching night and her empty dreams, but as night came my daily life with its bonds and shackles of work would appear a petty, false, ludicrous vanity.

After nightfall I was caught and overwhelmed in the snare of a strange intoxication, I would then be transformed into some unknown personage of a bygone age, playing my part in unwritten history; and my short English coat and tight breeches did not suit me in the least. With a red velvet cap on my head, loose paijamas, an embroidered vest, a long flowing silk gown, and coloured handkerchiefs scented with attar, I would complete my elaborate toilet, sit on a high-cushioned chair, and replace my cigarette with a many-coiled narghileh filled with rose-water, as if in eager expectation of a strange meeting with the beloved one.

I have no power to describe the marvellous incidents that unfolded themselves, as the gloom of the night deepened. I felt as if in the curious apartments of that vast edifice the fragments of a beautiful story, which I could follow for some distance, but of which I could never see the end, flew about in a sudden gust of the vernal breeze. And all the same I would wander from room to room in pursuit of them the whole night long.

Amid the eddy of these dream-fragments, amid the smell of henna and the twanging of the guitar, amid the waves of air charged with fragrant spray, I would catch like a flash of lightning the momentary glimpse of a fair damsel. She it was who had saffron-coloured paijamas, white ruddy soft feet in gold-embroidered slippers with curved toes, a close-fitting bodice wrought with gold, a red cap, from which a golden frill fell on her snowy brow and cheeks.

She had maddened me. In pursuit of her I wandered from room to room, from path to path among the bewildering maze of alleys in the enchanted dreamland of the nether world of sleep.

Sometimes in the evening, while arraying myself carefully as a prince of the blood-royal before a large mirror, with a candle burning on either side, I would see a sudden reflection of the Persian beauty by the side of my own. A swift turn of her neck, a quick eager glance of intense passion and pain glowing in her large dark eyes, just a suspicion of speech on her dainty red lips, her figure, fair and slim crowned with youth like a blossoming creeper, quickly uplifted in her graceful tilting gait, a dazzling flash of pain and craving and ecstasy, a smile and a glance and a blaze of jewels and silk, and she melted away.

A wild glist of wind, laden with all the fragrance of hills and woods, would put out my light, and I would fling aside my dress and lie down on my bed, my eyes closed and my body thrilling with delight, and there around me in the breeze, amid all the perfume of the woods and hills, floated through the silent gloom many a caress and many a kiss and many a tender touch of hands, and gentle murmurs in my ears, and fragrant breaths on my brow; or a sweetly-perfumed kerchief was wafted again and again on my cheeks. Then slowly a mysterious serpent would twist her stupefying coils about me; and heaving a heavy sigh, I would lapse into insensibility, and then into a profound slumber.

One evening I decided to go out on my horse—I do not know who implored me to stay-but I would listen to no entreaties that day. My English hat and coat were resting on a rack, and I was about to take them down when a sudden whirlwind, crested with the sands of the Susta and the dead leaves of the Avalli hills, caught them up, and whirled them round and round, while a loud peal of merry laughter rose higher and higher, striking all the chords of mirth till it died away in the land of sunset.

I could not go out for my ride, and the next day I gave up my queer English coat and hat for good.

That day again at dead of night I heard the stifled heart-breaking sobs of some one—as if below the bed, below the floor, below the stony foundation of that gigantic palace, from the depths of a dark damp grave, a voice piteously cried and implored me: "Oh, rescue me! Break through these doors of hard illusion, deathlike slumber and fruitless dreams, place by your side on the saddle, press me to your heart, and, riding through hills and woods and across the river, take me to the warm radiance of your sunny rooms above!"

Who am I? Oh, how can I rescue thee? What drowning beauty, what incarnate passion shall I drag to the shore from this wild eddy of dreams? O lovely ethereal apparition! Where didst thou flourish and when? By what cool spring, under the shade of what date-groves, wast thou born—in the lap of what homeless wanderer in the desert?

What Bedouin snatched thee from thy mother's arms, an opening bud plucked from a wild creeper, placed thee on a horse swift as lightning, crossed the burning sands, and took thee to the slave-market of what royal city? And there, what officer of the Badshah, seeing the glory of thy bashful blossoming youth, paid for thee in gold, placed thee in a golden palanquin, and offered thee as a present for the seraglio of his master? And O, the history of that place! The music of the sareng, the jingle of anklets, the occasional flash of daggers and the glowing wine of Shiraz poison, and the piercing flashing glance! What infinite grandeur, what endless servitude!

The slave-girls to thy right and left waved the chamar as diamonds flashed from their bracelets; the Badshah, the king of kings, fell on his knees at thy snowy feet in bejewelled shoes, and outside the terrible Abyssinian eunuch, looking like a messenger of death, but clothed like an angel, stood with a naked sword in his hand! Then, O, thou flower of the desert, swept away by the blood-stained dazzling ocean of grandeur, with its foam of jealousy, its rocks and shoals of intrigue, on what shore of cruel death wast thou cast, or in what other land more splendid and more cruel?

Suddenly at this moment that crazy Meher Ali screamed out: "Stand back! Stand back!! All is false! All is false!!" I opened my eyes and saw that it was already light. My chaprasi came and handed me my letters, and the cook waited with a salam for my orders.

I said; "No, I can stay here no longer." That very day I packed up, and moved to my office. Old Karim Khan smiled a little as he saw me. I felt nettled, but said nothing, and fell to my work.

As evening approached I grew absent-minded; I felt as if I had an appointment to keep; and the work of examining the cotton accounts seemed wholly useless; even the Nizamat of the Nizam did not appear to be of much worth. Whatever belonged to the present, whatever was moving and acting and working for bread seemed trivial, meaningless, and contemptible.

I threw my pen down, closed my ledgers, got into my dog-cart, and drove away. I noticed that it stopped of itself at the gate of the marble palace just at the hour of twilight. With quick steps I climbed the stairs, and entered the room.

A heavy silence was reigning within. The dark rooms were looking sullen as if they had taken offence. My heart was full of contrition, but there was no one to whom I could lay it bare, or of whom I could ask forgiveness. I wandered about the dark rooms with a vacant mind. I wished I had a guitar to which I could sing to the unknown: "O fire, the poor moth that made a vain effort to fly away has come back to thee! Forgive it but this once, burn its wings and consume it in thy flame!"

Suddenly two tear-drops fell from overhead on my brow. Dark masses of clouds overcast the top of the Avalli hills that day. The gloomy woods and the sooty waters of the Susta were waiting in terrible suspense and in an ominous calm. Suddenly land, water, and sky shivered, and a wild tempest-blast rushed howling through the distant pathless woods, showing its lightning-teeth like a raving maniac who had broken his chains. The desolate halls of the palace banged their doors, and moaned in the bitterness of anguish.

The servants were all in the office, and there was no one to light the lamps. The night was cloudy and moonless. In the dense gloom within I could distinctly feel that a woman was lying on her face on the carpet below the bed—clasping and tearing her long dishevelled hair with desperate fingers. Blood was tricking down her fair brow, and she was now laughing a hard, harsh, mirthless laugh, now bursting into violent wringing sobs, now rending her bodice and striking at her bare bosom, as the wind roared in through the open window, and the rain poured in torrents and soaked her through and through.

All night there was no cessation of the storm or of the passionate cry. I wandered from room to room in the dark, with unavailing sorrow. Whom could I console when no one was by? Whose was this intense agony of sorrow? Whence arose this inconsolable grief?

And the mad man cried out: "Stand back! Stand back!! All

is false! All is false!!"

I saw that the day had dawned, and Meher Ali was going round and round the palace with his usual cry in that dreadful weather. Suddenly it came to me that perhaps he also had once lived in that house, and that, though he had gone mad, he came there every day, and went round and round, fascinated by the weird spell cast by the marble demon.

Despite the storm and rain I ran to him and asked: "Ho, Meher Ali, what is false?"

The man answered nothing, but pushing me aside went round and round with his frantic cry, like a bird flying fascinated about the jaws of a snake, and made a desperate effort to warn himself by repeating: "Stand back! Stand back!! All is false! All is false!!"

I ran like a mad man through the pelting rain to my office, and asked Karim Khan: "Tell me the meaning of all this!"

What I gathered from that old man was this: That at one time countless unrequited passions and unsatisfied longings and lurid flames of wild blazing pleasure raged within that palace, and that the curse of all the heart-aches and blasted hopes had made its every stone thirsty and hungry, eager to swallow up like a famished ogress any living man who might chance to approach. Not one of those who lived there for three consecutive nights could escape these cruel jaws, save Meher Ali, who had escaped at the cost of his reason.

I asked: "Is there no means whatever of my release?" The

old man said: "There is only one, means, and that is very difficult. I will tell you what it is, but first you must hear the history of a young Persian girl who once lived in that pleasure-dome. A stranger or a more bitterly heart-rending tragedy was never enacted on this earth."

Just at this moment the coolies announced that the train was coming. So soon? We hurriedly packed up our luggage, as the tram steamed in. An English gentleman, apparently just aroused from slumber, was looking out of a first-class carriage endeavouring to read the name of the station. As soon as he caught sight of our fellow-passenger, he cried, "Hallo," and took him into his own compartment. As we got into a second-class carriage, we had no chance of finding out who the man was nor what was the end of his story.

I said; "The man evidently took us for fools and imposed upon us out of fun. The story is pure fabrication from start to finish." The discussion that followed ended in a lifelong rupture between my theosophist kinsman and myself.

The Auspicious Vision

Kantichandra was young; yet after his wife's demise he looked for no second accomplice, and gave all his attention to hunting animals and birds. His body was long and slim, hard and light-footed; his sight sharp; his aim impeccable. He dressed like a countryman, and took with him Hira Singh the wrestler, Chakkanlal, Khan Saheb the musician and performer, Mian Saheb, and numerous others. He had no shortage of idle supporters.

In the time of Agrahayan, Kanti had gone out shooting close to the swamp of Nydighi with a couple of active companions. They were in boats, and an group of servants who were also in boats, occupied the bathing-ghats. The village ladies thought that it was well-near difficult to bathe or to draw water. Throughout the day, land and water trembled to the discharging of the guns; and each night musicians killed the possibility of sleep.

One morning as Kanti was seated in his boat cleaning a favourite gun, he suddenly started at what he thought was the cry of wild duck. Looking up, he saw a village maiden, coming to the water's edge, with two white ducklings clasped to her breast. The little stream was almost stagnant. Many weeds choked the current. The girl put the birds into the water, and watched them anxiously. Evidently the presence of the sportsmen was the cause of her care and not the wildness of the ducks.

The girl's beauty had a rare freshness—as if she had just come from Vishwakarma's workshop. It was difficult to guess her age. Her figure was almost a woman's, but her face was so childish that clearly the world had left no impression there. She seemed not to know herself that she had reached the threshold of youth.

Kanti's gun-cleaning stopped for a while. He was fascinated. He had not expected to see such a face in such a spot. And yet its beauty suited its surroundings better than it would have suited a palace. A bud is lovelier on the bough than in a golden vase. That day the blossoming reeds glittered in the autumn dew and morning sun, and the fresh, simple face set in the midst was like a picture of festival to Kanti's enchanted mind. Kalidos has forgotten to sing how Siva's Mountain-Queen herself sometimes has come to the young Ganges, with just such ducklings in her breast.

As he gazed, the maiden started in terror, and hurriedly took back the ducks into her bosom with a half-articulate cry of pain. In another moment, she had left the river-bank and disappeared into the bamboo thicket hard by. Looking round, Kanti saw one of his men pointing an unloaded gun at the ducks. He at once went up to him, wrenched away his gun, and bestowed on his cheek a prodigious slap. The astonished humourist finished his joke on the floor. Kanti went on cleaning his gun.

But curiosity drove Kanti to the thicket wherein he had seen the girl disappear. Pushing his way through, he found himself in the yard of a well-to-do householder. On one side was a row of conical thatched barns, on the other a clean cow-shed, at the end of which grew a zizyph bush. Under the bush was seated the girl he had seen that morning, sobbing over a wounded dove, into whose yellow beak she was trying to wring a little water from the moist corner of her garment. A grey cat, its fore-paws on her knee, was looking eagerly at the bird, and every now and then, when it got too forward, she kept it in its place by a warning tap on the nose.

This little picture, set in the peaceful mid-day surroundings of the householder's yard, instantly impressed itself on Kanti's sensitive heart. The checkered light and shade, flickering beneath the delicate foliage of the zizyph, played on the girl's lap. Not far off a cow was chewing the cud, and lazily keeping off the flies with slow movements of its head and tail. The north wind whispered softly in the rustling bamboo thickets.

And she who at dawn on the river-bank had looked like the Forest Queen, now in the silence of noon showed the eager pity of the Divine Housewife. Kanti, coming in upon her with his gun, had a sense of intrusion. He felt like a thief caught red-handed. He longed to explain that it was not he who had hurt the dove. As he wondered how he should begin, there came a call of "Sudha!" from the house. The girl jumped up. "Sudha!" came the voice again. She took up her dove, and ran within. "Sudha," thought Kanti, "what an appropriate name!"

Kanti returned to the boat, handed his gun to his men, and went over to the front door of the house. He found a middle-aged Brahmin, with a peaceful, clean-shaven face, seated on a bench outside, and reading a devotional book. Kanti saw in his kindly, thoughtful face something of the tenderness which shone in the face of the maiden.

Kanti saluted him, and said: "May I ask for some water, sir? I am very thirsty." The elder man welcomed him with eager hospitality, and, offering him a seat on the bench, went inside and fetched with his own hands a little brass plate of sugar wafers and a bell-metal vessel full of water.

After Kanti had eaten and drunk, the Brahmin begged him to introduce himself. Kanti gave his own name, his father's name, and the address of his home, and then said in the usual way: "If I can be of any service, sir, I shall deem myself fortunate."

"I require no service, my son," said Nabin Banerji; "I have only one care at present."

"What is that, sir?" said Kanti.

"It is my daughter, Sudha, who is growing up" (Kanti smiled as he thought of her babyish face) "and for whom I have not yet been able to find a worthy bridegroom. If I could only see her well married, all my debt to this world would be paid. But there is no suitable bridegroom here, and I cannot leave my charge of Gopinath here to search for a husband elsewhere."

"If you would see me in my boat, sir, we would have a talk about the marriage of your daughter." So saying, Kanti repeated his salute and went back. He then sent some of his men into the village to inquire, and in answer heard nothing but praise of the beauty and virtues of the

Brahmin's daughter.

When next day the old man came to the boat on his promised visit, Kanti bent low in salutation, and begged the hand of his daughter for himself. The Brahmin was so much overcome by this undreamed-of piece of good fortune— for Kanti not only belonged to a well-known Brahmin family, but was also a landed proprietor of wealth and position— that at first he could hardly utter a word in reply. He thought there must have been some mistake, and at length mechanically repeated: "You desire to marry my daughter?"

"If you will deign to give her to me," said Kanti.

"You mean Sudha?" he asked again.

"Yes," was the reply.

"But will you not first see and speak to her——?"

Kanti, pretending he had not seen her already, said: "Oh, that we shall do at the moment of the Auspicious Vision."

In a voice husky with emotion the old man said: "My Sudha is indeed a good girl, well skilled in all the household arts. As you are so generously taking her on trust, may she never cause you a moment's regret. This is my blessing!"

The brick-built mansion of the Mazumdars had been borrowed for the wedding ceremony, which was fixed for next Magh, as Kanti did not wish to delay. In due time the bridegroom arrived on his elephant, with drums and music and with a torch-light procession, and the ceremony began.

When the bridal couple were covered with the scarlet screen for the rite of the Auspicious Vision, Kanti looked up at his bride. In that bashful, downcast face, crowned with the wedding coronet and bedecked with sandal paste, he could scarcely recognize the village maiden of his fancy, and in the fulness of his emotion a mist seemed to becloud his eyes.

At the gathering of women in the bridal chamber, after the wedding ceremony was over, an old village dame insisted that Kanti himself should take off his wife's bridal veil. As he did so he started back. It was not the same girl.

Something rose from within his breast and pierced into his brain. The light of the lamps seemed to grow dim, and darkness to tarnish the face of the bride herself.

At first he felt angry with his father-in-law. The old scoundrel had shown him one girl, and married him to another. But on calmer reflection he remembered that the old man had not shown him any daughter at all— that it was all his own fault. He thought it best not to show his arrant folly to the world, and took his place again with apparent calmness.

He could swallow the powder; he could not get rid of its taste. He could not bear the merry-makings of the festive throng. He was in a blaze of anger with himself as well as with everybody else.

Suddenly he felt the bride, seated by his side, give a little start and a suppressed scream; a leveret, scampering into the room, had brushed across her feet. Close upon it followed the girl he had seen before. She caught up the leveret in her arms, and began to caress it with an affectionate murmuring. "Oh, the mad girl!" cried the women as they made signs to her to leave the room. She heeded them not, however, but came and unconcernedly sat in front of the wedded pair, looking into their faces with a childish curiosity. When a maidservant came and took her by the arm to lead her away, Kanti hurriedly interposed, saying, "Let her be."

"What is your name?" he then went on to ask her.

The girl swayed backwards and forwards but gave no reply. All the women in the room began to titter.

Kani put another question: "Have those ducklings of yours grown up?"

The girl stared at him as unconcernedly as before.

The bewildered Kanti screwed up courage for another effort, and asked tenderly after the wounded dove, but with no avail. The increasing laughter in the room betokened an amusing joke.

At last Kanti learned that the girl was deaf and dumb, the companion of all the animals and birds of the locality. It was but by chance that she rose the other day when the name of Sudha was called.

Kanti now received a second shock. A black screen lifted from before his eyes. With a sigh of intense relief, as of escape from calamity, he looked once more into the face of his bride. Then came the true Auspicious Vision. The light from his heart and from the smokeless lamps fell on her gracious face; and he saw it in its true radiance, knowing that Nabin's blessing would find fulfilment.

The Home Coming

Phatik Chakravorti was the instigator among the young men of the village. Another mischief got into his head. There was an dense log lying on the mud-level of the river holding up to be molded into mast for a boat. He concluded that they should all cooperate to move the log by force from its place and move it away. The owner of the log would be furious and shocked, and they would all enjoy the sneer. Each one favored the proposition, and it was carried out collectively.

But just as the fun was going to start, Mākhan, Phatik's younger sibling, walked up and sat down on the log before them all without a word. The boys were bewildered for a minute. He was pushed, rather hesitantly, by one of the boys and advised to get up; however he remained very unconcerned. He seemed like a youthful rationalist reflecting on the worthlessness of pranks. Phatik was enraged. "Mākhan," he cried, "if you don't get down right now, I'll thrash you!"

Mākhan only moved to a more comfortable position. Now, if Phatik was to keep his regal dignity before the public, it was clear he ought to carry out his threat. But his courage failed him at the crisis. His fertile brain, however, rapidly seized upon a new manœuvre which would discomfit his brother and afford his followers an added amusement. He gave the word of command to roll the log and Mākhan over together. Mākhan heard the order and made it a point of honour to stick on. But he overlooked the fact, like those who attempt earthly fame in other matters, that there was peril in it.

The boys began to heave at the log with all their might, calling out, "One, two, three, go!" At the word "go" the log went; and with it went Mākhan's philosophy, glory and all.

The other boys shouted themselves hoarse with delight. But Phatik was a little frightened. He knew what was coming. And, sure enough, Mākhan rose from Mother Earth blind as Fate and screaming like the Furies. He rushed at Phatik and scratched his face and beat him and kicked him, and then went crying home. The first act of the drama was over.

Phatik wiped his face, and sat down on the edge of a sunken barge by the river bank, and began to chew a piece of grass. A boat came up to the landing and a middle-aged man, with grey hair and dark moustache, stepped on shore. He saw the boy sitting there doing nothing and asked him where the Chakravortis lived. Phatik went on chewing the grass and said: "Over there," but it was quite impossible to tell where he pointed. The stranger asked him again. He swung his legs to and fro on the side of the barge and said: "Go and find out," and continued to chew the grass as before.

But now a servant came down from the house and told Phatik his mother wanted him. Phatik refused to move. But the servant was the master on this occasion. He took Phatik up roughly and carried him, kicking and struggling in impotent rage.

When Phatik came into the house, his mother saw him. She called out angrily: "So you have been hitting Mākhan again?"

Phatik answered indignantly: "No, I haven't! Who told you that?"

His mother shouted: "Don't tell lies! You have."

Phatik said sullenly: "I tell you, I haven't. You ask Mākhan!" But Mākhan thought it best to stick to his previous statement. He said: "Yes, mother. Phatik did hit me."

Phatik's patience was already exhausted. He could not bear this injustice. He rushed at Mākhan and hammered him with blows: "Take that," he cried, "and that, and that, for telling lies."

His mother took Mākhan's side in a moment, and pulled Phatik away, beating him with her hands. When Phatik pushed her aside, she shouted out: "What! you little villain! Would you hit your own mother?"

It was just at this critical juncture that the grey-haired stranger arrived. He asked what was the matter. Phatik looked sheepish and ashamed.

But when his mother stepped back and looked at the stranger, her anger was changed to surprise. For she recognized her brother and cried: "Why, Dada! Where have you come from?"

As she said these words, she bowed to the ground and touched his feet. Her brother had gone away soon after she had married; and he had started business in Bombay. His sister had lost her husband while he was there. Bishamber had now come back to Calcutta and had at once made enquiries about his sister. He had then hastened to see her as soon as he found out where she was.

The next few days were full of rejoicing. The brother asked after the education of the two boys. He was told by his sister that Phatik was a perpetual nuisance. He was lazy, disobedient, and wild. But Mākhan was as good as gold, as quiet as a lamb, and very fond of reading. Bishamber kindly offered to take Phatik off his sister's hands and educate him with his own children in Calcutta. The widowed mother readily agreed. When his uncle asked Phatik if he would like to go to Calcutta with him, his joy knew no bounds and he said: "Oh, yes, uncle!" in a way that made it quite clear that he meant it.

It was an immense relief to the mother to get rid of Phatik. She had a prejudice against the boy, and no love was lost between the two brothers. She was in daily fear that he would either drown Mākhan some day in the river, or break his head in a fight, or run him into some danger. At the same time she was a little distressed to see Phatik's extreme eagerness to get away.

Phatik, as soon as all was settled, kept asking his uncle every minute when they were to start. He was on pins and needles all day long with excitement and lay awake most of the night. He bequeathed to Mākhan, in perpetuity, his fishing-rod, his big kite, and his marbles. Indeed, at this time of departure, his generosity towards Mākhan was unbounded.

When they reached Calcutta, Phatik made the acquaintance

of his aunt for the first time. She was by no means pleased with this unnecessary addition to her family. She found her own three boys quite enough to manage without taking any one else. And to bring a village lad of fourteen into their midst was terribly upsetting. Bishamber should really have thought twice before committing such an indiscretion.

In this world of human affairs there is no worse nuisance than a boy at the age of fourteen. He is neither ornamental nor useful. It is impossible to shower affection on him as on a little boy; and he is always getting in the way. If he talks with a childish lisp he is called a baby, and if he answers in a grown-up way he is called impertinent. In fact any talk at all from him is resented. Then he is at the unattractive, growing age. He grows out of his clothes with indecent haste; his voice grows hoarse and breaks and quavers; his face grows suddenly angular and unsightly. It is easy to excuse the shortcomings of early childhood, but it is hard to tolerate even unavoidable lapses in a boy of fourteen. The lad himself becomes painfully self-conscious. When he talks with elderly people he is either unduly forward, or else so unduly shy that he appears ashamed of his very existence.

Yet it is at this very age when, in his heart of hearts, a young lad most craves for recognition and love; and he becomes the devoted slave of any one who shows him consideration. But none dare openly love him, for that would be regarded as undue indulgence and therefore bad for the boy. So, what with scolding and chiding, he becomes very much like a stray dog that has lost his master.

For a boy of fourteen his own home is the only Paradise. To live in a strange house with strange people is little short of torture, while the height of bliss is to receive the kind looks of women and never to be slighted by them.

It was anguish to Phatik to be the unwelcome guest in his aunt's house, despised by this elderly woman and slighted on every occasion. If ever she asked him to do anything for her, he would be so overjoyed that he would overdo it; and then she would tell him not to be so stupid, but to get on with his lessons.

The cramped atmosphere of neglect oppressed Phatik so much that he felt that he could hardly breathe. He wanted to go out into the open country and fill his lungs with fresh air. But there was no open country to go to. Surrounded on all sides by Calcutta houses and walls, he would dream night after night of his village home and long to be back there. He remembered the glorious meadow where he used to fly his kite all day long; the broad river-banks where he would wander about the live-long day singing and shouting for joy; the narrow brook where he could go and dive and swim at any time he liked. He thought of his band of boy companions over whom he was despot; and, above all, the memory of that tyrant mother of his, who had such a prejudice against him, occupied him day and night. A kind of physical love like that of animals, a longing to be in the presence of the one who is loved, an inexpressible wistfulness during absence, a silent cry of the inmost heart for the mother, like the lowing of a calf in the twilight,—this love, which was almost an animal instinct, agitated the shy, nervous, lean, uncouth and ugly boy. No one could understand it, but it preyed upon his mind continually.

There was no more backward boy in the whole school than Phatik. He gaped and remained silent when the teacher asked him a question, and like an overladen ass patiently suffered all the blows that came down on his back. When other boys were out at play, he stood wistfully by the window and gazed at the roofs of the distant houses. And if by chance he espied children playing on the open terrace of any roof, his heart would ache with longing.

One day he summoned up all his courage and asked his uncle: "Uncle, when can I go home?"

His uncle answered: "Wait till the holidays come."

But the holidays would not come till October and there was a long time still to wait.

One day Phatik lost his lesson book. Even with the help of books he had found it very difficult indeed to prepare his lesson. Now it was impossible. Day after day the teacher would cane him unmercifully. His condition became so abjectly miserable that even his cousins were ashamed to own him. They began to jeer and insult him more than the other boys. He went to his aunt at last and told her that he had lost his book.

His aunt pursed her lips in contempt and said: "You great clumsy, country lout! How can I afford, with all my family, to buy you new books five times a month?"

That night, on his way back from school, Phatik had a bad headache with a fit of shivering. He felt he was going to have an attack of malarial fever. His one great fear was that he would be a nuisance to his aunt.

The next morning Phatik was nowhere to be seen. All searches in the neighbourhood proved futile. The rain had been pouring in torrents all night, and those who went out in search of the boy got drenched through to the skin. At last Bishamber asked help from the police.

At the end of the day a police van stopped at the door before the house. It was still raining and the streets were all flooded. Two constables brought out Phatik in their arms and placed him before Bishamber. He was wet through from head to foot, muddy all over, his face and eyes flushed red with fever and his limbs trembling. Bishamber carried him in his arms and took him into the inner apartments. When his wife saw him she exclaimed: "What a heap of trouble this boy has given us! Hadn't you better send him home?"

Phatik heard her words and sobbed out loud: "Uncle, I was just going home; but they dragged me back again."

The fever rose very high, and all that night the boy was delirious. Bishamber brought in a doctor. Phatik opened his eyes, flushed with fever, and looked up to the ceiling and said vacantly: "Uncle, have the holidays come yet?"

Bishamber wiped the tears from his own eyes and took Phatik's lean and burning hands in his own and sat by him through the night. The boy began again to mutter. At last his voice became excited: "Mother!" he cried, "don't beat me like that.... Mother! I am telling the truth!"

The next day Phatik became conscious for a short time. He turned his eyes about the room, as if expecting some one to come. At last, with an air of disappointment, his head sank back on the pillow. He turned his face to the wall with a deep sigh.

Bishamber knew his thoughts and bending down his head whispered: "Phatik, I have sent for your mother."

The day went by. The doctor said in a troubled voice that the boy's condition was very critical.

Phatik began to cry out: "By the mark—three fathoms. By the mark—four fathoms. By the mark——." He had heard the sailor on the river-steamer calling out the mark on the plumb-line. Now he was himself plumbing an unfathomable sea.

Later in the day Phatik's mother burst into the room, like a whirlwind, and began to toss from side to side and moan and cry in a loud voice.

Bishamber tried to calm her agitation, but she flung herself on the bed, and cried: "Phatik, my darling, my darling."

Phatik stopped his restless movements for a moment. His hands ceased beating up and down. He said: "Eh?"

The mother cried again: "Phatik, my darling, my darling."

Phatik very slowly turned his head and without seeing anybody said: "Mother, the holidays have come."

The Patriot

I am certain that Chitragupta, who keeps strict record at the entryway of Death, probably noted down in huge letters allegations against me, which had gotten away from my attention altogether. Then again a considerable lot of my wrongdoings, that have passed unnoticed by others, pose a potential threat in my own memory. The account of my transgression, that I will relate, has a place with the last kind, and I trust that a straight to the point admission of it, before it is at last entered in the Book of Doom, may diminish its culpability.

Everything happened yesterday evening, on a day of celebration for the Jains in our neighborhood. I was going out with my wife, Kalika, to tea at the place of my friend Nayanmohan.

My wife's name means literally a 'bud.' It was given by my father-in-law, who is thus solely responsible for any discrepancy between its implication and the reality to which it is attached. There is not the least tremor of hesitancy in my wife's nature; her opinions on most subjects have reached their terminus. Once, when she had been vigorously engaged in picketing against British cloth in Burrabazar, the awe-struck members of her party in a fit of excessive admiration gave her the name, Dhruva-vrata, the woman of unwavering vows.

My name is Girindra, the Lord of the Rocks, so common among my countrymen, whose character generally fails to act up to it. Kalika's admirers simply know me as the husband of my wife and pay no heed to my name. By good luck inherited from my ancestors I have, however, some kind of significance, which is considered to be convenient by her followers at the time of collecting subscriptions.

There is a greater chance of harmony between husband and wife, when they are different in character, like the shower of rain and the dry earth, than when they are of a uniform constitution. I am somewhat slipshod by nature, having no grip over things, while my wife has a tenacity of mind which never allows her to let go the thing which it has in its clutches. This very dissimilarity helps to preserve peace in our household.

But there is one point of difference between us, regarding which no adjustment has yet become possible. Kalika believes that I am unpatriotic.

This is very disconcerting, because according to her, truth is what she proclaims to be true. She has numerous internal evidences of my love for my country; but as it disdains to don the livery of the brand of nationalism, professed by her own party, she fiercely refuses to acknowledge it.

From my younger days, I have continued to be a confirmed book-lover: indeed, I am hopelessly addicted to buying books. Even my enemies would not dare to deny that I read them; and my friends know only too well how fond I am of discussing their contents. This had the effect of eliminating most of my friends, till I have left to me Banbihari, the sole companion of my lonely debates. We have just passed through a period, when our police authorities, on the one hand, have associated the worst form of sedition with the presence of the Gita in our possession; and our patriots, on their side, have found it impossible to reconcile appreciation of foreign literature with devotion to one's Motherland.

Our traditional Goddess of culture, Saraswati, because of her white complexion, has come to be regarded with-suspicion by our young nationalists. It was openly declared, when the students shunned their College lectures, that the water of the divine lake, on which Saraswati had her white lotus seat, had no efficacy in extinguishing the fire of ill-fortune that has been raging for centuries round the throne of our Mother, Bharat-Lakshmi. In any case, intellectual culture was considered to be a superfluity in the proper growth of our political life.

In spite of my wife's excellent example and powerful urgings I do not wear Khaddar,—not because there is anything wrong in it, nor because I am too fastidious in the choice of my wardrobe. On the contrary, among those of my traits, which are not in perfect consonance with our own national habits, I cannot include a scrupulous care as to how I dress.

Once upon a time, before Kalika had her modern transformation, I used to wear broad-toed shoes from Chinese shops and forgot to have them polished. I had a dread of putting on socks: I preferred Punjabis to English shirts, and overlooked their accidental deficiency in buttons. These habits of mine constantly produced domestic cataclysms, threatening our permanent separation. Kalika declared that she felt ashamed to appear before the public in my company. I readily absolved her from the wifely duty of accompanying me to those parties where my presence would be discordant.

The times have changed, but my evil fortune persists. Kalika still has the habit of repeating: 'I am ashamed to go out with you.' Formerly, I hesitated to adopt the uniform of her set, when she belonged to the pre-nationalist age; and I still feel reluctant to adopt the uniform of the present regime, to which she owns her allegiance.

The fault lies deep in my own nature. I shrink from all conscious display of sectarian marks about my person. This shyness on my part leads to incessant verbal explosions in our domestic world, because of the inherent incapacity of Kalika to accept as final any natural difference, which her partner in life may possess. Her mind is like a mountain stream, that boisterously goes round and round a rock, pushing against it in a vain effort to make it flow with its own current. Her contact with a different point of view from her own seems to exercise an irresistible reflex action upon her nerves, throwing her into involuntary convulsions.

While getting ready to go out yesterday, the tone with which Kalika protested against my non-Khaddar dress was anything but sweet. Unfortunately, I had my inveterate pride of intellect, that forced me into a discussion with my wife. It was unpleasant, and what more, futile.

'Women find it convenient,' I said to her, 'to veil their eyes and walk tied to the leading strings of authority. They feel safe when they deprive their thoughts of all freedom, and confine them in the strict Zenana of conformity. Our ladies today have easily developed their devotion to Khaddar, because it has added to the over-burdened list of our outward criterion's of propriety, which seem to comfort them.'

Kalika replied with almost fanatical fury: 'It will be a great day for my country, when the sanctity of wearing Khaddar is as blindly believed in as a dip in the holy water of the Ganges. Reason crystallised becomes custom. Free thoughts are like ghosts, which find their bodies in convention. Then alone they have their solid work, and no longer float about in a thin atmosphere of vacillation.'

I could see that these were the wise sayings of Nayanmohan, with the quotation marks worn out; Kalika found no difficulty in imagining that they were her own.

The man who invented the proverb, 'The silent silence all antagonist', must have been unmarried. It made my wife all the more furious, when I offered her no answer. 'Your protest against caste', she explained, 'is only confined to your mouth. We, on the contrary, carry it out in practice by imposing a uniformly white cover over all colour distinctions.'

I was about to reply, that my protest against caste did truly have its origin in my mouth, whenever I accepted with relish the excellent food cooked by a Muhammadan. It was certainly oral, but not verbal; and its movements were truly inward. An external cover hides distinctions, but does not remove them.

I am sure my argument deserved utterance, but being a helpless male, I timidly sought safety in a speechless neutrality; for, I knew, from repeated experience, that such discussions, started in our domestic seclusion, are invariably carried by my wife, like soiled linen, to her friendly circle to be ruthlessly beaten and mangled. She has the unpleasant habit of collecting counter-arguments from the mouth of Professor Nayanmohan, exultantly flinging them in my face, and then rushing away from the arena without waiting for my answer.

I was perfectly certain about what was in store for me at the Professor's tea-table. There would be some abstruse dissertation on the relative position in Hindu culture of tradition and free thought, the inherited experience of ages and reason which is volatile, inconclusive, and colourlessly universal. In the meanwhile, the vision floated before my mind's eye of the newly-brought books, redolent of Morocco leather, mysteriously veiled in a brown paper cover, waiting for me by my cushions, with their shy virginity of uncut pages.

All the same, I was compelled to keep my engagement by the dread of words, uttered and unuttered, and gestures suggestive of trouble.

We had travelled only a short distance from our house. Passing by the street-hydrant, we had reached the tiled hut occupied by an up-country shopkeeper, who was giving various forms to indigestibility in his cauldron of boiling mustard oil, when we were obstructed by a fearful uproar.

The Marwaris, proceeding to their temple, carrying their

costly paraphernalia of worship, had suddenly stopped at this place. There were angry shouts, mingled with the sound of thrashing, and I thought that the crowd were dealing with some pickpocket, enjoying the vigour of their own indignation, which gave them-the delightful freedom to be merciless towards one of their own fellow beings. When, by dint of impatient footing of horn, our motor car reached the centre of the excited crowd, we found that the old municipal sweeper of our district was being beaten. He had just taken his afternoon bath and was carrying a bucket of clean water in his right hand with a broom under his arm. Dressed in a check-patterned vest, with carefully combed hair still wet, he was walking home, holding his seven-year-old grandson by his left hand, when accidentally he came in contact with somebody, or something, which gave rise to this violent outburst. The boy was piteously imploring everybody not to hurt his grandfather; and the old man himself with joined hands uplifted, was asking forgiveness for his unintentional offence. Tears were streaming from his frightened eyes, and blood was smeared across his grey beard.

The sight was intolerable to me. I decided at once to take up the sweeper into my car and thereby demonstrate to the pious party, that I was not of their cult.

Noticing my restlessness, Kalika guessed what was in my mind. Griping my arm, she whispered: 'What are you doing? Don't you see he is a sweeper?'

'He maybe a sweeper,' said I, 'but those people have no right to beat him in this brutal manner.'

'It's his own fault.' Kalika answered, 'Would it have hurt his dignity, if he had avoided the middle of the road?'

'I don't know', I said impatiently. 'Anyhow, I am going to take him into my car.'

'Then I leave your car this moment,' said Kalika angrily. 'I refuse to travel with a sweeper.'

'Can't you see,' I argued, 'that he was just bathed, and his clothes are clean,—in fact, much cleaner than those of the people who are beating him?'

"He's a sweeper!" She said decisively. Then she called to the chauffeur, 'Gangadin, drive on'.

I was defeated. It was my cowardice.

Nayanmohan, I am told, brought out some very profound sociological arguments, at the tea-table, specially dealing with the inevitable inequality imposed upon men by their profession and the natural humiliation which is inherent in the scheme of things. But his words did not reach my ears, and I sat silent all through the evening.

The Child's Return

I

Raicharan was twelve years of age when he came as a servant to his lord's home. He was from the same caste as his master and was his duty was to nurse his master's little son. As time went on thc kid left Raicharan's arms to go to school. From school he went ahead to college, and after college he entered the legal administration. Continuously, until the point when he married, Raicharan was his sole chaperon.

But when a mistress came into the house, Raicharan discovered two bosses rather than one. All his former impact went to the new lady. This was rcompensated by a new arrival. Anukul had a son born to him and Raicharan by his sincere attention soon got a total hold over the child. He used to hurl him up in his arms, call to him in absurd kiddish talk, put his face close to the baby's and draw it away again with a snicker.

Presently the child was able to crawl and cross the doorway. When Raicharan went to catch him, he would scream with mischievous laughter and make for safety. Raicharan was amazed at the profound skill and exact judgment the baby showed when pursued. He would say to his mistress with a look of awe and mystery: "Your son will be a judge some day."

New wonders came in their turn. When the baby began to toddle, that was to Raicharan an epoch in human history. When he called his father Ba-ba and his mother Ma-ma and Raicharan Chan-na, then Raicharan's ecstasy knew no bounds. He went out to tell the news to all the world.

After a while Raicharan was asked to show his ingenuity in other ways. He had, for instance, to play the part of a horse, holding the reins between his teeth and prancing with his feet. He had also to wrestle with his little charge; and if he could not, by a wrestler's trick, fall on his back defeated at the end a great outcry was certain.

About this time Anukul was transferred to a district on the banks of the Padma. On his way through Calcutta he bought his son a little go-cart. He bought him also a yellow satin waistcoat, a gold-laced cap, and some gold bracelets and anklets. Raicharan was wont to take these out and put them on his little charge, with ceremonial pride, whenever they went for a walk.

Then came the rainy season and day after day the rain poured down in torrents. The hungry river, like an enormous serpent, swallowed down terraces, villages, cornfields, and covered with its flood the tall grasses and wild casuarinas on the sandbanks. From time to time there was a deep thud as the river-banks crumbled. The unceasing roar of the main current could be heard from far away. Masses of foam, carried swiftly past, proved to the eye the swiftness of the stream.

One afternoon the rain cleared. It was cloudy, but cool and bright. Raicharan's little despot did not want to stay in on such a fine afternoon. His lordship climbed into the go-cart. Raicharan, between the shafts, dragged him slowly along till he reached the rice-fields on the banks of the river. There was no one in the fields and no boat on the stream. Across the water, on the farther side, the clouds were rifted in the west. The silent ceremonial of the setting sun was revealed in all its glowing splendour. In the midst of that stillness the child, all of a sudden, pointed with his finger in front of him and cried: "Chan-na! Pitty fow."

Close by on a mud-flat stood a large Kadamba tree in full flower. My lord, the baby, looked at it with greedy eyes and Raicharan knew his meaning. Only a short time before he had made, out of these very flower balls, a small go-cart; and the child had been so entirely happy dragging it about with a string, that for the whole day Raicharan was not asked to put on the reins at all. He was promoted from a horse into a groom.

But Raicharan had no wish that evening to go splashing knee-deep through the mud to reach the flowers. So he quickly pointed his finger in the opposite direction, calling out: "Look, baby, look! Look at the bird." And with all sorts of curious noises he pushed the go-cart rapidly away from the tree.

But a child, destined to be a judge, cannot be put off so easily. And besides, there was at the time nothing to attract his eyes. And you cannot keep up for ever the pretence of an imaginary bird.

The little Master's mind was made up, and Raicharan was at his wits' end. "Very well, baby," he said at last, "you sit still in the cart, and I'll go and get you the pretty flower. Only mind you don't go near the water."

As he said this, he made his legs bare to the knee, and waded through the oozing mud towards the tree.

The moment Raicharan had gone, his little Master's thoughts went off at racing speed to the forbidden water. The baby saw the river rushing by, splashing and gurgling as it went. It seemed as though the disobedient wavelets themselves were running away from some greater Raicharan with the laughter of a thousand children. At the sight of their mischief, the heart of the human child grew excited and restless. He got down stealthily from the go-cart and toddled off towards the river. On his way he picked up a small stick and leant over the bank of the stream pretending to fish. The mischievous fairies of the river with their mysterious voices seemed inviting him into their play-house.

Raicharan had plucked a handful of flowers from the tree and was carrying them back in the end of his cloth, with his face wreathed in smiles. But when he reached the go-cart there was no one there. He looked on all sides and there was no one there. He looked back at the cart and there was no one there.

In that first terrible moment his blood froze within him. Before his eyes the whole universe swam round like a dark mist. From the depth of his broken heart he gave one piercing cry: "Master, Master, little Master."

But no voice answered "Chan-na." No child laughed

mischievously back: no scream of baby delight welcomed his return. Only the river ran on with its splashing, gurgling noise as before,—as though it knew nothing at all and had no time to attend to such a tiny human event as the death of a child.

As the evening passed by Raicharan's mistress became very anxious. She sent men out on all sides to search. They went with lanterns in their hands and reached at last the banks of the Padma. There they found Raicharan rushing up and down the fields, like a stormy wind, shouting the cry of despair: "Master, Master, little Master!"

When they got Raicharan home at last, he fell prostrate at the feet of his mistress. They shook him, and questioned him, and asked him repeatedly where he had left the child; but all he could say was that he knew nothing.

Though every one held the opinion that the Padma had swallowed the child, there was a lurking doubt left in the mind. For a band of gipsies had been noticed outside the village that afternoon, and some suspicion rested on them. The mother went so far in her wild grief as to think it possible that Raicharan himself had stolen the child. She called him aside with piteous entreaty and said: "Raicharan, give me back my baby. Give me back my child. Take from me any money you ask, but give me back my child!"

Raicharan only beat his forehead in reply. His mistress ordered him out of the house.

Anukul tried to reason his wife out of this wholly unjust suspicion: "Why on earth," he said, "should he commit such a crime as that?"

The mother only replied: "The baby had gold ornaments on his body. Who knows?"

It was impossible to reason with her after that.

II

Raicharan went back to his own village. Up to this time he had had no son, and there was no hope that any child would now be born to him. But it came about before the end of a year that his wife gave birth to a son and died.

An overwhelming resentment at first grew up in Raicharan's heart at the sight of this new baby. At the back of his mind was resentful suspicion that it had come as a usurper in place of the little Master. He also thought it would be a grave offence to be happy with a son of his own after what had happened to his master's little child. Indeed, if it had not been for a widowed sister, who mothered the new baby, it would not have lived long.

But a change gradually came over Raicharan's mind. A wonderful thing happened. This new baby in turn began to crawl about, and cross the doorway with mischief in its face. It also showed an amusing cleverness in making its escape to safety. Its voice, its sounds of laughter and tears, its gestures, were those of the little Master. On some days, when Raicharan listened to its crying, his heart suddenly began thumping wildly against his ribs, and it seemed to him that his former little Master was crying somewhere in the unknown land of death because he had lost his Chan-na.

Phailna (for that was the name Raicharan's sister gave to the new baby) soon began to talk. It learnt to say Ba-ba and Ma-ma with a baby accent. When Raicharan heard those familiar sounds the mystery suddenly became clear. The little Master could not cast off the spell of his Chan-na and therefore he had been reborn in his own house.

The three arguments in favour of this were, to Raicharan, altogether beyond dispute:

The new baby was born soon after his little master's death.

His wife could never have accumulated such merit as to give birth to a son in middle age.

The new baby walked with a toddle and called out Ba-ba and Ma-ma.—There was no sign lacking which marked out the future judge.

Then suddenly Raicharan remembered that terrible accusation of the mother. "Ah," he said to himself with amazement, "the mother's heart was right. She knew I had stolen her child."

When once he had come to this conclusion, he was filled with remorse for his past neglect. He now gave himself over, body and soul, to the new baby and became its devoted attendant. He began to bring it up as if it were the son of a rich man. He bought a go-cart, a yellow satin waistcoat, and a gold-embroidered cap. He melted down the ornaments of his dead wife and made gold bangles and anklets. He refused to let the little child play with any one of the neighbourhood and became himself its sole companion day and night. As the baby grew up to boyhood, he was so petted and spoilt and clad in such finery that the village children would call him "Your Lordship," and jeer at him; and older people regarded Raicharan as unaccountably crazy about the child.

At last the time came for the boy to go to school. Raicharan sold his small piece of land and went to Calcutta. There he got employment with great difficulty as a servant and sent Phailna to school. He spared no pains to give him the best education, the best clothes, the best food. Meanwhile, he himself lived on a mere handful of rice and would say in secret: "Ah, my little Master, my dear little Master, you loved me so much that you came back to my house! You shall never suffer from any neglect of mine."

Twelve years passed away in this manner. The boy was able to read and write well. He was bright and healthy and good-looking. He paid a great deal of attention to his personal appearance and was specially careful in parting his hair. He was inclined to extravagance and finery and spent money freely. He could never quite look on Raicharan as a father, because, though fatherly in affection, he had the manner of a servant. A further fault was this, that Raicharan kept secret from every one that he himself was the father of the child.

The students of the hostel, where Phailna was a boarder, were greatly amused by Raicharan's country manners, and I have to confess that behind his father's back Phailna joined in their fun. But, in the bottom of their hearts, all the students loved the innocent and tender-hearted old man, and Phailna was very fond of him also. But, as I have said before, he loved him with a kind of condescension.

Raicharan grew older and older, and his employer was continually finding fault with him for his incompetent work. He had been starving himself for the boy's sake, so he had grown physically weak and no longer up to his daily task. He would forget things and his mind became dull and stupid. But his employer expected a full servant's work out of him and would not brook excuses. The money that Raicharan had brought with him from the sale of his land was exhausted. The boy was continually grumbling about his clothes and asking for more money.

III

Raicharan made up his mind. He gave up the situation where he was working as a servant, and left some money with Phailna and said: "I have some business to do at home in my village, and shall be back soon."

He went off at once to Baraset where Anukul was magistrate. Anukul's wife was still broken down with grief. She had had no other child.

One day Anukul was resting after a long and weary day in court. His wife was buying, at an exorbitant price, a herb from a mendicant quack, which was said to ensure the birth of a child. A voice of greeting was heard in the courtyard. Anukul went out to see who was there. It was Raicharan. Anukul's heart was softened when he saw his old servant. He asked him many questions and offered to take him back into service.

Raicharan smiled faintly and said in reply: "I want to make obeisance to my mistress."

Anukul went with Raicharan into the house, where the mistress did not receive him as warmly as his old master. Raicharan took no notice of this, but folded his hands and said: "It was not the Padma that stole your baby. It was I."

Anukul exclaimed: "Great God! Eh! What! Where is he?"

Raicharan replied: "He is with me. I will bring him the day after to-morrow."

It was Sunday. There was no magistrate's court sitting. Both husband and wife were looking expectantly along the road, waiting from early morning for Raicharan's appearance. At ten o'clock he came leading Phailna by the hand.

Anukul's wife, without a question, took the boy into her lap and was wild with excitement, sometimes laughing, sometimes weeping, touching him, kissing his hair and his forehead, and gazing into his face with hungry, eager eyes. The boy was very good-looking and dressed like a gentleman's son. The heart of Anukul brimmed over with a sudden rush of affection.

Nevertheless the magistrate in him asked: "Have you any proofs?"

Raicharan said: "How could there be any proof of such a deed? God alone knows that I stole your boy, and no one else in the world."

When Anukul saw how eagerly his wife was clinging to the boy, he realised the futility of asking for proofs. It would be wiser to believe. And then,—where could an old man like Raicharan get such a boy from? And why should his faithful servant deceive him for nothing?

"But," he added severely, "Raicharan, you must not stay here."

"Where shall I go, Master?" said Raicharan, in a choking voice, folding his hands. "I am old. Who will take in an old man as a servant?"

The mistress said: "Let him stay. My child will be pleased. I forgive him."

But Anukul's magisterial conscience would not allow him. "No," he said, "he cannot be forgiven for what he has done."

Raicharan bowed to the ground and clasped Anukul's feet. "Master," he cried, "let me stay. It was not I who did it. It was God."

Anukul's conscience was more shocked than ever when Raicharan tried to put the blame on God's shoulders.

"No," he said, "I could not allow it. I cannot trust you any more. You have done an act of treachery."

Raicharan rose to his feet and said: "It was not I who did it."

"Who was it then?" asked Anukul.

Raicharan replied: “It was my fate.”

But no educated man could take this for an excuse. Anukul remained obdurate.

When Phailna saw that he was the wealthy magistrate’s son, and not Raicharan’s, he was angry at first, thinking that he had been cheated all this time of his birthright. But seeing Raicharan in distress, he generously said to his father: “Father, forgive him. Even if you don’t let him live with us, let him have a small monthly pension.”

After hearing this, Raicharan did not utter another word. He looked for the last time on the face of his son. He made obeisance to his old master and mistress. Then he went out and was mingled with the numberless people of the world.

At the end of the month Anukul sent him some money to his village. But the money came back. There was no one there of the name of Raicharan.

Once There was a King

"Once upon a time there was a king."

When we were kids there was no compelling reason to know who the king in a fairytale was. It didn't make a difference whether he was called Shiladitya or Shaliban, regardless of whether he lived in Kashi or Kanauj. The thing that made a seven-year-old kid's heart pound, pound with excitement and charm was this one sovereign truth, this reality of all substances: "Once there was a king."

But the readers of this modern age are significantly more exact and demanding. When they hear such an opening to a story, they are at once suspicious and skeptical. They apply the searchlight of science to its traditional haze and ask: "Which king?"

The story-tellers have become more precise in their turn. They are no longer content with the old indefinite, "There was a king," but assume instead a look of profound learning and begin: "Once there was a king named Ajatasatru."

The modern reader's curiosity, however, is not so easily satisfied. He blinks at the author through his scientific spectacles and asks again: "Which Ajatasatru?"

When we were young, we understood all sweet things; and we could detect the sweets of a fairy story by an unerring science of our own. We never cared for such useless things as knowledge. We only cared for truth. And our unsophisticated little hearts knew well where the Crystal Palace of Truth lay and how to reach it. But to-day we are expected to write pages of facts, while the truth is simply this:

"There was a king."

I remember vividly that evening in Calcutta when the fairy story began. The rain and the storm had been incessant. The whole of the city was flooded. The water was knee-deep in our lane. I had a straining hope, which was almost a certainty, that my tutor would be prevented from coming that evening. I sat on the stool in the far corner of the verandah looking down the lane, with a heart beating faster and faster. Every minute I kept my eye on the rain, and when it began to diminish I prayed with all my might: "Please, God, send some more rain till half-past seven is over." For I was quite ready to believe that there was no other need for rain except to protect one helpless boy one evening in one corner of Calcutta from the deadly clutches of his tutor.

If not in answer to my prayer, at any rate according to some grosser law of nature, the rain did not give up.

But, alas, nor did my teacher!

Exactly to the minute, in the bend of the lane, I saw his approaching umbrella. The great bubble of hope burst in my breast, and my heart collapsed. Truly, if there is a punishment to fit the crime after death, then my tutor will be born again as me, and I shall be born as my tutor.

As soon as I saw his umbrella I ran as hard as I could to my mother's room. My mother and my grandmother were sitting opposite one another playing cards by the light of a lamp. I ran into the room, and flung myself on the bed beside my mother, and said:

"Mother, the tutor has come, and I have such a bad headache; couldn't I have no lessons to-day?"

I hope no child of immature age will be allowed to read this story, and I sincerely trust it will not be used in text-books or primers for junior classes. For what I did was dreadfully bad, and I received no punishment whatever. On the contrary, my wickedness was crowned with success.

My mother said to me: "All right," and turning to the servant added: "Tell the tutor that he can go back home."

It was perfectly plain that she didn't think my illness very serious, as she went on with her game as before and took no further notice. And I also, burying my head in the pillow, laughed to my heart's content. We perfectly understood one another, my mother and I.

But every one must know how hard it is for a boy of seven years old to keep up the illusion of illness for a long time. After about a minute I got hold of Grandmother and said: "Grannie, do tell me a story."

I had to ask this many times. Grannie and Mother went on playing cards and took no notice. At last Mother said to me: "Child, don't bother. Wait till we've finished our game." But I persisted: "Grannie, do tell me a story." I told Mother she could finish her game to-morrow, but she must let Grannie tell me a story there and then.

At last Mother threw down the cards and said: "You had better do what he wants. I can't manage him." Perhaps she had it in her mind that she would have no tiresome tutor on the morrow, while I should be obliged to be back at those stupid lessons.

As soon as ever Mother had given way, I rushed at Grannie. I got hold of her hand, and, dancing with delight, dragged her inside my mosquito curtain on to the bed. I clutched hold of the bolster with both hands in my excitement, and jumped up and down with joy, and when I had got a little quieter said: "Now, Grannie, let's have the story!"

Grannie went on: "And the king had a queen."

That was good to begin with. He had only one!

It is usual for kings in fairy stories to be extravagant in queens. And whenever we hear that there are two queens our hearts begin to sink. One is sure to be unhappy. But in Grannie's story that danger was past. He had only one queen.

We next hear that the king had not got any son. At the age of seven I didn't think there was any need to bother if a man had no son. He might only have been in the way.

Nor are we greatly excited when we hear that the king has gone away into the forest to practise austerities in order to get a son. There was only one thing that would have made me go into the forest, and that was to get away from my tutor!

But the king left behind with his queen a small girl, who grew up into a beautiful princess.

Twelve years pass away, and the king goes on practising austerities, and never thinks all this while of his beautiful daughter. The princess has reached the full bloom of her youth. The age of marriage has passed, but the king does not return. And the queen pines away with grief and cries: "Is my golden daughter destined to die unmarried? Ah me, what a fate is mine!"

Then the queen sent men to the king to entreat him earnestly to come back for a single night and take one meal in the palace. And the king consented.

The queen cooked with her own hand, and with the greatest care, sixty-four dishes. She made a seat for him of sandal-wood and arranged the food in plates of gold and cups of silver. The princess stood behind with the peacock-tail fan in her hand. The king, after twelve years' absence, came into the house, and the princess waved the fan, lighting up all the room with her beauty. The king looked in his daughter's face and forgot to take his food.

At last he asked his queen: "Pray, who is this girl whose beauty shines as the gold image of the goddess? Whose daughter is she?"

The queen beat her forehead and cried: "Ah, how evil is my fate! Do you not know your own daughter?"

The king was struck with amazement. He said at last: "My tiny daughter has grown to be a woman."

"What else?" the queen said with a sigh. "Do you not know that twelve years have passed by?"

"But why did you not give her in marriage?" asked the king.

"You were away," the queen said. "And how could I find her a suitable husband?"

The king became vehement with excitement. "The first man I see to-morrow," he said, "when I come out of the palace shall marry her."

The princess went on waving her fan of peacock feathers, and the king finished his meal.

The next morning, as the king came out of his palace, he saw the son of a Brahman gathering sticks in the forest outside the palace gates. His age was about seven or eight.

The King said: "I will marry my daughter to him."

Who can interfere with a king's command? At once the boy was called, and the marriage garlands were exchanged between him and the princess.

At this point I came up close to my wise Grannie and asked her eagerly: "When then?"

In the bottom of my heart there was a devout wish to substitute myself for that fortunate wood-gatherer of seven years old. The night was resonant with the patter of rain. The earthen lamp by my bedside was burning low. My grandmother's voice droned on as she told the story. And all these things served to create in a corner of my credulous heart the belief that I had been gathering sticks in the dawn of some indefinite time in the kingdom of some unknown king, and in a moment garlands had been exchanged between me and the princess, beautiful as the Goddess of Grace. She had a gold band on her hair and gold earrings in her ears. She had a necklace and bracelets of gold, and a golden waist-chain round her waist, and a pair of golden anklets tinkled above her feet.

If my grandmother were an author, how many explanations she would have to offer for this little story! First of all, every one would ask why the king remained twelve years in the forest? Secondly, why should the king's daughter remain unmarried all that while? This would be regarded as absurd.

Even if she could have got so far without a quarrel, still there would have been a great hue and cry about the marriage itself. First, it never happened. Secondly, how could there be a marriage between a princess of the Warrior Caste and a boy of the priestly Brahman Caste? Her readers would have imagined at once that the writer was preaching against our social customs in an underhand way. And they would write letters to the papers.

So I pray with all my heart that my grandmother may be born a grandmother again, and not through some cursed fate take birth as her luckless grandson.

With a throb of joy and delight, I asked Grannie: "What then?"

Grannie went on: Then the princess took her little husband away in great distress, and built a large palace with seven wings, and began to cherish her husband with great care.

I jumped up and down in my bed and clutched at the bolster more tightly than ever and said: "What then?"

Grannie continued: The little boy went to school and learnt many lessons from his teachers, and as he grew up his class-fellows began to ask him: "Who is that beautiful lady living with you in the palace with the seven wings?"

The Brahman's son was eager to know who she was. He could only remember how one day he had been gathering sticks and a great disturbance arose. But all that was so long ago that he had no clear recollection.

Four or five years passed in this way. His companions always asked him: "Who is that beautiful lady in the palace with the seven wings?" And the Brahman's son would come back from school and sadly tell the princess: "My school companions always ask me who is that beautiful lady in the palace with the seven wings, and I can give them no reply. Tell me, oh, tell me, who you are!"

The princess said: "Let it pass to-day. I will tell you some other day." And every day the Brahman's son would ask: "Who are you?" and the princess would reply: "Let it pass to-day. I will tell you some other day." In this manner four or five more years passed away.

At last the Brahman's son became very impatient and said: "If you do not tell me to-day who you are, O beautiful lady, I will leave this palace with the seven wings." Then the princess said: "I will certainly tell you to-morrow."

Next day the Brahman's son, as soon as he came home from school, said: "Now, tell me who you are." The princess said:

"To-night I will tell you after supper, when you are in bed."

The Brahman's son said: "Very well"; and he began to count the hours in expectation of the night. And the princess, on her side, spread white flowers over the golden bed, and lighted a gold lamp with fragrant oil, and adorned her hair, and dressed herself in a beautiful robe of blue, and began to count the hours in expectation of the night.

That evening when her husband, the Brahman's son, had finished his meal, too excited almost to eat, and had gone to the golden bed in the bedchamber strewn with flowers, he said to himself: "To-night I shall surely know who this beautiful lady is in the palace with the seven wings."

The princess took for her food that which was left over by her husband, and slowly entered the bedchamber. She had to answer that night the question, who was the beautiful lady that lived in the palace with the seven wings. And as she went up to the bed to tell him she found a serpent had crept out of the flowers and had bitten the Brahman's son. Her boy-husband was lying on the bed of flowers, with face pale in death.

My heart suddenly ceased to throb, and I asked with choking voice: "What then?"

Grannie said: "Then ..."

But what is the use of going on any further with the story? It would only lead on to what was more and more impossible. The boy of seven did not know that, if there were some "What then?" after death, no grandmother of a grandmother could tell us all about it.

But the child's faith never admits defeat, and it would snatch at the mantle of death itself to turn him back. It would be outrageous for him to think that such a story of one teacherless evening could so suddenly come to a stop. Therefore the grandmother had to call back her story from the ever-shut chamber of the great End, but she does it so simply: it is merely by floating the dead body on a banana stem on the river, and having some incantations read by a magician. But in that rainy night and in the dim light of a lamp death loses all its horror in the mind of the boy, and seems nothing more than a deep slumber of a single night. When the story ends the tired eyelids are weighed down with sleep. Thus it is that we send the little body of the child floating on the back of sleep over the still water of time, and then in the morning read a few verses of incantation to restore him to the world of life and light.

Bankim Chandra Chattopadhyay

(1838-1894)

The Globe of Gold

On Koylas Peak, underneath the sprouting Deodars, sat Mahadev and his life partner Parvati, on tiger skins, tossing the dice. The stake was a globe of gold. The flaw in Mahadev's play was that he couldn't win the stake. Had he possessed the capacity to do as such at the churning of the sea, the venom would not have held up in his throat.

In any case, Parvati was shrewd at winning the stake; in verification of which, witness her yearly three days' worship on earth. However it may be with the dice, at crying she was unrivaled, having phenomenal capacity in it. Accordingly, if a high toss tumbled to Mahadev she awaken the neighbourhood with her wails, and when a low number tumbled to herself she would cast at the three-eyed Mahadev a look meant to demolish the universe, so that however he got the winning toss, he acted up not to see it, and lost the stake. This was the perpetual outcome.

So Mahadev consented to bestow upon Parvati the golden ball, which she had no sooner obtained than she threw it down upon the earth: whereupon the five-faced god demanded with a frown, "Why have you thrown away my gift?"

Parvati replied, "Lord! your ball must certainly possess some wonderfully beneficent property. I have cast it down to benefit mankind."

The god made answer, "Lady, no good can result from opposing the laws by which Prajâpati, Vishnu and I have framed the universe. Prosperity can come only from obedience to these laws. A golden ball can serve no purpose. If it have any beneficent property, the laws being broken, it will injure mankind. At your suggestion I have endued it with a special quality. Sit here, and watch how it works."

Kali Kanta Babu was a man of good position, in age about thirty-five, of a goodly presence. Some years earlier he had contracted a second marriage, and he was now on his way to visit his wife, Kama Sundari, a girl about eighteen, now staying at her father's house. His father-in-law was a wealthy man, residing at a village on the banks of the Ganges.

Kali Kanta, fastening his boat to the Ghāt, set out on foot for the house of his father-in-law, attended by his servant, Rama, bearing his portmanteau. Kali Kanta Babu noticed a golden ball lying in the path. Picking it up in astonishment, he found it was indeed of fine gold. Much pleased, he handed it to his servant, saying, "I see this is golden; some one must have lost it. If it is inquired for I will produce it, otherwise, I will take it home with me. For the present, keep it carefully."

In order to conceal the ball in his dress, Rama put down the portmanteau, then taking the golden thing from his master's hand he hid it in his garments. But Rama did not again place the portmanteau on his head. Kali Kanta took it up and placed it on his own head. Rama went on in front, the Babu followed with his load. Presently Rama called out "Hi, you Rama!"

Babu. "What do you wish, Sir?"

Rama. "You are an ill-mannered fellow. Take care that you are guilty of no rudeness in my father-in-law's house. They are gentlefolk."

Babu. "Could I possibly commit any rudeness in your presence?"

In Koylas, Parvati was saying, "My lord! I can't understand this at all. What is this property in your golden ball?"

Mahadev answered, "Its property is exchange of mental personality. If I were to place this ball in Nandi's hand he would think 'I am Mahadev,' and would take me to be Nandi. I should think myself Nandi and fancy Nandi to be Mahadev. Rama thinks, 'I am Kali Kanta Babu,' and takes the Babu to be the servant Rama. Kali Kanta thinks, 'I am Rama Khansama,' and fancies Rama to be Kali Kanta Babu."

When Kali Kanta Babu arrived at the house, his father-in-law was in the inner apartments. But the confusion began outside. The gatekeeper, Ram Din Panre, said, "Hi, Khansamaji, don't sit there, come and sit with us." Whereupon Rama replied angrily, "Go, go you rustic fellow, mind your own business."

The gatekeeper took down the portmanteau from the head of Kali Kanta Babu, who said, "Do not insult the Babu in that manner. He will become angry and go away."

The gatekeeper was acquainted with the son-in-law, but not with the servant, so when he heard Kali Kanta Babu speak thus he thought, "Since the son-in-law speaks of this person as 'Babu,' he must be some great man in disguise." In this faith he addressed Rama humbly, with joined hands, entreating pardon for his fault. To which Rama answered, "Well, well, send some tobacco."

Udbhab Khansama was an ancient servant of the father-in-law's household. He brought a handsomely mounted huka prepared for use, which Rama, reclining among the cushions, began to smoke. Kali Kanta, seeking the servants' rooms, enjoyed his modest hubble-bubble. Greatly amazed, Udbhab exclaimed, "What is this, Sir? why do you do thus?" Kali Kanta replied, "How can I smoke in his presence?"

Udbhab going to the inner apartments, said to his master: "The Jamai Babu (son-in-law) has arrived, Sir, and a gentleman in disguise has come with him. The Jamai Babu honours him so highly that he will not even smoke before him."

The head of the house, Nil Ratan Babu, came out in haste. Kali Kanta, seeing him, prostrated himself in the distance and moved away. Rama, coming forward, took a pinch of dust from Nil Ratan Babu's feet, and they mutually embraced. Nil Ratan thought "The companion is certainly a well-bred man, but why does the son-in-law act so strangely?"

Nil Ratan Babu sat down to address the usual welcoming inquiries to his visitor, but could make nothing at all of his replies. Meantime, lunch having been prepared in the inner apartments, a female attendant appeared to call the son-in-law to partake of it. Kali Kanta said, "Good gracious!

How can I take food before the Babu has eaten? Let him be served first, then my turn will come; I will eat in your mess, Ma Thakurun."

The maidservant, hearing herself addressed in this respectful manner, thought to herself, "The Jamai Babu takes me for one of the family! Why should he not? I come of respectable people and show it in my looks. He sees all sorts and can distinguish, not like the stupid people in this house, who don't know a gentlewoman when they see one." So, greatly pleased, the maid, Bindi, went inside and reported that the Jamai Babu's scruple was admirable, that it would not be suitable for him to eat until his companion had eaten, that the friend should be served first.

The mistress thought, "This is some stranger, so let him be served outside, and the son-in-law in the inner apartments." Rama, seeing preparations for his lunch in the outer apartments, was much incensed, thinking "What a strange proceeding is this."

In the meantime the maid called Kali Kanta to lunch. All was ready within, but Kali Kanta, standing in the courtyard, said, "Why should I go in? Give me a little pulse and treacle in my hand to eat here."

The sister-in-law said, "What a lot of funny ways you have learned."

Distressed, Kali Kanta replied, "Why do you make fun of me? Am I a fit object for your sport?"

An elder lady said, "Why an object of sport to us? Go to her who has the right to jest with you." And taking his hand, stumbling as she went, she pulled him into the room.

Kali Kanta's wife, Kama Sundari, was standing there. Kali Kanta, taking her to be the wife of his master, prostrated himself before her. At this, Kama Sundari's lovely face broke into smiles. "What game is this?" she asked. "What new jest have you learned?"

Troubled by these words, Kali Kanta said, "Oh! why will you speak to me thus? I am your servant, you are my lord."

"You are servant, I am master? not for to-day or tomorrow only—so long as I live that relation shall continue. Now eat your lunch."

Kali Kanta. "If anyone has represented me to you in that light he has lied. Humbly I beg of you, as my preceptress, to let me go."

Jest-loving Kama Sundari thought this was indeed a new sort of game. She said, "Dearer than life, I begin to see that you have learned some fine jokes this time," and taking his two hands, she again pulled him towards the seat.

No sooner had she caught him by the hand than he, thinking all was over with him, shouted out, "Help! help I am done for! she is killing me!"

The frightened family came running at these cries. Kama Sundari, at the sight of her mother, sister, and aunt, released her husband's hands, and he, seizing this opportunity, with a long breath, escaped.

The mistress asked her daughter, "What is the matter, Kami? Why has the son-in-law gone in this way? Did you strike him?"

Amazed and wounded to the heart, Kama Sundari answered, "I strike him! why should I strike him—with so evil a fate as mine?" Gradually her voice was lost in sobs. "My evil destiny—some wretch has destroyed me—has bewitched him." These cries attracted a crowd around her. They said, "Yes, you must have struck him, else why should he call out so piteously?" And they called her names—"sinful one," "witch," "ogress," &c., scolding her. The innocent Kama Sundari, thus reproached, went weeping to her room, closed the door, and laid herself down on her bed.

Meantime, Kali Kanta, coming out, saw that a great commotion had arisen. Nil Ratan Babu himself, the gate keeper, and Udbhab, were all belabouring Rama wherever they chanced to find him. Amid the shower of slaps and cuffs raining upon him, Rama kept saying, "Let me go, I never heard of a son-in-law being beaten so; it does not matter to me, but do you want to make your daughter a widow?"

Near by stood Taranga, the maid servant, laughing. She was accustomed to go to the son-in-law's house, and told her master that she recognised the man as being the Babu's servant, Rama. Kali Kanta Babu, seeing the beating going on, paced the courtyard like one distraught, crying, "How dreadful! they are beating the Babu!"

At this, Nil Ratan Babu, yet more enraged, said to Rama, "You, fellow! what have you given the son-in-law to eat to madden him? Beat the rascal with a shoe!"

At this command, as rain follows rain in August, so on the guiltless Rama fell the rain of blows. In the pain of the beating, the ball hidden in his garments fell to the ground. The maid, Taranga, picking it up, offered it to her master, saying, "This good-for-nothing fellow is a thief! See, Sir, he has stolen a golden ball." "Let me see it," said Nil Ratan Babu, taking it from her. Then, letting Rama go, he stood aside, opened the pleated fold of his upper garment, and cast it over his head (like a woman's veil), while Taranga, letting her sari fall from her head, tucked it up like a man's, and was about to beat Rama with the slipper, when Udbhab said to her, "You, woman, why are you again mixing yourself up with this?"

Taranga. "Whom are you calling woman?"

Udbhab. "You!"

Taranga. "You mock at me!" and, with the slipper in her hand, she struck Udbhab. He, greatly incensed, but unwilling to strike a woman, looked towards his master, saying, "See, Sir, the impudence of this woman, she is striking me with a shoe!"

But the master, pulling his veil a little more over his face, with a merry smile, said, sweetly, "Yes, he is striking you; but do not be angry. He is the master, and may do so."

Whereat Udbhab, yet more incensed, replied, "How is she my master? She is a servant, I also am a servant. How can you talk like this? I am your servant; how can I be hers? I don't serve on those terms."

Again, smiling merrily, the master said, in the same gentle

voice, "What curious fancies we see in old men! My servant! how can you be that?"

Speechless with amazement, Udbhab thought, "Have we got into a lunatic neighbourhood to-day?" And in his surprise he let go Rama, and remained standing.

At this moment, Gobordhan Ghosh, keeper of the household cows, came up—he was Taranga's husband. He was astonished at Taranga's condition and behaviour, also she took no notice of him: while, on the other hand, the master of the house, seeing Gobordhan, again drew the veil off his face and stood aside. Looking sideways at Gobordhan, he whispered, "Don't mix yourself up in that."

Gobordhan, witnessing Taranga's conduct, became enraged; the master's words did not reach his ear. He went to seize Taranga by the hair, "Vile woman!" he exclaimed; "have you no shame?" Seeing him coming, Taranga said, "Gobordhan! are you also out of your senses? go and feed the cows!"

At this Gobordhan seized her by the hair, and began to abuse her roundly, whereupon Nil Ratan Babu exclaimed, "Heavens! that ill-fated wretch is murdering the master."

Taranga, also becoming furious, said, "Do you dare to touch the person of your master?" and began to strike Gobordhan.

Then the uproar became general. At the sound of it the neighbours, Ram Mukherji, Gobind Chatterji, &c., came up to see what was going on. Ram Mukherji, seeing a golden ball lying about, took it up and gave it to Gobind

Chatterji, saying, "See, Sir, what is this?"

In Koylas, Parvati now said, "Oh, my lord! take back your golden ball, only see! Gobind Chatterji has gone into old Ram Mukherji's inner apartments, and taking the old man's old wife to be his own young wife is addressing sportful speeches to her; and Ram Mukherji's scandalised maid servants are beating the intruder with a broom. Meanwhile, old Ram Mukherji, fancying himself the youthful Gobind Chatterji, has gone to Gobind's inner rooms, and is singing songs to Gobind's wife. Should that ball remain a moment longer in the world there will be confusion in every house. Therefore take it back."

Mahadev answered, "Oh, mountain born! what is the fault in my ball? Is this a new condition of things on earth? Do you not constantly observe the old setting the young in order, the young doing the same by the old? The master behaving like the servant, the servant in his master's seat? Do you never see a man behaving like a woman, or a woman like a man? All these things are constantly happening on the earth, but no one seems to see how ludicrous it is. I have for once made it evident to the senses of all. Now, I take back the ball. At my wish each shall return to his own nature, and no one shall remember what has occurred."

Sarat Chandra Chattopadhyay

(1876-1938)

Lalu

1

I had a childhood friend who was lovingly called Lalu. About 50 years prior – truth be told, such a long time ago that you can't discover it properly – we were classmates in a little Bangla school. We were around ten or eleven years of age at that time. There was no limit to the quantity of pranks Lalu had in his mind by which he would either scare people or overwhelm them.

When, he had bothered his mother with an elastic snake in such a way that she needed to limp alonga sprained lower leg for around seven or eight days. She was annoyed to the point that she requested a mentor to be arranged for him. Each evening the mentor would keep him involved so he would not have time to bug people any more.

Lalu's father disagreed and said no: he himself had never studied under a tutor. It was through sheer perseverance in his studies and after enduring a lot of hardship that he was a successful lawyer today. He wished his son would also study in the same manner. Of course, there was one condition. A tutor would be appointed for Lalu only when he failed to be the first in his class. Though he was relieved at this occasion, Lalu was secretly very cross with his mother. The reason was that she had tried to force a tutor upon him and calling a tutor at home was similar to calling the police.

Lalu's father was a rich householder. A few years back he renovated his old house into a huge three-storied building. Since then, Lalu's mother had kept wishing that the family gurudev would come to their house and bless them. All this time the old man was reluctant to travel so far from Faridpur, but now the opportunity presented itself. Smritiratna had come to Kashi for the solar eclipse and had sent a letter from there stating that he would come to bless Nandarani on his return journey. Joy and excitement were boundless for Lalu's mother. She started the preparations in full swing. After all, gurudev's visit to the house would make it holy.

All the furniture from the big room on the ground floor was removed. A new taped bed with new furnishings arrived for the gurudev to sleep in. Because he would find it difficult to climb up to the puja room on the top floor, a corner of the same room was specified for his puja and rituals.

A few days later, gurudev arrived. But what bad weather! The sky was overcast with dark clouds accompanied by storm and incessant rain. In the meantime, Lalu's mother was so busy preparing sweets and arranging for fruits and flowers that she hardly found any time to breathe. Even with all that she managed to clean up the bed and fix up the mosquito net for the gurudev. After a lot of discussion, the tired guru finished his dinner and went to bed. The servants also retired. Lying down in that neat and comfortable bed, the guru could not help blessing Nandarani once again.

But suddenly in the middle of the night he woke up. Drops of water were falling over his stomach from the ceiling and through the mosquito net. Oh! How cold that water was!

Hurriedly he came out of the bed and wiped his stomach. Then he said to himself, "Even though Nandarani built a new house, the roof has already developed cracks under the strong western sunrays."

The taped bed was not heavy, so the guru dragged it to the other side of the room along with the mosquito net and again lay down to sleep. Just as he closed his eyes, within half a minute a few drops of cold water fell upon his stomach once again. Smritiratna got up again, and dragging the cot to another end of the room once again exclaimed, "I see, the cracks on the terrace seem to have spread from one end to another."

Again he lay down and once again water started dripping on his stomach. Dragging the cot to another corner did not help matters in any way. Water started dripping again. Then he realized that the bed was so wet that he could no longer sleep in it. Smritiratna was in trouble. He was an old man, and although staying in the room was risky, at the same time he was too scared to go out of the room in this unknown place. What would happen if the cracked roof collapsed upon his head? Scared to death, he opened the door and came out to the verandah. Though a lantern was lit there, it was pitch dark outside and no one was in sight.

The storm was raging in full swing accompanied by incessant rain. It was difficult to stand still. He did not know in which room the servants slept. He shouted for them, but there was no answer. There was a wooden bench in one corner of the verandah on which the poor clients of Lalu's father sat prior to their consultation. Gurudev sat down there. Though he felt that it was beyond his dignity to do so, there were no other means left. The cold north wind sprayed some rain water on him and made him shiver with cold. Lifting his feet upon the bench, he pulled one end of his dhoti over his body and tried to make himself as comfortable as he could. Tired after the whole day, his body feeling numb, bitter at heart, with sleepy eyelids, and with the indigestion that had been caused by the rich food and sleepless night, the gurudev was really perturbed. All of a sudden there was a new botheration. Huge mosquitoes started singing in his ears. Worried about the number of mosquitoes that were attacking him, at first he could not shut his eyes. But within two minutes he realized that the mosquitoes were innumerable. There was no brave man in the world who could counter such an army. The biting became unbearable, as did the scratching.

Smritiratna quickly left the place, but the mosquitoes followed him. The water in the room and the mosquitoes outside it really disturbed him. He started flapping his hands and feet, and even tried to hit them with his gamchha, but to no avail. Running around from one end of the room to another, he perspired a lot even on such a cold night. He felt like shouting at the top of his voice but restrained from committing such a childish act. He imagined that Nandarani was fast asleep in her comfortable bed inside a mosquito net and that everyone else in the house was also sleeping peacefully. Only he had no end to his running about. Somewhere a clock struck four, and resigning himself to his fate he said, "Go on biting as much as you can – I can't stand it anymore."

Going to one corner of the verandah he squatted on the floor, saving himself with his back as much as possible.

"If I survive till morning, I'm not going to stay in this horrible place anymore. I will take the first train available for home," he promised himself.

Now he realized why he did not want to visit this place. But soon deep sleep erased all the sorrows of the night and he was nearly senseless in deep slumber.

Nandarani in the meantime woke up at dawn --- she had to look after her gurudev. Though he had had a heavy meal at night, she felt that the food was not sufficient. She even resolved to compensate for it with different items throughout the day. Upon coming downstairs, she found his door open. She felt ashamed that gurudev had woken up before her. Peeping into the room, she found that he was not inside. But what was wrong? The cot on the southern side was now placed north, gurudev's canvas bag which was near the window was now in the middle of the room, and all the utensils used for his pujas were scattered around the room. She could not comprehend what had happened. Coming outside, she called the servants but none of them had woken up. Where did gurudev go alone? Suddenly she saw something – what was it? In one corner of the dark verandah, wasn't it something like a man sitting there? Gathering courage she moved closer and bent down to find her gurudev. In an unexplained fear she shouted, "Thakurmoshai! Thakurmoshai!"

Smritiratna woke up, opened his eyes and sat up straight very slowly. Distressed with fear, worry and shame,

Nandarani started crying. She asked him, "Thakurmoshai, why are you here?"

Smritiratna stood up and said, "There was no end to my misery all night, Ma."

"Why, Baba?"

"You have built a new house no doubt, but the roof is damaged everywhere. All the rain throughout the night did not fall outside but upon my body. Wherever I pulled the bed, water kept falling. I came outside in case the whole roof collapsed upon my head. But here too the huge armies of mosquitoes kept biting me the whole night. I ran from here to there, again from there to here. I think half the blood in my body is no longer there, Ma."

Seeing the pitiable condition of the old gurudev whom she could bring home only after a lot of effort, coaxing and cajoling, Nandarani was moved to tears.

"But Baba," she said, "the house is three-storied. There are two more rooms above yours, so how could rain water pierce through three floors?"

Then suddenly she realized that there might be the handiwork of her wicked Lalu behind it. She rushed to the bed and found that the sheet was totally wet at the center, and drops of water were still falling from the mosquito net. Quickly taking it down, she found a slab of ice wrapped up in a piece of cloth – part of it had not melted and a little piece of it was still left.

Running out wildly, she shouted at whichever servant she

saw, "Where is that wicked Lelo? Leave all your work, go look for him, and wherever you find that devil, beat him, and bring him back."

Lalu's father was just coming downstairs. Perplexed at his wife's condition, he asked, "What are you doing? What happened?"

Bursting into tears Nandarani said, "Either you throw your Lelo out of the house or else I shall go and drown myself in the Ganga today to redeem this sinner."

"What has he done?"

"Go and see for yourself what he has done to gurudev for no reason."

They all went into the room. Nandarani narrated everything, showed him everything. Then she said to her husband, "Tell me, how can I run this house with such a wicked boy?"

Gurudev understood everything. Realizing his own stupidity, he burst out in laughter. Lalu's father turned his face the other way.

The servants came and reported, "Lalu is nowhere in the house."

Another one informed that Lalu was having food at his mashi's house. Mashi did not let him come home. Mashi was Nandarani's younger sister. Her husband was a lawyer too and they lived in another locality. After this incident, Lalu did not dare to come near his house for about fifteen days.

2

His nickname was Lalu. He had a formal, official name yet I don't recollect it. Maybe you realize that "lal" in Hindi means the favourite. I don't know who had given him such a name however such an evenness between a man and his name is not really found. He was universally adored.

Subsequent to leaving school we got admitted to college. Lalu said that he would go for some business. He loaned ten rupees from his mother and began business as a contractor."Lalu, your capital asset is just ten rupees," we let him know. He would smile and say, "Do I need more? This is enough."

Everyone loved Lalu. So he always got the contracts easily. After that, on my way to college, I would often see Lalu standing with an umbrella over his head supervising a few labourers undertaking road repair. Making fun of us he would say, "Go, run –- or you will be marked absent in the attendance register."

Much earlier, when we were younger and studied in a Bangla school, he was everyone's mechanic. He always had several instruments in his schoolbag – the handle of a mortar and pestle, a nail cutter, a broken knife, a carpenter's drill to make holes with, and a horseshoe. I do not know from where he had accumulated these things, but there was no work that he could not do with them. He would do many things for his schoolmates. This included repairing broken umbrellas, fixing the wooden frames of slates, stitching clothes torn while playing games, etc. Moreover, Lalu never declined any work. And he would do it efficiently. Once on the Chhawt festival day, he bought a few paise worth of coloured paper and Indian cork and made some toys with them. Then he went and sold them near the bank of the river for two and a half rupees and with that money fed us a lot of chickpeas.

As the years went by, we all grew up. There was no one in the gymnastics club to compete with Lalu. Both his physical strength and courage were endless. He would turn up whenever anyone called him or whenever anyone was in trouble perhaps because he did not know what fear meant. He had only one serious vice: he could not control himself whenever he found an opportunity to frighten or terrify people. This he did to all men irrespective of their age. How he could invent such plans for frightening people within seconds was beyond our imagination. Let me narrate one or two such incidents.

Kalipuja was being celebrated in our locality at Manohar Chatterjee's house. At midnight, the auspicious time for animal sacrifice was waning away but the man to do it was still absent. People who went to fetch him found him unconscious with stomach ache. When they came back and broke the news, everyone was upset and worried. How could they arrange for another person to do the sacrifice in the middle of the night? The puja for the goddess would be ruined. Someone said, "Lalu can slaughter lambs. He has done this job many times before."People ran for Lalu. He woke up from his sleep and just said "No."

"How can you say no? It would be dangerous if there were

impediments in the puja."

"Let it be interrupted," replied Lalu. "I did all that in childhood but I will not do it now."

Those who had come to call him started scratching their heads. There was hardly ten to fifteen minutes left for the auspicious moment to be over and after that no one would escape from the wrath of the goddess. Lalu's father came and ordered him to go."Since they have come to you in desperation, it would not be good to refuse. You better go" he said. Lalu had no power to disobey his father's command.

Mr. Chatterjee was relieved after seeing Lalu. Time was running short. The sacrificial lamb was hurriedly decorated with sindoor and a red garland of hibiscus and led to the stocks. The loud shouts in unison of "Ma, Ma" by all the members present there subdued the last cries of the helpless animal. The large falchion in Lalu's hand was raised and came down instantly. The spurt of blood from the beheaded beast painted the dark ground in red. For some time Lalu stood with his eyes closed. Gradually the loud noise of drums and cymbals subsided. Again sindoor was smeared on the second lamb's forehead, a red garland hung on his neck, again the stocks and the shouting of "Ma, Ma" in unison. Lalu lifted the blood-smeared falchion once again and brought it down instantly. The severed body of the animal shook for some time before it became still and the animal's blood stained the ground even further.

The drummer kept on beating the drum in full swing, the people stood crowded upon the front verandah, Manohar Chatterjee sat on a carpet seat praying with his eyes closed, when suddenly Lalu delivered a menacing shout. In an instant all the noise subsided and everyone was astonished at his behaviour. Opening his eyes as widely as possible, his eyeballs roving, Lalu shouted, "Where are more lambs?" Someone from the house replied in a scared tone, "There are no more lambs. We just offer only two per year."

Swinging the blood-stained falchion twice above his head, Lalu roared in a rough voice, "No more lambs? That will not do. I want to kill. Either give me lambs or I will get hold of anyone and slaughter him – Ma! Ma! Jai Kali!"

Uttering these words he gave a huge leap over the stocks with the falchion still spinning above his head.

What followed next defies description. Everyone started rushing towards the front door before Lalu could catch them. The rush to escape resulted in a stampede. Some rolled down, some crawled between the legs of other people, some people whose necks were caught under the arms of others were nearly suffocating to death, some even tried to climb above other people's shoulders and fell flat upon the floor. All these lasted for a moment and soon it was empty everywhere.

"Where is Manohar Chatterjee? Where is the purohit?" roared Lalu.

The purohit was a lean man and right at the beginning he had hid himself behind the idol. The gurudev who was sitting on the floor and reciting from the holy scriptures quickly got up and hid behind a huge pillar near the puja pavilion. But it was very difficult for Manohar to run away with his huge body. Lalu came up, caught his arm with his left hand and said, "Come and rest your neck in the stocks."

The firm grip of his arm and the sight the falchion scared Chatterjee to death. In a soft and entreating manner he begged, "Lalu! Dear! Look patiently – I am not a lamb, but a human being. I am your uncle, so to say, dear. Your father is like my younger brother."

"I don't know about that. I want to slaughter. So come and I will sacrifice you. It is the order of the goddess."

"No, dear, it cannot be the dictates of the goddess." Chatterjee sobbed loudly. "It cannot be so – she is the Mother of the world."

"Mother of the world? Do you have that much knowledge? Will you sacrifice lambs again? Will you send for me again to do the slaughter? Answer me."

Chatterjee replied in tears, "No, never again. I am promising before the goddess that from this day onwards there shall not be any more sacrifices in my house."

"Promise?"

"Yes, I promise. Not again. Now dear, let go of my hand. I want to go to the toilet."

Releasing his hand Lalu said, "OK, go, I am letting you off for today. But where did the purohit escape? Where is the gurudev?"

With a menacing shout he rushed towards the goddess. Suddenly cries in two different voices came out from behind the pillar. The combined cries of a thin and a hoarse voice resulted in such a strange and funny situation that Lalu could not control himself anymore. He burst out laughing – Ha, ha, ha! And dropping the falchion upon the floor, scampered away from that house.

It was only then that everyone regained their senses and realized that Lalu was just playing tricks with them. The murderous frenzy was just a part of his deliberate plan to fool everyone. Everyone who had run away assembled back within five minutes. The puja was still incomplete and things had already been delayed for quite some time. Amidst all that hustle and bustle Mr. Chatterjee kept on promising to himself, "If I cannot make that boy's father give him at least fifty blows with a sandal by tomorrow morning, I shall no longer be called Manohar Chatterjee."

But Lalu did not have to undergo that ordeal. He escaped somewhere early in the morning so quietly that no one could find him for about seven or eight days. About a week later he quietly sneaked into Manohar Chatterjee's house one evening and begged forgiveness by touching his feet. So for that instance at least, he was saved from his father's wrath. But whatever it might be, because he had sworn before the goddess, the practice of sacrificing lambs during Kalipuja was forever stopped in the Chatterjee household.

3

With the onset of winter in our city, cholera broke out. The very mention of cholera in those days would make people petrified with fear. If anyone heard that cholera had broken out in one area, they would not stay there anymore. If anyone died, it would be difficult to find people to cremate him. But even in such difficult times, there was one person in our locality who never objected to it. His name was Gopal-khuro and his aim in life was cremating the dead. If anyone was seriously ill, he would go to the doctor everyday and find out about his condition. As soon as he heard that there was no hope left, he would arrive there at least two hours ahead, barefooted and with a gamchha on his shoulders. A few of us were his disciples. He would tell us with a serious face, "Be a bit careful tonight. You should respond instantly if I call you. Do you remember the scriptures? "Rajadware smashane cha….."

Yes, we do remember it. We will come with our gamchas as soon as you call us."

"Ok, Ok, This is what we want. There is no more virtuous deed in the world than this.

Lalu was also part of our group. Except when he was going out on his contractor's job, he never refused. That evening, a morose looking khuro came and told us, "I think Bishtu Pundit's wife will not be saved this time."

All of us were shocked. In our childhood days we had all studied under this very poor schoolmaster. He was congenially sick and always depended on his wife. He had no one else in the world to call his own and I have never seen any more timid and helpless person other than him.

It was around eight at night when the pundit's wife was carried in a rope cot from the bedroom into the courtyard.

The pundit stared at us vacantly and nothing in the world can be compared to such a look. One can never forget it for a whole life.

While we were lifting up the dead body, the pundit asked us very slowly, "If I do not go with you, who will singe the mouth of the dead at cremation?"

Before anyone could reply, Lalu said, "I will do that job, Punditmoshai. You are our guru and in that sense, she is our mother." We all knew that it was impossible for the pundit to walk all the way to the cremation ground. Our Bangla school was hardly a five-minutes walk but he would take more than half an hour's time to come panting all the way.

After remaining quiet for some time Panditmoshai said, "Won't you put some sindoor upon her head before taking her, Lalu?"

"Of course I'll do, Punditmoshai." Saying this, he gave a big leap into the room, brought out the container full of sindoor and emptied it on the corpse's head.

Chanting religious intonations we left the house with its mistress's dead body departing forever while the punditmoshai stood quietly with his hands resting on the panel of the open door.

The cremation ground was situated about six miles away on the banks of the Ganges. When we reached there and placed the cot with the dead body on the floor, it was two o'clock at night. Lalu held on to the cot and squatted on the floor with his feet spread out. In order to ward off their tiredness, some of the others just lay down here and there.

It was a bright lunar fortnight and the empty stretches of the sandy cremation ground spread out endlessly in the moonlight. A cold north wind across the Ganges gave rise to big waves, some of which were breaking almost near Lalu's feet. There was still no sign of the burning logs which usually came from the city by bullock carts. We had already informed the domson our way here. They lived about a mile away and no one knew how long they would take to arrive.

All of a sudden thick grey clouds rose from the horizon across the river and strong northerly winds started blowing towards this side of the riverbank. Warily Gopal-khuro said, "The signs are not good – it might rain. We shall be in trouble if we are drenched in this winter night." There were no shelters nearby, not even a big tree. In the mango orchard at some distance there were a few gardeners' huts but it was not an easy job to run so far out there.

Dark clouds gradually covered the whole sky, the moonlight disappeared in the darkness, and we could hear the hissing sound of fast-falling rain. Like sharp arrows, a few drops first pierced us and by the time we could make up our minds as to what should be done, heavy downpour began. To save themselves, everyone ran helter-skelter leaving the dead body behind.

When the rain stopped about an hour later, we all came back one by one. The sky had cleared, the moonlight reappeared as clear as day. The cartload of firewood and other ingredients had arrived in the meantime and they were preparing to leave. But the domes were nowhere in sight.

"These people are always like that," said Gopal Khuro. "They do not like to come out of their houses in winter."

Moni said, "But why didn't Lalu return till now? He said he would light the pyre. Has he run away home in fear?"

Annoyed with Lalu, Khuro replied," He is like that. If he was so frightened, why was he sitting down holding the dead body? Even if thunder and lightening had struck me, I would not have left the dead body."

"What happens when one leaves the dead body, Khuro?"

"What happens? A lot of things happen. After all this is the cremation ground."

"Would you not feel scared to wait alone in the cremation ground?"

"Scared? Me? Do you know that I have cremated at least a thousand dead bodies?"

Moni could not say anything else after this. Really, Khuro had reasons to be proud.Picking up a shovel that was lying on the floor, Khuro said, "I am digging the pit. You all give a hand in bringing the wood."

Khuro was busy digging, we were carrying the wood, when suddenly Noru said, "Hasn't the dead body swollen up to double its size?"

"Without looking anywhere Khuro replied, "Won't it swell? All the blankets and quilts have been drenched in the rain."

"But cotton is supposed to squeeze smaller when wet, not swell up."

"You have too much of intelligence. Do what you are doing," replied Khuro in anger.

The job of collecting the wood was almost done. Noru had kept a constant watch over the cot of the dead body. He stopped suddenly and said, "Khuro, the dead body seems to be moving."

Khuro had finished his work. Throwing the spade away he said, "I have never seen such a coward like you, Noru. Why do you volunteer for such work? Go and fetch the remaining wood. Let me arrange the pyre. You donkey!"

A couple of minutes elapsed. Now Moni suddenly jumped a few steps back and warily said, " No, Khuro. Things don't seem to be all right. The dead body really seemed to move."

Giving out a loud laugh Khuro smiled and said, "You youngsters, do you want to scare me? Someone who has cremated over a thousand dead bodies?"

"See it's moving again," said Noru.

"Yes, moving. It has become a ghost to eat you up". But even before he could finish his sentence, the wrapped up dead body sat up kneeling on the cot and shouted in a shrill, fearful voice, "No, no. Not Noru. I will eat Gopal."

Scared to death, we started running as fast as we could. There was a huge pile of wood in front of Gopal-khuro. Unable to run behind us, he went and jumped into the Ganges. Standing abreast in that cold water, he kept on shouting, "Oh my God, I'm going to die. The ghost is going to eat me up. Ram –Ram- Ram-"

The ghost on the other hand uncovered his face and kept on shouting, "Hey Nirmal, hey Moni, hey Noru, don't run away. I am Lalu. Come back, come back—"

Lalu's voice reached us. Ashamed at our stupidity, all of us came back. Shivering in the cold, Gopal-khuro also came up to the embankment.

Lalu paid obeisance to him and added in a shy tone, "Everyone left in fear of the rain. But I could not leave the dead body and go, so I had gone under the quilt."

"Very good, dear. You've done a wise job. Now go, smear yourself with the holy mud and take a dip in the Ganges. I've never seen such a wicked boy in my life."

But actually he had forgiven him wholeheartedly. He realized that displaying such fearlessness was impossible for him. Actually, staying alone at night with a dead body inflicted by cholera, amidst all the infected bedding was no mean feat.

While lighting the pyre, Khuro objected, "No, this cannot be done. If she comes to know about it, his mother will never see me again."

The cremation was over. After a dip in the Ganges, the sun was just rising when we headed home.

Devdas

Summary

In the mid 1900s, Kaushalya hears that her younger child, Devdas, is to return home after he had left at an early age for graduate school in England. Kaushalya reveals to her neighbor Sumitra, who is thrilled. Sumitra's daughter, "Paro" Parvati Chakraborty and Devdas have shared a profound friendship since adolescence. At the point when Devdas went to England, Paro had lit an oil lamp wishing for his early return and never lets it smother.

When Devdas returns home, the friendship between him and Paro progresses towards affection. Everybody looks forward to the notion of Devdas and Paro getting married. However Devdas' plotting sister-in-law Kumud helps Kaushalya to remember Paro's maternal heredity of nautch girls and nautanki entertainers, unsuitable for the Mukherjee family. Sumitra freely declares her craving for Devdas and Paro to wed, and Kaushalya rejects and embarrasses her out in the open by saying that she is from a lower class in the public arena. Crushed, Sumitra quickly masterminds Paro's marriage to a man from a wealthier family than the Mukherjees: Thakur Bhuvan Chaudhry, a forty-year-old widowed blue-blood with three grown children.

When Devdas' father also rejects Paro, Devdas leaves his

parents' house and takes refuge at a brothel. He leaves a letter for Paro, falsely stating that love had never existed between them. At the brothel, he meets a good-hearted tawaif (courtesan) named Chandramukhi, who falls in love with him. Soon, Devdas realizes his mistake in abandoning Paro. He returns to her during her wedding and asks her to elope but Paro refuses, reminding him of the way he had discarded her so easily.

Paro learns from her new husband that he has married her only to be mother to his children and lady of the estate, but that his love is only for his late first wife. She dutifully fulfills her responsibilities, while Devdas, heartbroken at having lost Paro, permanently moves to Chandramukhi's brothel and becomes an alcoholic. When Devdas' father is on his deathbed, he asks to see his son Devdas, but Devdas arrives later, at his father's funeral, drunk.

Eventually, Devdas becomes so ill that the slightest dose of alcohol could kill him. He returns to the family home to heal, and discovers that his sister-in-law has stolen his mother's keys to the family safe. He confronts her but Kumud tells his mother that Devdas had stolen the keys. His mother believes her and Devdas leaves, banished. Paro arrives at Chandramukhi's brothel, accusing her of driving Devdas to drink, but soon realizes that Chandramukhi loves Devdas. Paro urges Devdas to stop drinking, but Devdas remains stubborn. He promises Paro that before he dies, he will come to her doorstep one last time.

Paro invites Chandramukhi to a celebration of Durga Puja at her husband's home and introduces her to her in-laws without revealing Chandramukhi's profession. However, Bhuvan's ill-natured son-in-law Kalibabu, a frequent visitor to the brothel, reveals Chandramukhi's background and humiliates her in front of the guests. He also tells Bhuvan of Paro's relationship with Devdas. As a result, Bhuvan permanently forbids Paro from leaving the mansion. Devdas tells Chandramukhi that she must let him go, and decides to travel the country; on a train, he meets his old college friend Chunnibabu, who urges him to drink in the name of friendship. Devdas drinks, knowing full well it will be fatal.

On the verge of death, Devdas travels to Paro's house to honor his promise, collapsing under a tree in front of the main gate. Paro runs through the mansion, attempting to reach him. Bhuvan sees this and orders the servants to shut the gates. Devdas sees a blurred image of Paro running towards him, but the gates close just before she can reach him, leaving her sobbing inside. Devdas dies, whispering Paro's name with his last breath. At the same time, the lamp that Paro had lit for him flickers out forever for all eternity.

Excerpt from Devdas

In this passage from a novel by Sarat Chandra Chattopadhyay, a man visits Calcutta after his father's demise and stumbles upon a courtesan he knows who has fallen on difficult circumstances.

Devdas was aggravated after spending half an year at home after his father's demise. No joys, no peace, an altogether dull existence. To add to everything, constant musings of Parvati, whom he remembered regardless of what he was doing. What's more, his sibling, Dwijdas, and Dwijdas' devoted wife exasperated Devdas' misery in no little measure.

His mother was in a similar difficulty, all her joys departed along with her husband. An existence without freedom was becoming unbearable. She had for quite a while set out to spend whatever remains of her days with different widows in Kashi, yet she couldn't go till she had arranged for wife for Devdas. Her constant grumble: Get married, Devdas, I need to see you wedded before I go. Be that as it may, how could this be conceivable? Not only did their religion not allow a wedding just after a demise in the family, however a suitable woman additionally must be looked for. No wonder Kaushalya was overwhelmed with regret and repented her decision of not having allowed Devdas and Parvati to marry, when they had wanted it with all their heart.

One day she summoned Devdas to tell him of her decision: I cannot bear it here any longer, Devdas. I wish to go to Kashi for some time. Devdas was of the same opinion. I agree, he replied. I can bring you back after six months.

Yes, that's best. When I'm back, after your father's last rites are complete, I'll get you married and then go away to Kashi for good.

Concurring, Devdas escorted his mother to Kashi and then departed for Calcutta. There he spent three or four days looking for his old friend Chunilal. His friend was not to be found, having moved houses and disappeared. One evening Devdas remembered Chandramukhi. Should he not meet the dancing girl? He had not thought of her at all following his father's death. Embarrassed by his own neglect of her, Devdas hired a carriage and appeared before her house soon after dusk. After he had called out her name several times, a woman's voice answered from within, She isn't here.

Devdas moved closer to a lamppost and asked, Can you tell me where she has gone?

The woman opened a window to look at him. Are you Devdas, she asked?

Yes.

Wait, let me open the door.

Come in, she said.

The voice appeared familiar, but he failed to recognize her in the darkness. Do you know where Chandramukhi is, he inquired hesitantly.

With a smile the woman said, I do. Come upstairs.

Finally Devdas recognized her. Is it really you?

Yes, it is. Have you forgotten me completely, Devdas?

Upstairs, Devdas discovered that Chandramukhi was dressed in a plain white sari with a black border. She was wearing no ornaments besides a pair of bangles. Her hair was disheveled. In astonishment, Devdas said, It is you. Looking closely, he found that Chandramukhi had become considerably thinner. Were you indisposed? he asked.

Smiling, Chandramukhi responded, Physically, not at all. Make yourself at home.

Settling himself on the bed, Devdas observed that the room had changed. Like its owner's, its circumstances seemed strained too. Not an item of furniture remained—the spaces where the cupboard, the desk, and the chair had stood were empty now. Only a bed remained, its sheets dirty. The paintings had been removed from the walls, but the nails were still there, as were the red cords in one or two places. The clock still hung on the bracket, but in silence. Spiders had spun webs to their heart's content. In one corner, a dim glow emanated from an oil lamp, enabling Devdas to see the room in its new appearance. With a mixture of surprise and unhappiness he inquired, Why this wretched state of affairs, Chandra?

Smiling dejectedly, Chandramukhi said, Who says it's wretched? My luck has turned.

Not understanding, Devdas said, And what has happened to all your jewelry?

Sold it.

The furniture?

Sold it, too.

Did you sell the paintings as well?

Smiling, Chandramukhi pointed to the house across the road. I gave them away to Khetromoni there.

Gazing at her for a while, Devdas asked, Where's Chuni-babu?

Can't say. He went away after a quarrel two months ago, never came back.

Devdas was even more surprised.Quarreled? Why?

Don't people quarrel?

They do. But why?

He was here as a middleman, so I threw him out.

Middleman for what?

Chandramukhi smiled.

For jute. Is it so hard to understand? He got hold of a rich man, two hundred rupees a month, a box full of ornaments, and a guard at the door. Do you understand now?

Devdas understood. He smiled.

But I don't see any of it.

You would if they were there. I sent them away.

What was their crime?

Nothing much, but I didn't like it.

After a great deal of thought, Devdas said, Hasn't anyone else been here since then?

No. In fact, no one has been here since you left. Only Chuni would turn up now and then, but that too has stopped for two months now.

Devdas stretched out on the bed. Sunk in thought, he was silent for some time. Then he said, So you've closed up shop, Chandramukhi?

Yes, I am penniless.

Without responding to this, Devdas said, How do you propose to survive?

As I told you, I've sold my jewelry.

How much can that have got you?

Not a great deal. I have about eight or nine hundred. I've deposited it with a moneylender, he gives me twenty a month.

Twenty was never enough for you.

It isn't enough now, either. I owe three months' rent. So I've decided to sell these bangles, pay all my creditors, and go away.

Go where?

I haven't decided. Somewhere cheap, a village perhaps, where I can survive on twenty rupees a month.

Why didn't you go earlier? If indeed you do not want anything here, why did you have to prolong your stay and get deeper into debt?

Chandramukhi lowered her eyes. She searched for an answer, embarrassed for the first time in her life at having to say what she was about to. Well? Devdas said.

Sitting down diffidently on one corner of the bed, Chandramukhi slowly began her story.

Don't be angry. I stayed here in the hope of meeting you before leaving. I kept thinking maybe you would visit me once more. Now that you are here, I will make preparations to leave tomorrow. But can you tell me where I should go?

Devdas sat up in astonishment.In the hope of meeting me? But why?

A whim. You hated me so much. Perhaps because no one has ever hated me quite so much. I don't know if you can remember now, but I do, clearly—you had my attention from the day of your very first visit. I knew you were a rich man's son, but your wealth was not what attracted me to you. Many others had been here before you, but in none of them did I see a spirit such as yours. And you hurt me as soon as you arrived—your behavior was undeserved, uncalled-for, and unsuitable. You kept your face averted in disgust, and farcically left some money for me at the end. Do you remember any of this?

Devdas was silent. Chandramukhi continued, You have held my attention since then. Not out of love, and not out of revulsion. Just as one cannot forget something new, I too could not forget you. I was afraid, on my guard when you came, but I hated it when you did not come. And then I don't know what madness took hold of me—I began to look at everything differently. I changed so much that I no longer remained who I was. Then you started drinking. I hate it. I think it's disgusting when someone gets drunk. But in your case I would be upset, not angry.Stopping, Chandramukhi put her hand on Devdas's feet. Tearfully, she said, I am a nobody, do not be angry with me. You used to be so harsh with your words, brush me aside with such revulsion, and the more you did that, the more I wanted to go to you. Then you would finally fall asleep . . . but let me not get into that, I don't want you to get angry again.

Devdas said nothing. These new revelations troubled him. Covertly wiping her eyes, Chandramukhi began to speak once again. Do you remember the day you spoke to me about how much we put up with? Humiliation, disgrace, torment, persecution—I was so upset when you said this that I stopped everything that very same day.

But what will you live on? Devdas asked.

I told you already.

But what if he cheats you out of all your money . . .

Chandramukhi showed no signs of worry. That's not impossible, she said calmly, but I've considered that likelihood too. I will ask you for some money if I get in trouble.

After some thought, Devdas replied, Very well. Now make your arrangements and get out of this place.

Tomorrow. After I've sold these bangles. I'll meet the moneylender.

Taking five one hundred-rupee notes out of his pocket and putting them beneath the pillow, Devdas said, Don't sell the bangles, though you should meet the moneylender. But where will you go? To go to one of those holy places?No, Devdas. I have no faith in holy places. I don't want to live very far from Calcutta, I'll find a village nearby.

Are you thinking of working as a maid for a decent family?

Tears welled up in Chandramukhi's eyes again. Wiping them away, she said, I am not inclined to. I will live independently, in my own way. Why should I put myself through that? I have never had to endure physical suffering before, and I cannot face it now. Any more might tear me apart.

Devdas smiled wanly. But if you remain near the city, he said, you might give in to temptation again. The human heart cannot be trusted.

Chandramukhi's expression changed now. Smiling, she said, That is true, the human heart cannot be trusted, but I won't give in to temptation. I realize that women always desire certain things, but since I have chosen to give up the things I desire on my own, I'm no longer afraid of anything. Had I given all this up on an impulse, perhaps a little more caution might be necessary, but I have not felt a moment's regret in all this time. I'm quite happy, you see.

Still Devdas shook his head, saying, Women are far too fickle, far too untrustworthy.

Chandramukhi stepped close to him. Devdas, she said, taking his hand.

Devdas looked at her. This time he could not tell her not to touch him.

Her eyes brimming with affection, her voice trembling, Chandramukhi drew his hands into her own, saying, It's our last day together, don't be angry today. There's something I've been wanting to ask you.

She gazed at him for a few moments before putting forth her question: Has Parvati hurt you deeply?

Devdas frowned.

Why this question?

Chandramukhi was not discouraged. Quietly and firmly, she replied, I have a reason for asking. I will not lie, it hurts me when you suffer. And besides, I think I know a great deal, I've heard you say many things when you were drunk. Still, I do not believe that Parvati betrayed you.

On the contrary, I believe you have deceived yourself. I am older than you, Devdas, and I have seen a great many things in this world. Do you know what I think? I think it's you who are mistaken. I do not think women deserve this reputation for being fickle and inconstant. It is men like you who praise them, and men like you who criticize them too. You can say what you want to without any consequences, but they cannot. They can't express what's in their hearts, and even when they do, not everyone understands. They are incoherent, and silenced by men.

And yet their infamy only grows.

Pausing, Chandramukhi continued in a clearer voice, I have been in the business of love for a long time, but I have loved only once. I cherish that love. I've learned a lot, you know, love is one thing, and infatuation, another. These two things are often in conflict, and it's men who create the conflict. We are far less attracted by beauty than you men, which is why we do not lose our heads in an instant the way you do. When you come to us and declare your love, expressing it in so many different ways, with so many different words, we stay silent. Often we feel embarrassed or afraid to hurt you, so we hold back. Even when we are repulsed by your very appearance, we cannot bring ourselves to say we do not love you. Then begins the whole charade of love, a mere show, and when it ends, the man says in a fury, You lying slut! That is what everyone hears, that is what everyone believes. And still we remain silent. We suffer so much, but no one seems to care.

Devdas did not reply. Chandramukhi gazed at him in silence for a while and then said, Perhaps a tenderness develops between man and woman. The woman thinks, this is love. She performs her duties quietly and resolutely, provides all the support she can in times of crisis, and you men praise her to the skies. But possibly even at this time she has not learned the alphabet of love. And then, at some dark hour, when she feels an indescribable agony in her heart—Chandramukhi cast a piercing glance at Devdas—that is when you scream, Traitor! Shame!

Suddenly Devdas touched Chandramukhi's mouth with his

hand. What's all this, Chandramukhi?

As he slowly removed his hand, Chandramukhi said, Don't worry, I'm not talking of your Parvati.

Stories from the Ramayana

Jatayu's sacrifice in fight with Ravana

In Ramayan, Jatayu was a very old and loyal vulture.

When he met king Ravana, he was very old. He was the King of the vultures but not very strong that time due to old age. He saw that Sita mata was in trouble and she was calling when Ravana abducted her. Jatayu did not hesitate a moment to serve her. Not to save her but to serve her. Jatayu did not think he could save Sita mata. He wanted to serve her.

There is a difference. We always think that we are saving the satsang program with all our association, but says it is good to remember that you are just a servant not a saviour. We cannot do anything except to serve. So Jatayu flew off into the sky to fight Ravana because he wanted to serve Lord Rama.

He said, "My body is of no value if it is not used in the service of the Lord. The Lord's most precious mother Sita is being kidnapped. It is my duty to stop this."

So Jatayu fought with Ravana and gave him a good run for his money. He made it so difficult for Ravana for a while that he thought that mother Sita is going to be out of this demon king's claws.

But then Ravana's strength came into play. Ravana chopped and somehow severed the wings and limbs of Jatayu.

Jatayu fell in the midst of heap of blood and his life was slowly going away.

When he was dying, Lord Rama and Lakshmana arrived there. Seeing Jatayu, they thought that he must be the demon who is trying to catch Sita. So they approached with caution. When they saw Jatayu actually dying because of Ravana, Lord Rama's heart was in pain.

Jatayu praised Rama, "My dear Lord please forgive me that I could not execute my service to the best of my ability. I failed in my service. But I tried and I could tell you from my knowledge of shastra, the time in which she is leaving now is an auspicious time. Whatever you have lost in this time, you will gain back."

Jatayu even in that condition tried to serve Lord by uttering sweet words to pacify the Lord. He didn't have to because he is already dying. Even then he did not think, "My Lord I tried to serve you, now I am dying, what kind of a Lord you are?"

It is stated in shastras that Jatayu did a nice service to the Lord Ram. At that point Lord decided to conduct funeral of Jatayu just like he is His father and they are his sons.

Lord Ram with Lakshman did the funeral and as the body of Jatayu was being burnt, Rama said, "Today the loss of Jatayu is more painful to Me than the loss of Sita."

This is how Lord Rama values the service of His devotees.

And that service was done with eagerness. Jatayu fought like a young man.

It was done with devotion and meditation of Lord Rama and the result of that was Jatayu did not die in vain but pacified by the darshan of Rama. How many of us can claim to have darshan of the Lord at the point when we leave our body? We don't know. But Jatayu had that. So what appeared to be a failure of effort materially is actually a great success spiritually and the reason for that is remembrance of Krishna.

Ravana, not being in the feet of Lord, lost everything.

Srimad Bhagavatam verse 3.29.39:

na caasya kaschid dayito / na dveshyo na ca baandhavah

aavishaty apramatto 'sau / pramattam janam anta-krt

"No one is dear to the Supreme Personality of Godhead, nor is anyone His enemy or friend. But He gives inspiration to those who have not forgotten Him and destroys those who have."

Service without expectation would please the Lord: The word inspiration means also 'sacrifice'. There is a very subtle link between inspiration and sacrifice.

A devotee who wants to be in the service of the Lord will get inspiration because of his eagerness to do whatever is necessary for devotional service.

Why did Lord Shiva allow Mother Sati to give up Her body?

It is said that when Ravana abducted Mother Sita, and Lord Ram was roaming around looking for Her, He was crying, shouting and moaning as He was so sad to have lost Her.

Of course, the Lord was playing a role on earth as a human, so He had to display human emotions.

Lord Shiva and Mother Sati came across this scene. Lord Shiva from far bowed down to His Lord. Mother Sati said, "why are you bowing down?" Lord Shiva said because He is the Supreme Lord! Mother Sati said that He is crying like humans, how can He be God? I want to test Him. So Lord Shiva said go ahead and test Him, but stay within your principles.

But Mother Sati changed Her form into the form of Mother Sita and went in front of Lord Ram, trying to confuse and fool Him.

Of course, Lord Ram knew she was Mother Sati and greeted Her and asked Her where is Lord Shiva?

She was ashamed and closed Her eyes. But even as Her eyes were closed, Lord Ram gave Her His Darshan along with Mother Sita in Her mind.

She went back to Lord Shiva but did not tell Him how She had tested Lord Ram. But Lord Shiva knew.

And so He thought to Himself, that today She took the form of Mother Sita, whom I worship! So from today I have to look at Sati as a Mother. So He did not let Her sit next to Him anymore. Sati could not bear it and always came in front of Lord Shiva with a crying face. He got tired of seeing this and went into meditation for 87000 years!

And then, as we know, Sati went to the house of Her father, Daksh Prajapati, to attend a Yajna even though She and Lord Shiva were not invited.

When She heard Her Lord Shiva being insulted in that Yajna assembly, She could not take it and jumped into the fire and gave up Her life.

Moral of the story:

So the real reason that Lord Shiva let this happen, because She had not recognized Lord Ram, She had not listened to Him, and She had taken on the form of Mother Sita.

Of course, as we know, in a future birth Mother Sati did come back as Mother Parvati and attained Her beloved Lord Shiva after years of penance.

But let us keep in mind, that Sati did not actually doubt Lord Ram or Lord Shiva. She just put on this act to prove to the world that Lord Ram was not a human because seeing how He went around crying for Mother Sita people might doubt His divinity.

Rama becomes disciple of Ravana learning from him on his deathbed

After airing fatal arrow on the battlefield of Lanka, Lord Rama told his brother Lakshman: Go to Ravana quickly before he dies and request him to share whatever knowledge he can. A brute he may be, but he is also a great scholar!

The obedient Lakshmana rushed across the battlefield to Ravana side and wispread in his ears: Oh demon king, do not let your knowledge die with you. Share it with us and wash away your sins!

Ravana responded by simply turning away his head. An angry Lakshman went back to Lord Rama and said: He is arrogant as he always was, too proud to share anything!
Rama conformed his brother and asked him softly: Where did you seat while asking Ravana for knowledge?

Next to his head so that I hear what he had to say clearly! – spoke Lakshman.

Lord Rama smiled, placed his bow on the ground ansd walked to where Ravana lay. Lakshmana watched in astonishment as his divine brother knelt at Ravanas feet. With palms joined with extreme humility, Lord Rama said:

Lord of Lanka, you abducted my wife, a terrible crime for which I have been forced to punish you. Now, you are no more my enemy. I bow to you and request you to share your wisdom with me. Please do that, for if you die without doing so, all your wisdom will be lost forever to the world.

To Lakshmana's surprise Ravana opened his eyes and raised his arms to salute Lord Rama: If only I had more time as your teacher than as your enemy. Standing at my feet as a student should, unlike your rude younger brother, you are worthy recipient of my knowledge.

Moral:

1. "Things that are bad for you seduce you easily; you run towards them impatiently. So you must defer the bad action as much as you can and avoid them.

2. Things that are actually good for you, fail to attract you; you shun them creatively, finding powerful excuses to justify your procrastination. So you must do good action without any delay and as much early as you can.

This is why I was impatient to abduct Sita but avoided meeting you. This is wisdom of my life, Lord Rama. My last words. I give it to you!" said Ravana and died.

Lord Rama meeting Shabari

There was a young woman named Shabari who was a daughter of a hunter. She wasn't a good looking woman, but her heart was pure. Before the day of her wedding she saw thousands of goats and sheep that her father had brought to sacrifice, as it was a custom among the hunters of that time.

She couldn't bear to see those animals being killed, so she ran away into the forest early in the morning to avoid the killing of those animals.

She went to many teachers and asked them to take her as their disciple and teach her 'true wisdom' (Brahma Jnana), but all the teachers rejected her because she was of a low caste and wasn't worthy to learn Brahma Jnana.

Sage Matanga welcomed her and took her as his disciple. But other rishis and yogis condemned him for taking an outcaste as the disciple, they criticized him, called him fallen, impure.

Sage Matanga told Shabari "Oh my daughter, stay in my Ashram, clean the place, take care of the chores, serve, it will do good to you."

"But other rishis in the forest are not happy about you taking me as your disciple" said Shabari.

"You have come to me seeking the greatest, I'll give you shelter", Sage was firm in his decision.

She was living peacefully in the Ashram, doing her daily duties, taking cows to the pastures and so on. Those rishis who were still ignorant and rejected Shabari's Guru, calling him an impure one.

One day when Sage Matang was very old he called his disciple Shabari and said "My Daughter, I'm leaving this body, is there anything you want me to do for you?"

Shabari prayed "Lord take me with you to the highest abode you are going. I can not live without you."

Sage Matanga said "Dear, One day Lord Rama will come to see you, until then stay alive, after that you can come to me."

Shabari stayed alive in anticipation of Lord Rama, She would get up early morning every day and go to the forest to collect the berries to serve Lord Rama, she didn't know when Rama would come, she would go to the forest and collect berries every day. In that manner she spent many years.

There was a beautiful and grand lake called Pampasar near her Guru's Ashram. Shabari who was now very old went to the lake with her pot made up of mud to collect water. There was a rishi sitting there with long beard and matted hairs chanting mantras, he was old and was reciting mantras wrongly. He heard this outcaste woman filling the divine water of the lake.

He thought "This low caste woman is making the water impure for our use." He threw a stone at her in anger which hit her leg and blood came out. A drop of blood fell into the lake, within seconds all the water in the lake turned into blood. Rishi started shouting loudly, "Look, a drop of this outcaste's blood has turned the whole lake into blood, what should we do now?"

Shabari went to her Ashram with her filled pot, still crying with pain. Rishis had no water to drink or to use for the sacred rites. They started chanting purification mantras, doing Yagnas and Havanas, throwing holy powders into the lake but nothing helped. Water still remained bloody. They brought water from Yamuna and Ganga which was of no use.

Someone in the group said, "Lord Rama has come, he is wandering in the forest, he can help us. Let's go to him and pray him to turn this blood into water again."

Rama came upon their request to Pama sarovar. The lake was red everywhere; rishis were all standing around him.

Rama asked "What can I do for you now?"

"Lord, touch of your feet will change this into water back" said the rishis.

Rama walked into the lake but the blood still stayed blood.

"Take a dip in it Lord" said the rishis gathered there.

Rama took a dip in it, but nothing changed..

"Lord, it is our last wish. Would you please clean your

mouth with it and spit back into it" they requested.

Rama took the blood with both hands, "But this is blood brother" said Lakshman, Rama took blood in his mouth and spit it back, but that did not change the lake.

Rama asked them "Tell me How did it become blood?"

One of the rishis said "There was a sage living here, he had an outcaste disciple Shabari, he has died but she still lives. She came to fetch water from this lake, a rishi threw a stone at her, it injured her and a drop of her blood fell into the river. It turned all the water into blood."

Rama on hearing the name of Shabari placed both of his hands on his heart and said "Oh rishis that was not Shabari's blood, that was the blood from my heart, I can not clean this."

"Lord our life has become difficult, we can not live without this water."

"I have come to see her, bring her to me, send someone to bring her."

One of them went to Shabari and said "Lord Rama has come and he is requesting you."

Shabari on hearing Lord Rama's name came running to see him. Rishis thought her impure shadow should not touch the Lord and tried to stop her. The soil from her feet fell into the water as she was running hastily, blood turned back into water. Everyone was surprised and were asking themselves "What just happened?"

Lord Rama said "Did you see, dust from Shabari's feet has purified the lake. I bathed in it, cleaned my mouth but nothing changed. Dust from the feet of a pure devotee purified the lake."

Shabari prayed to Lord Rama "Now, please come to my hut Lord, I have decorated it with flowers for you, I have brought sweet berries for you. Please come my Lord."

Rama and Lakshman followed her to her hermitage. She brought them sweet berries in a bowl she had made with the leaves of a tree. Rama was pleased with the hard work she had gone through to bring him berries.

"Lord I have selected only the sweet berries for you, I tasted every berry to make sure I have only brought the sweetest berries, please take it my Lord."

When Rama was about to take a berry Lakshman said "Brother these are half eaten, no good to eat". Rama took a fruit and ate it, he said to Lakshman "Brother, these berries are so sweet, I have never tasted berries as sweet as Shabari's berries. Whomsoever offers a fruit, a leaf, a flower or water with love, I take it with great joy."

Rama was touched by her love. He saw the leaves she had used to make the bowl, he blessed the tree that the leaves naturally grow to become like bowls. Rama asked her "Ask me anything you wish, I'm pleased by your devotion."

Shabari prayed only for pure devotion to Lord Rama. Rama blessed her and left. After this darshan Shabari's bodily life ended and she achived Spiritual world and eternal abode of Sri Rama.

Moral of the story:

From this story we can learn few things:

1. No mater who is one and what is his origin he can achieve great spiritual advancement.

2. We should be careful in dealing with everyone, especially with the devotees of the Lord. Offending them can bring many problems in life. And pleasing them will bring many blessing in our life and ultimately Lord will be happy with us.

3. It is not what we do or offer to the Lord, how big or small things and projects we do. What matter is with how much devotion we offer it to Him.

Hanuman and the pearl necklace of mother Sita

Great rejoicings and festivities followed the return of Sri Rama to Ayodhya and his crowning as the King. Lord Rama distributed gifts to all the monkeys who had served as warriors in his army. Sri Rama noticed his fervent devotee, Hanumanji and asked:

"O mighty hero how am I to compensate you for all you have done for me and my family?"

Many would have wanted wealth, name or fame, approbation or recognition or VIP line in return for their services. But Sri Hanuman was above all these:

"I desire nothing, Prabhu!"

Then, Maa Sita removed a valuable necklace of pearls from her neck and offered it to the humble Sri Hanuman.

Sri Hanuman received the necklace with great respect from Mata Sita, but began to break the pearls with His teeth.

Sita, and other ministers who were sitting in the council-hall, were quite astonished at this queer act of Sri Hanuman. Some wondered why the noble and great warrior Sri Hanuman was behaving like a monkey. Was it the monkey mind?

Sita asked Hanuman, "O mighty Hero! What are You doing? Why do you break the pearls?"

Sri Hanuman said, "O venerable Mother! It is the most valuable necklace, indeed, as it has come to me through Thy holy hand. But I want to find out whether any of the pearls contains my beloved Lord Rama. I do not keep a thing devoid of Him. I do not find Him in any of the pearls."

At this, one of the assembly members ironically remarked, "You would not wear any thing that has not got in it the Name of Rama. Well, You are wearing your body. You are carrying it about with you. Prove to us that you have the Name in it."

Hanuman laughed aloud; he said, "I shall prove, See!"

Sri Hanuman then tore his chest open with his mighty hands and Lo! Sri Rama and Maa Sita were seated in his heart!

Lord Rama came down the throne and embraced Hanuman and blessed Him. He asked him, "Hanuman! What can I offer you on this occasion? I have no gift worthy to be given to you. I am giving you myself as my gift to you." Then, he offered his body to be clasped by Hanuman's hands. The assembly was moved into shouts of "Jai ho" at this unique act of Grace. They praised Hanuman and declared that there was no one to equal him in all the worlds. They praised the devotion and dedication of Hanuman.

When Sri Rama ascended to His Supreme abode, Hanuman also wished to follow Him. But the Lord asked him to remain in this world as His representative, and attend the assemblies of saints where discourses (katha) on His deeds were held and heard, and help His devotees in cultivating devotion.

Hanumanji is a Chiranjeevi (immortal). He is everywhere. He who has devotion beholds Him, and receives His blessing.

Surya and Moon desire to see Lord Rama

When Lord Ram killed Ravan and handed over the Lanka kingdom to Sri Vibhisan, everywhere it was joy and gaiety, Lord Ram decided to return to Shri Ayodhya puri with his confident companions and friends.

When Lord Rama reached Ayodhya, it was celeberation all over, after all for the residents of Ayodhya Lord Ram was not just a King but He was their life and soul, for them each moment was like a 12 year span. They did not enjoy any luxury, sacrificing all the comfort because their Supreme father was in exile.

So when they got the news they forgot themselves, the entire Ayodha was jubilant, not only the people but also the demigods were celebrating the moment.

At that time the Sun God was about to set, when He saw the all attractive and all pleasing Lord Ram, He was so much attracted that he just stood gazing and felt in trance and forgot that it was his setting time.

In this way a month passed away and it was day all over and people were so much enjoying the celebration that they did not feel that a month has passed, they never wanted this celebration to end, and on the other side the moon god was nervous and impatient to have a glimpse of Lord Ram.

Lord Ram was just smiling at all this.

Only He knew that 30 days have passed. Sun god came to his consciousness and hurriedly left on his chariot toward west, and by the mercy of Lord that 30 day duration just turned into a 24 hours duration day, and no one felt it.

Lord was about to proceed toward His palace. Up in the sky the moon god was very sad and pale, because He missed this spellbound Lila of Lord Ram.

Lord Ram knew the desire of moon god, so He asked what was the matter.

At this, Moon replied, "My Lord what sin I have done that everyone else enjoyed your arrival except me, you are Karunasindhu, and you give equality to all, then why sun got opportunity to have your darshan and why not me?"

At this Lord Ram replied, "My dear Moon,I know your wish. Don't lament I will certainly fulfil your desire, but not this time. In my next incarnation, as Krishna, I will appear on full moon day, and then you can satisfy your desire by enjoying my all attractive and all pleasing appearance, and also you will be glorified."

Moral of the story:

Just see how merciful Lord is. He cares even for a small wish of His devotees, and fulfills it by all means. Isn't it astonishing to see the supreme personality of Godhead caring for His devotees wish?

Lord Ram came in Suryavanshi kul, where as Lord Krishna appeared in Chandravansh. What a mercy!

Lord Rama and boatmen Kevat

When Lord Sri Ramachandra reached the forest with Sita and Lakshmana, they had to cross the river Ganga.

Guha had heard about the banishment of Lord Rama and came running to help Him. One of his boatmen was unloading people on the opposite bank and Guha said to Kevat to bring the boat and take divine personalities on other side of mother Ganga.

Kevat brought the boat near Lord Rama, got down and did namaskaar with intense devotion to Lord Rama. He started and ended his days with prayers to Lord Rama and throughout the day he was well known for talking about the glories of Lord.

Kevat asked Guha whether he could wash Lord's feet before He stepped into the boat. Guha told him to wash His feet after seating Him in the boat.

But Kevat was adamant and told Guha that he would like to wash Lord's feet before he got into the boat. Guha was a little angry at his stubbornness and was about to loose temper.

Then Kevat decided to explain his point to Lord Rama himself. "Lord, the limited income I have as a boatman is just enough to make both ends meet in life and I am afraid that I cannot afford any more boats. So let me please wash the dust on your feet before you step into my boat."

Lord Rama smiled looking at Sita devi and remained silent.

Kevat continued: "Lord, I have heard that the dust from your feet embraced a stone in the forest and it became a woman. My boat is made of several pieces of wood and if the dust of your feet fell on my boat, I am afraid the boat would turn into several women corresponding to each piece of wood.. I sincerely cannot take care of any more members in my household. That is why I am requesting to wash the feet and make it dust free before you step into the boat. Please be kind to me."

Lord Rama appreciated his pure and innocent faith.

After washing their feet Kevat place his hands on earth and asked Lord to first step on his hand before stepping into the boat. This way he washed all his sins by having a touch of Lords feet.

After washing the Lord's feet, Kevat ferried them across the river. As soon as they alighted from the boat, Ma Sita immediately withdrew a ring from her finger and handed it over to Lord Rama, signaling to him to pass it on to the boatman.

Lord Rama: Here Brother, that is all we can pay you for your kind service. Please accept it.

Kevat: (Shaking his head). No, My Lord! I can not possibly accept this from you.

Lord Rama: Why?

Kevat: Because people of the same profession do not charge each other for their services. A barber never takes payment, when he gives a haircut to another barber. Even a washer-man never charges a fellow washer-man.

Lord Rama: Brother, how can you and I be of the same profession? You are a boatman and I am...

Kevat: Lord, both of us do the same work. I ferry people from this shore of the Ganges to the other. You ferry people across the ocean of Samsaara (Bhav-sagar),through the journey of life.

How can I accept payment from you? Prabhu! I don't want anything. But please, as I have made you cross this river today, when my time comes, take me across sansaar saagar [the ocean of material existence]. That would be your return to me.

The Lord was so overwhelmed at this devotional request from Kevat, that he held out his arms and embraced the boatman. Later, the expert ferryman was delivered from the cycle of birth and death just because of this little service done unto the Supreme Lord.

He also asked Lord for endless devotion to the feet of Lord Rama. Lord Rama said that from today you do not need to take another birth, and granted Kevat – Mukti from material world.

punarapi jananam punarapi maranam

punarapi jananii jathare shayanam

iha samsaare bahudustaare

kripayaa apaare paahi muraare

Moral of the story:

We all ask God for material elements and temporary material pleasure. This is just like asking a rupee to a benevolent who has ability to give you whole world.

How foolish are we, who runs after the world leaving the loving supreme soul.

Let's act smartly like this expert ferryman. Let's do some devotional service unto the Supreme Lord.

That way reaching the ultimate perfection in life would be assured.

The Merciful Lord comes Himself or sends His devotees (saints) to show us the right direction. As soon as Arjuna accepted Lord Krishna as his guide, Lord's perfect instructions lead him to victory and fame. Little service rendered to the merciful Supreme Lord would please Him and He would hold the reins of the chariot of our life. And, when the Supreme Lord would be our guide, would there be any doubt in our victory on the path of life?

Little squirrel who helped Lord Rama!

Here in a story from the Ramayana, Lord Rama and his army of monkeys were preparing for war with Ravana.

Rama asked his army to build the bridge over the sea. Work began at once on a stone bridge. The monkeys pulled out rocks and heavy stones from the mountains, and carried them to the sea. They cut them into shape and began to build the bridge. All this was very difficult work and it took a long time. Thousands of monkeys worked night and day.

Rama felt happy. "How hard they work! Their love for me makes them work like this," thought Rama.

One day, Rama saw a small brown squirrel. He was going up and down the seashore with little pebbles in his mouth. The little squirrel could carry only little pebbles at a time in his small mouth. He carried the pebbles from the seashore and dropped them into the sea.

A great monkey was carrying a large heavy stone on his back and the squirrel came in his way.

The monkey jumped back. "Here, you little thing," shouted the monkey in a voice like thunder, "you're in my way, I stepped back and you're alive now. But I nearly fell. And what are you doing here?"

The little squirrel looked up at the great monkey.

"I'm sorry you nearly fell, Brother Monkey," he said in his small voice, "but please always look where you are going. I'm helping Rama build the bridge. And I want to work hard for him."

"You, what?" shouted the monkey and laughed aloud. "Did you hear that!" he said to the other monkeys. "The squirrel is building a bridge with his pebbles. Oh dear! Oh dear! I've never heard a funnier story." The other monkeys laughed too.

The squirrel did not think this funny at all. He said, "Look, I can't carry mountains or rocks. God gave me only a little strength. I can only carry pebbles. My heart cries out for Rama and I'll do all I can for him."

The monkeys said, "Don't be foolish. Do you think you can help Rama? Do you think we can build a bridge with pebbles? He has a big army to help him. Go home and don't get in our way."

"But I want to help, too," said the squirrel and would not go.

He carried the pebbles again from the shore to the sea. The monkeys were angry and one of them picked up the squirrel by his tail and threw him far away. The squirrel, crying out the name of Rama, fell into his hands.

Then Rama held the squirrel close to him.

He said to the monkeys, "Do not make fun of the weak and the small. Your strength or what you do is not important.

What matters is your love. This little squirrel has love in his heart."

"O Vanaras, you are brave and strong, and are doing a wonderful job bringing all these huge boulders and stones from far and dropping them in the ocean.

But did you notice that it is the tiny pebbles and stones brought by this small squirrel and some of the other smaller creatures which are filling the small gaps left between the huge stones?

Further, do you not realize that the tiny grains of sand brought by this squirrel are the ones which bind the whole structure and make it strong? Yet you scold this small creature and fling him away in anger!"

Hearing this, the Vanaras were ashamed, and bowed down their heads.

Rama continued, "Always remember, however small, every task is equally important. A project can never be completed by the main people alone. They need the support of all, and however small, an effort should always be appreciated!"

Rama then turned to the squirrel and said softly, "My dear squirrel, I am sorry for the hurt caused to you by my army, and thank you for the help you have rendered to me. Please go and continue your work happily." Saying this, he gently stroked the back of the squirrel with his fingers, and three lines appeared where the Lord's fingers had touched it.

Rama held the squirrel closer to him and said. "Little one, your love touches my heart." He said these words and passed his fingers gently over the little squirrel's back.

And when he put him down there were three white stripes on his back. These were the marks of Lord Rama's fingers.

Moral of the story:

No task and service to the Lord, however small, is unimportant. Every task should be looked upon as service to the Lord, and his blessings will always be with us. We should never forget that love and dedication is what matters to Lord Rama and not big services and show we make for our prestige.

Lord Rama and the Crow

In the earlier Kali yuga, there was a shudra, who was by nature jealous and highly egostic. Somehow he was a devotee of Lord Shiva but envious of Lord Vishnu.

He used to worship by his own whims. He used to travel from place to place to find a guru who would give him "Shiva mantra". Being naturally envious he could not approach humbly to any guru.

At last he met one Brahmana who was by nature very humble and caring. This sudra took shelter in his ashram and started serving him, although not with full heart as this sadhu was a Brahmana as well as worshiper of Lord Vishnu.

The Brahamna knew the envious nature of this shudra but being a pure Vaishnava he never saw his bad quality and always tried to convince him to give up the bad quality. One day the Brahmana gave him "Shiva mantra" as per shudra's desire, but also advised him the truth about Lord Narayana, but all in vain.

As days passed the shudra chanted the mantra of Lord Shiva but at the same time his hatred toward his own guru increased. His guru being merciful never cared for his behavior, on other hand always tried for his upliftment.

One day as the shudra was chanting his mantra in Lord

Shiva's temple, his guru maharaj visited the temple. Seeing his guru maharaj, he turned his face otherside and did not bother to pay obeisances pretending as if he was deeply meditating.

His guru being a pure sadhu did not mind for this disrespect but this behavior of the shudra was not tolerated by Lord Shiva.

With a thunderous roar Lord Shiva appeared from his diety form, with his eyes burning like red fire, holding His trishul, he was about to kill the shudra.

Seeing the situation, the guru fell down at the feet of Lord Shiva, and with tears in his eyes, the guru started pleading to Lord Shiva, by offering him prayers and singing his glories. He prayed for forgiveness of the shudra and in turn offering his own head, and in this way he was able to cool down Lord Shiva.

Lord Shiva then cursed the shudra saying, "You only pretend to worship me and did not offer any respect to your guru. Being a pure Vaishnava he did not mind it, but I could not tolerate this insult of a pure Vaishnava. Therefore I curse you to become a python and you will have to take 1000 birth in low species form."

Hearing this curse the guru again fell at the Lord's feet and said, "Oh! Mahadev you are called 'Bhole Shankar'! You are so merciful. Please forgive my disciple, and sow the seed of Lord Narayan bhakti in his heart."

Lord Shiva being pleased with the guru again said, "As my curse won't go in vain but seeing the love of your guru maharaj, I bless you that although you will have to change your body 1000 times you will never feel any pain while taking birth nor at the time of death and in your last birth you will become a brahmana and will attain pure bhakti at the feet of Lord Ram and you will be able to remember all your past." Saying this the Lord Shiva blessed the shudra and dissappeared.

Being cursed and blessed by Lord Shiva, he fell down at the feet of his guru maharaj and with tears in his eyes he begged his forgiveness.

Soon, he took the form of python and kept changing his body without any pain (as per the blessing) and in his last birth he was born in a brahmana family.

In his early age he lost his parents. Taking this as the mercy of the Lord he left in search of Lord Ram's mantra.

Whomever he met he use to ask about Lord Ram and nothing else. At the end he met a Rishi from whom he enquired about Lord Ram.

After a lot of argument about Lord's niraakaar(Impersonal) and saakaar (Personal) forms, the rishi being under the influence of Lord Ram's maya, tried to convince the superiority of Lord's niraakaar form.

The brahmana with having no interest at all in Niraakaar form, debated and asked again the mantra of Lord Ram.

At this the muni got furious and cursed him to at once become a crow.

This curse was taken as blessing by the brahmana boy, and

with folded hand he again asked the mantra of Lord Ram.

Seeing his firm devotion, the Lord situated in everyones heart removed the influence of His maya from the rishi.

Immediately the rishi realized his mistake, deeply repenting for it, he asked forgivness and at once gave him Ram mantra. Obtaining the mantra for which he waited so many lives, the crow knew no sorrows. He thanked the rishi and flew away.

Lord Ram appeared in front of this crow and asked the crow to ask for any benediction. The Lord said take riddhi, siddhi, wealth, beauty or any thing you name I shall give to you." The crow being smart by nature thought that Lord offered me everything but He never ever mentioned to give His unflinching devotional service.

The crow said, "What I will do with all this ? I want nothing, oh! Lord of universe, If You are really pleased with me then give me Your loving bhakti of which Lord Shiva had talked about."

In the entire Ramayana Lord Ram has never given so many boons along with His unflinching bhakti except for Hanuman.

Lord Ram even made him immortal, and whenever Treta Yug comes this crow along with Lord Shiva, visits Ayodha dham to enjoy the "Bal Lila" of Lord Ram.

This crow's name was "Kak Bhusundi" (Kak means crow) and even today he is present in man-sarovar where he constantly chants the glories of Lord Ram and all the liberated souls visit him to hear the nectar of Ramayana.

And he never changed his body of crow. The crow's rendition of Ramayana is very famous as bhusundi-ramayana.

Moreover, Lord's dear devotee Sri Garudaji comes to this kak-bhusundi and hears his sweet singing of the Lord's pastimes.

Moral of the story:

Just imagine the fate of the shudra, what he was and what he became, and all this is because of a mercy of a pure vaishnava, a true sadhu, a real guru maharaj, who is many many times more merciful than a true father.

The spiritual master is rightly called Karuna Sindhu who liberated his disciple who was not at all qualified and who insulted him. When we think of such Sadhu, a Param Vaishnava, a real loving father, then at once our spiritual master comes in our mind, so much caring for fallen souls like us, he extends his strong hand and pulls us out of the blind well of ignorance.

A relevant verse from the scripture that highlights the quality of a spiritual master:

mukham karoti vacalam pangum langayate girim

yat kripa tamaham vande sri gurum deena taarinam paramaananda madhavam

"By the mercy of the all-blissful Lord and the Spiritual Master, even a dumb can speak eloquent poetic verses and a lame can climb mountains."

Sita devi tells story of compassion to Hanuman

In the Ramayana, we find that after Ravana was killed, Sri Hanuman went to the Ashoka vana to meet Sitadevi and inform her of the good news of Sri Ramas victory.

Srimati Sita was extremely delighted on hearing the news and asked Hanumanji to ask for any boon he desired.

Sri Hanuman was full of anger against the deamoness who were guarding Sita devi because they were always causing trouble and fear to her. So he wanted Sitadevis permission to kill them.

Mother Sita exhibited her unlimited compassion and magnanimity when She said that those Raksasis were simply and helplessly working under the instructions of the evil Ravana as his servants and it is not right to punish them. At that time, she told the following story:

Once a hunter in the forest tripped and fell down while hunting a lion and lost his weapons.

The lion then started chasing the hunter. The hunter ran and he climbed upon a tree. On the tree he could see that there was a bear sitting. The man was completely helpless and he took shelter of the bear requesting the bear to spare his life.

Meanwhile the lion came to the bottom of the tree and instigated the bear to push the man down so that they can both eat the man.

The bear refused saying that the man has taken shelter of him and hence he would not push him down.

After sometime the bear started sleeping and the lion told the hunter, I am feeling very hungry. So you push the sleeping bear down from the tree so that I can kill and eat him and you can be relieved.

The ungrateful hunter, so much concerned about his own life, pushed the sleeping bear.

The bear somehow woke up while falling down and caught hold of a branch of the tree and was saved.

The lion told the bear that even though the bear tried to save the hunter, he was so ungrateful as to push him down. Hence the bear should now help the lion by pushing the hunter.

The saintly bear replied that great souls never have the inimical attitude towards others and it is their nature to be compassionate even if the others are of a bad nature. Thus the bear stood by its principles and did not harm the hunter who was greatly ashamed seeing the behaviour of the bear.

Moral of the story:

In the Srimad Bhagavatam we find that saintly Vidura gave good counsel to his brother Dhritarashtra and asked him to get rid of Duryodhana, the source of all trouble.

Hearing this, Duryodhana insulted Vidura very badly calling him a spy, infidel and he desired that Vidura be immediately put out of the palace. Thus being pierced by arrows through his ears and afflicted to the core of his heart, Vidura quit his brothers palace and went on a pilgrimage.

Dhritarashtra could not speak anything against his son.

It is unimaginable for any other person who has been subjected to such an insult to come back and do good for such a brother. But we find that Mahatma Vidura came back after having already adopted the renounced order of life, just for only one purpose and that is to deliver his elder brother.

Srimad Bhagavatam says,

kancit kaalam athaavaatsit sat-krto devavat sukham

bhraatur jyesthasya sreyas-krt sarvesaam sukham aavahan

Thus Mahatma Vidura, being treated just like a godly person by his kinsmen, remained there for a certain period just to rectify the mentality of his eldest brother and in this way bring happiness to all the others.

Such is the compassion of the great souls for all the conditioned living entities who have turned their faces away from the Lord. It is what the compassionate spiritual master does for all of us.

THE END